CHANGING

LANDSCAPE

a novel

Olivia Valentine

Trafford
PUBLISHING™

ACKNOWLEDGMENTS

I would like to thank those who have made this book possible.

Firstly my parents, my mother for encouraging me to read and who read many wonderful stories to my sister and I when we were young. My father for enchanting us with his own stories, many of which I still remember today.

My sister who read the first draft and was a valuable critique.

Paula Readman who gave me equally valuable advice and information.

Dominic Read for painstakingly proof reading and editing.

Edward Middleton for designing the cover.

To all my friends who have encouraged me.

The Gallery tea room for endless cups of tea and delicious indulgencies.

I would like to thank all at Trafford Publishing and in particular Nickie Claassens for all their advice and patience.

Finally my husband Ian, for his love, encouragement and support without which this book would not have been written.

For my sons and my step children
Dominic, Alistair, Oliver, Jo, Stephen, Kerry, Marc and Sarah.

To Kerry

Changing Landscape

Written by Olivia Valentine

Best wishes

Olivia Valentine

ONE

Rosie looked at herself in the small hand mirror, just as she would be asking her pupils to do later that morning. A self-portrait from memory in half an hour was not an easy task but a valuable lesson in observation and quick interpretation.

She observed herself dispassionately. A mass of unruly golden amber hair (not quite ginger) twisted in a bun on top of her head. An oval shaped face with a high forehead, which her mother had always told her was a sign of intelligence, in her case, she was not so sure.

She looked straight into her own wide green eyes, her favourite feature. She stared at her reflection for a minute or more and found it quite surprisingly disconcerting. It felt as if she was looking deep into herself and wasn't sure who was there. She had read somewhere that one eye was the kind eye the other the hard, she had dismissed it as rubbish then but now looking at her eyes one was more intent, more glaring than the other. She did not like to think she could be cruel in any way, she tried to be kind but if she was honest, she had a determined streak especially when it came to protecting her family. She laughed and growled at herself, yes she could see a pussycat with a lioness interior waiting to pounce if necessary.

She rarely looked for long in the mirror, merely a cursory glance and a short-sighted attempt at makeup occasionally. She blinked and looking further down noted her nose with its sprinkling of freckles and remembered what she had told Ben, her son who had inherited her colouring, a face without freckles is like a sky without stars. Fine lines were evident around her eyes and horror of horrors a hint of wrinkles. They appeared to travel all the way down from her eyes to her mouth they must be laughter lines. She laughed experimentally, yes definitely laughter lines.

She noted her slightly crooked front teeth, which two years in braces as a teenager had only marginally improved. Moving swiftly on, she looked then at a rather pleasing long elegant neck where her silver cross from Bulgaria rested. The rest of her once very slim, now softly rounded body was encased in a light white cotton shift, bespattered with paint, and baggy green trousers, perhaps not the latest fashion but cool and unrestricting nonetheless.

Making faces at herself she laughed, "Oh well I am thirty-nine after all."

She put the mirror down, picked up a paintbrush and dipped it into the watery burnt sienna paint she had already prepared. Then from memory, she expertly painted herself on the blank canvas in front of her. Using only one brush and one colour, she deftly produced in half an hour a good recognisable self-portrait.

As she painted, she thought of her classes and smiled with pleasure. She remembered how thrilled she had been when after only a week of the poster being up in the local post office advertising an art class in the village hall she had received more than twenty enquiries from residents and their friends. Now ten months later, she not only taught that class but an evening one too with a waiting list for both.

One of the delights for her was the age range of her students; the eldest was Violet at eighty-nine whose paintings were becoming more abstract as the arthritis in her hands made free movement difficult. Rosie laughed at the memory of Violet's comment the previous week "I am concentrating on colour from now on, forget the form!" The wonderful fluid mix of watercolour without strict definition produced paintings which Rosie thought quite lovely.

She remembered Violet mentioning that it was her birthday and Rosie thought she would buy some fresh cream cakes to have in their tea break in celebration. She had grown fond of Violet and admired her tenacity to paint despite her disability.

Her youngest was Sasha who was an A level student trying to achieve a good grade in art. She spent a lot of time with this shy girl in an attempt to boost her confidence. She had a lot of natural talent but lacked the courage to experiment. It was so rewarding seeing the results of her efforts as Sasha's confidence grew.

Rosie had put Violet and Sasha side-by-side last week and had taken a photo; she would paint them one day. There was something she found touching about the very old and young together. She remembered her Father visiting her in hospital a few hours after she had given birth to Grace, he had taken her tiny newborn hand in his and the touching beauty of it had made her cry.

From several of her students she had had commissions one of which was propped up against the wall and was nearly finished, she told herself that she must get on with it later that day.

It was four thirty in the afternoon before Rosie was back in her studio finishing her painting as she had promised herself she would. She was humming to herself and feeling happy, the class had gone well and dear Violet had been pleased with the delicious cream cakes she had bought for her.

Just as she was standing back to take a critical look at her finished work she heard the sound of a car on the drive. She looked out of her upstairs studio window and smiled, delighted that Tom was home early, and watched her tall good looking husband as he walked from his car to the house.

It was a balmy summer's afternoon with just enough of a breeze to stop it feeling oppressive. The sweet smell of the climbing Compassion rose wafted in through the open window.

She called out a welcome "Hello my handsome" and waved but when he looked up she noticed that instead of his usual smiley face a very grim one looked back up at her, he walked with heavy steps and appeared to be talking to himself. She wondered what could be the matter and ran downstairs to meet him.

Charlie their retriever, arrived at the door before her ready to give his usual exuberant welcome, which he gave to all who came through the door. For those he loved best he would roll on his back offering his tummy for a rub.

Rosie arrived at the front door just as Tom opened it.

"What's the matter Tom, you look utterly miserable"

It was only once Charlie had received enough attention that Tom could give Rosie his usual perfunctory kiss.

"I am, it has been a devil of a day". Then without saying a word, he took her hand and led her into the sitting room and they sat down on their comfy but faded linen sofa.

Tom took off his shoes, leaned back on the sofa, and sighed deeply "Oh it is good to be home"

Rosie normally so chatty with the telling of the days events instinctively knew to say nothing. Looking at her husband's face in the way as she had done hers a few hours earlier she saw his face also showing signs of middle age, his jaw a little heavier than in his youth, crows feet lines around his eyes, his hair receding slightly and she saw that grey hairs were just beginning to appear at his temples, why hadn't she noticed that before? She loved his thick and wavy hair, dark with chestnut tinges. Age had improved his looks; he had always been handsome but had sharper angular features when she had first met him all those years ago.

She saw how weary he looked, and hated to see it.

"You look so tired and tense Tom, would you like me to massage your head for you"

He nodded, Rosie stood up and moved around behind the sofa then reached over and ran her fingers through his hair. She massaged his head, neck and shoulders, he smiled up at her.

While she gently massaged his temples Rosie optimistically thought that Tom had simply had a bad day probably interviewing ill prepared and unsuitable youngsters that the employment agency had blithely sent along for a post that none of them were qualified for.

After a short while, Tom said, "I have some bad news, I have been asked if I will transfer to the same post in the American branch or face redundancy."

Rosie stopped her massage and came round to face Tom

"Oh no you can't mean it, move to America?"

Rosie felt her stomach churn.

"Well either that or nothing but a lump sum and the dole."

Sitting down Rosie tried to take in what Tom had just said

"What a shock tell me what happened Tom."

"Yes it is a shock, I am reeling, I can't quite believe it. Nothing happened as such, I was just sent for. I didn't think anything of it. Paul did a spiel about dissolving company investments and relocation of assets and then simply said Tom I am afraid you are one of the assets we have to relocate. He actually had the audacity to laugh."

"You have worked so hard for that Company and helped it develop into the company it is now. It seems so unfair, Paul has only been there for a couple of years and you have been there nearly twenty. He should be going not you!"

"It doesn't work like that, we do different jobs."

"Well why should you go when you have worked so long and hard for them?"

"Exactly, so damned if I am going to leave now!"

Rosie suddenly realised what this might mean, "What do you mean Tom, can you appeal?"

"No, I will relocate."

"You want to go to America and work?" Rosie looked incredulous.

Tom did not answer; they both sat there in their own private thoughts allowing the enormity of the news to penetrate and emerge in to some kind of tangible hurdle that they would be able to cross.

Rosie was the first to surface and said "We would have to move, leave this house" brokenly she continued "Oh Tom it took us so long to find it!"

Suddenly Tom turned to her and angrily said, "The house for crying out loud is that all you are worried about?"

Rosie felt aggrieved at his attitude "Of course not, this is a shock for me too. What concerns me more are Grace and Ben, they are at a critical stage in their schooling Tom. They will hate to leave their schools and their friends"

Tom raised his voice again "Ok, ok hang on for goodness sake, Rosie. I knew you wouldn't want to go. I understand, but it's not my fault. I don't want to go either, but I can't see what choice we have."

Rosie saw that he was utterly miserable and felt guilty at her reaction.

"I am sorry, this is such a shock, and I know it's not your fault."

Tom said nothing more but put his head in his hands and groaned loudly

"Tom, why don't you go and change while I pour us a glass of wine and we can have it in the garden and talk this through." she smiled reassuringly at him.

He rose to go and as he did Rosie saw his trousers covered in cat's hairs, she laughed.

"What can you possibly find to laugh at?"

"You have a hairy behind; the cat has been sleeping in here all day."

"Well thank you, but I thought you didn't like hairy bottoms" smiled Tom regaining a little of his usual good humour. Rosie brushed the hairs off grinning, "There are always exceptions"

"You know Rosie it was strange, I had an uncanny feeling this morning that life was about to change"

"That is unlike you, it is normally me who has premonitions. Had this been on the cards?"

"We had been given no indication of redundancies at all. I feel particularly angry about that.

"No hint at all?"

"None whatsoever. I'm not the only one of course; twenty-four employees are to be offered redundancy packages. Only myself and one other have been offered a post in America, the other poor chap has only three years to go before retirement and has a handicapped wife to care for. He wont go to America."

"Why just you two I wonder?"

"Because we have been there over fifteen years and they have to abide by the company policy of redeployment. Hell I even wrote the policy. To cap it all it's our job to interview all those facing redundancy."

"Perhaps they will change their minds."

"I very much doubt it, apparently the powers that be have decided to minimise the British concern and sell off some of the property then invest more in the American market."

Rosie who was ever the optimist said "Tom, you never know this might be the beginning of something really good, something around the corner that you wouldn't have done without the threat of redundancy."

Little did Rosie know how prophetic that statement was. Tom chose to ignore it and simply said, "A cold glass of wine sounds great, I'll go and change."

Upstairs in their bedroom, that they had just finished decorating, Tom suddenly felt full of anger, kicked out at the door, forgetting he had taken his shoes off, and swore.

He didn't like swearing and wasn't tolerant of it in others but the moment was a swearing sort of moment.

Downstairs Rosie poured the wine and thought of Tom and how he always hated change. He felt safe in the stability of the same routines.

Tom had moved schools several times as a child. His Father had been in the RAF all his working life.

Both he and his brother James had hated having to continually change schools, leave old friends and make new ones.

When Rosie met Tom at university, he had found the fact that she had grown up on a farm and lived in the same village, in the same house all her life refreshing. She was confident yet had a naivety, which had aroused Tom's protective masculinity and arousal of another kind.

Rosie had experienced the sort of childhood that they both wanted for their children.

Tom laid on the bed for a few minutes feeling exhausted by the days events and also feeling wretched at having to tell Rosie of his news, her happiness and their children's was so important to him, it was why he worked. It was for them he continued in a job which after eighteen years had ceased to appeal to him. He was sick to the eye teeth of company policy, corporate plans, budgets and public accountabilities.

Through the open door he could hear Grace in her room chatting to one of her friends, she seemed to spend hours most evenings speaking on the phone to friends she had spent the day with at school. A phenomena Tom had never understood.

Ben on the other hand only used the phone to make football arrangements with his friends, short and to the point.

"Hi, tomorrow, at three, Fairways Park, see ya." That was the conversation he had heard Ben have with two of his friends the previous day. Only eight words, so impressed he had told Grace and she had given him a look that had clearly said you can't be serious. Tom smiled ruefully at the thought of it.

Having changed into beige cotton shorts and a white polo shirt he made his way down stairs calling out "Hi" to Grace as he passed her room. Walking out of the French doors, he stopped to look at their garden. Although still a little overgrown despite Rosie and him spending many weekends weeding, cutting and trimming, it looked beautiful. They had decided to keep the rambling look; it suited the ancient crooked house. In fact Tom suspected that the rambling plants and ivy kept the old wall surrounding half the garden standing.

Rosie was sitting under the big old apple tree on the wrought iron furniture her parents had given them for a wedding present.

While she was waiting for Tom, she had prayed for a solution. She most definitely did not want to leave and could tell that Tom didn't want to either.

As Tom emerged from the house their son, Ben arrived home and rushed out behind him. Ben dressed in his football kit, having not bothered to change in his hurry to get home, whooped in the air and yelled, "I'm on the team! I'm on the team!"

Both Tom and Rosie looked at each other appalled, "Oh great

timing." mumbled Tom. Rosie quickly recovered and trying to sound pleased said, "Well done."

Ben had been trying for a place on the school football team for five long years; he thought his parents would be chuffed.

Visibly deflated by his parent's lack of response, he looked from one to the other. "What the hells the matter with you?" not waiting for an answer he ran indoors slamming the door as he went.

"Look what we have done now." said Tom, glaring at Rosie.

"Me, that's rich at least I congratulated him, you didn't even say well done."

Tom sat down taking a large gulp of wine, "Okay sorry, I will go and see him in a minute and explain"

"And say what Tom? That we are all leaving England to go and live in America, therefore he can't play on the football team. I think it is ridiculous we shouldn't even contemplate it."

Tom wearing an I will try and be patient look, which always irritated Rosie, said

"Try and understand Rosie it isn't just a matter of going or staying. It is job or no job, survive or go under."

"Tom, that is so melodramatic. Of course, we won't go under as you put it. We will just find other employment."

"That is the royal we is it? I don't recall you having much paid employment."

"That is so unfair, I have just sold one of my paintings and have a commission for another or have you conveniently forgotten that? I also have my art classes."

"Rosie you know as well as I do that I appreciate your talent but be realistic what you make from selling an occasional picture does not make a great deal of difference to the household finances".

Rosie was indignantly about to retort but held back and realised that arguing about money was pointless and wasn't truly the issue anyway.

"Did you see Grace when you were upstairs?"

"No but I heard her on the phone"

"I think she's infatuated with a boy called Carl. She drops his name into almost every conversation at the moment."

Tom laughingly dismissed it. "It is just a crush, aren't all girls supposed to have crushes? Anyway she is far too young."

"Oh Tom, Grace is sixteen and it is very real for her I am sure. I remember my first love; it was all consuming, wonderful and terrible at the same time also agonisingly painful when it ended."

Tom was hardly listening, he was suddenly remembering when Grace was little, just yesterday it seemed, she would climb onto his lap then snuggle down under his embracing arm and beg for a story. She had loved to hear about the antics he and his brother got up to when they were young boys. Then she went through a stage of near permanent angst only punctuated by moments of what only can be described as baby clinging, needing cuddles and reassurance, not easy when five minutes previously she had yelled that she hated everyone and everything. Now he hardly saw her, she was busy doing her own thing and spent hours it seemed in her room, thankfully in better temper.

This made him think of Ben, he was genuinely pleased that at last he had succeeded in getting a place on the school team. Somehow that and now Grace being "in love" made it even more difficult though to tell them that they may well be leaving England, and their life as they knew it.

Rosie had got up and was miserably de-heading the roses, how she loved them, she had tried when they first moved in to identify each one. She bent down and gently held the perfect bloom of

Alec's Red, smelling its exquisite scent and admiring the way it contrasted beautifully with the white Rambling Rector, which had festooned itself amongst the sturdy branches of the old lilac tree. So engrossed she hadn't heard Tom's approach, suddenly she felt Tom's arms around her waist; she twisted round to see him smiling down at her.

Smiling back, she said with conviction, "We will find a way to stay here, I know it Tom."

Tom said nothing just bent down and gave her a tender kiss, he didn't share her faith but they had argued enough.

"I am going in to see Ben; I am not going to mention the job. Let's celebrate Ben's success and all go out for dinner together at Marno's."

When Tom found Ben he was engrossed in sorting out his Warhammer models. Ben's room was its usual mess and there was literally nowhere for Tom to stand without stepping on something, he stood in the doorway. He looked at his gangly thirteen-year-old son so like Rosie to look at yet far more like him in temperament. Ben was full of jokes one minute and down in the dumps the next. Grace on the other hand looked more like him; and had Rosie's even temperament.

"Ben, I am sorry, we are thrilled for you of course."

"What were you arguing about?" asked Ben without looking up, ignoring Tom's apology.

"Well it is nothing for you to worry about Ben. I have had a difficult day at work, there are many changes going on and they may involve me. Changing the subject quickly Tom went on to say, "Mum and I thought it would be a good idea for us all to go out for dinner to Marno's tonight, what do you think?"

"What's the big occasion we only go there for birthdays?"

"Ben I think we have some celebrating to do don't you?"

Ben looked up and grinned at his Father. Tom felt forgiven.

He then went to knock on Grace's door; she called out "Who is it?"

"It's Dad."

"Hang on I'm just changing, what are you doing home so early?"

With that, the door opened and Grace stood there, not looking a bit like she had when he had seen her that morning "What have you done to your hair?"

"I have streaked it, and before you freak out Dad it isn't permanent."

"I am glad to hear it, I'm not sure that you should be sporting pink and green stripes for school."

"Mum liked it, she said it was creative and showed my individuality."

Tom inwardly admired Rosie's sang-froid.

"I hope you are spending as much time on revision as you are on your hair."

Grace rolled her eyes "Yes, of course don't be a bore Dad." she grinned at him and as always his heart melted.

He told her of the dinner plans "Oh right great I had better change then"

Tom with a confused look on his face said "You have just changed."

"I can't wear these jeans to Marno's"

Tom looked down at her long legs encased in perfectly ordinary looking jeans.

Rosie arrived at that moment and said, "Yes let's dress up and make a real occasion of it."

Ben hearing that called out "I am starving, it will be ages before dinner."

"Go and get a yoghurt or a banana." said Rosie putting her head around Ben's door. Glancing around Ben's room she added "I am averting my eyes from the mess for tonight, perhaps tomorrow you would like to have your pocket money tidy up. Tonight we are going to have some fun all together."

"I am being creative and expressing my individuality," replied Ben with a cheeky grin.

Everyone laughed and Tom said in an aside to Rosie, "Get out of that one."

The evening went well. Later when they were alone Tom talked about America and had begun to think positively about the possibilities there. Rosie sensed that he was keen to convince her and she so wanted to make it easier for him. Nothing in their marriage so far had shaken her sense of stability and rightness, they had the usual disagreements about minor things. The battle of wills, Tom usurping his authority, she determined to express her opinions. Nothing had truly shaken the foundation on which their marriage stood, surely, she thought, this won't.

She wanted to say wherever you go we go too and that is what she did feel in theory but faced with the reality, it felt too momentous a thought.

She decided before drifting off to sleep that Tom himself was bound to come to the conclusion that America was not truly an option.

T W O

——

en days later Rosie was running late for her art club. The time went far too quickly as it was, and she loved every minute. David, who led the class, preferred everyone to arrive ten minutes early he called it settling down time. Although she taught her own classes, she enjoyed belonging to an art club where she could mix with like-minded people. It was fun experimenting with different mediums and exchanging ideas with other artists.

She was relieved to see that she was not the only late one, she spotted John across the other side of the car park and she ran to catch him up. Breathlessly she called his name as she caught up with him, "Hi there Rosie" he gave her his lopsided smile, "Were you held up by the road works too?"

"Yes and I was running a bit late, I had to drop Ben off at football training, and I couldn't resist staying and watching for a few minutes."

By the time, they had arrived at the art room they had swapped news about their prospective families and entered quietly.

John and Rosie had been attending the same art club for five years and had become very relaxed together, they shared a love of water colour and although had very different styles they valued each others opinion on their work.

Rosie's expertise was flower painting within landscape. Her paintings were very loose and fluid which gave them a romantic look. Her weakness was light or not enough of it in her paintings. David was often advising her to leave more of the canvass bare.

John had decided lately to change style and had started to try pen and ink sketches with colour washes. Rosie thought they were atmospheric and beautiful. He managed to put a lot of light into his paintings, which bought them to life.

Perspective was something that he did not always have right; David had given him many exercises to improve this. He found that using pen and ink had made him more aware of perspective and he felt he had cracked it now.

Both typical artists they were rarely satisfied with their work and valued each other's constructive criticism. Never the less in the bi-annual art shows it was John and Rosie who invariably sold the most.

Today Rosie was thankful for the time to lose herself in her art.

She had met Tom for lunch, something she often did on Tuesdays as she helped voluntarily with art therapy at the local hospice, which was near Tom's office. He had told her he was going to New York for a week to meet the American team; he had seemed excited at the thought.

He had promised her he would not commit himself to anything until he had taken a good look at what the new post would entail.

She would have preferred it if he had said he would not commit himself to anything unless she and the children had agreed to it wholeheartedly. She also knew she would not honestly be able to.

She loved Tom dearly, he was a good husband and father but he was definitely the boss in their marriage. The fact that he was dominant had always felt rather sexy and he made her feel safe.

She had to admit that he rarely made decisions without her agreement, but this felt different; she feared she could be railroaded into moving to New York.

Rosie was well aware of Tom's dislike of change but it seemed that Tom felt he had no choice in the matter, in fact she wondered whether he was being objective about it all.

It had taken a while to persuade Tom to move from Victoria Crescent, he had come up with all sorts of objections. They had lived there since they had married, seventeen years ago, in the centre of Norwich in a small town house. The house had been perfect but grew smaller and smaller as the children grew bigger and bigger.

Tom himself made the decision after someone had scratched his car.

He had stormed in shouting, "That's it we are moving, we have to have a proper drive."

Once they had found Oak Cottage in Little Norseford he had said how glad he was to be away from city streets and traffic noise, surely he loved the cottage as much as she and the children did didn't he?

Rosie sighed deeply, she told herself she was getting things out of perspective, she must try and see the bigger picture and get her priorities right. In fact, she was at risk of becoming an absolute whinging bore to herself never mind anyone else. With a sigh, she decided she must forget her worries and enjoy the painting.

John hearing her sigh looked at Rosie's worried face and said, "Come for a drink after class and talk about it." Rosie smiled and said, "Thanks John I'd like that and I promise not to bore the pants off you."

"Rosie I would be delighted if you bored the pants off me but perhaps a little undignified in the pub."

Rosie laughed, already feeling better.

After lunch with Rosie Tom had hurried back to work, to meet with his line manager. Before that, he needed to make final arrangements with Sally, his personal assistant, for his trip to New York. He needed to make sure Sally knew exactly what she had to do while he was away. Sally was a pretty, pencil slim, brown-haired girl who tried very hard to be super efficient but would sometimes be distracted and forget to pass on messages or miss great chunks out of dictation. Generally, though Tom was pleased with her, she was young and quick to learn and had a determination to climb the corporate ladder.

As Tom entered the office Sally said, "I have four messages for you Mr Holden."

"Thank you Sally, would you bring them in and take some dictation, there will be a lot for you to do while I'm away I'm afraid. Have you booked the flight and a hotel?"

"Yes, ten o clock tomorrow from Heathrow. Lucky you, I wish I was flying off abroad. I have always wanted to go to New York." Tom just smiled, he did not have time for chat today, as it was he would not be getting home until after eight.

He rang home and left a message on the answer phone saying he would bring fish and chips home with him at eight.

He always cooked on Tuesday nights, since Rosie did not arrive home from her art club until after eight. He had decided that tonight he must talk to Rosie and the children about the future. Sally's comment pleased him, hopefully Grace and Ben would feel the same and if the children liked the idea then Rosie would be happier.

Tom felt in a buoyant mood when he went to his meeting, he had to stay focused on the job and surprisingly he found he was beginning to enjoy the thought of a new challenge. Perhaps there was more of his father in him than he had thought.

Whilst everyone was packing up their paints and easels David announced that the Art and Drama Centre was having an open day on the eleventh of July and the art department had been asked to put on an exhibition of work in the main foyer. He wanted each student to submit two pieces of work by 26th June and the department would then choose which pieces to exhibit. Immediately everyone started speaking at once, all trying to decide which pieces to put forward.

"I am ready for that drink Rosie how about you?" said John smiling.

"Absolutely I'll just pop my things in the car and meet you at the main gate, are we drinking at the usual hole?" said Rosie smiling back at him.

John laughed, "How about the new place in Station Street? I have not tried it yet."

"Ok, see you in a minute."

Rosie rang home to leave a message for Tom and Grace answered. "Hi Grace, have you had a good day darling?"

"Hi Mum good and bad I suppose, I handed in my geography course work and Mr Warsop gave me a £10 book token, apparently I was the first to hand it in. The bad thing is I am not speaking to Carl, he is a pig; he asked Kelly out in front of me in study period. I felt so embarrassed I could have died. I hate him and Kelly."

"Oh darling I am so sorry, I am sure you don't hate them you are just feeling very hurt at the moment. If he can do that to you then he was not worth going out with. You are so lovely, someone special will be along soon I am sure. Don't worry about it and well done with the course work you have worked so hard you deserve that. I will add another ten pounds and you will have enough to buy that book on the Impressionists you saw the other day."

"Thanks Mum."

"I am just ringing to say that I won't be back until later as I am going for a drink with John. Could you tell Dad that I won't want any dinner, I will grab a bite to eat at the pub."

"Okay say Hi to him for me and ask how Daniel is and when is he going to notice me?"

Grace had met John and his family several times through the years at the various art shows and had recently taken a liking to John's elder son Daniel.

Rosie laughed, "Okay I will see what I can do."

Well Grace cannot be too heart broken she thought, relieved. The last thing Grace needs is a broken heart whilst taking her GCSEs.

"Alice is dropping Ben home from football practise by the way. I must dash as John is waiting, Bye darling."

Alice was Rosie's closest friend, she made a mental note to organise an evening out with her soon.

Rosie walked quickly; it was her only exercise besides gardening so she walked with determined strides. Although she swam, she enjoyed the steam room, sauna and Jacuzzi too much for it to count as exercise.

Just thinking of going to the gym, which everybody seemed to do these days, was boring. Walking Charlie was much more therapeutic and a wonderful way to start each day. She felt she experienced the seasons more, she often saw foxes and many different birds. The wild flowers too were so abundant now farmers were not spraying the verges.

"You look a lot happier than you did at the beginning of the evening" greeted John.

Rosie smiled, "Painting always de-stresses me. Thank you for asking me for a drink John, I do need someone outside the family to talk to."

"That sounds serious but I am a good listener and I have plenty of time."

Once they had their drinks and found a quiet corner, Rosie

told John all about Tom's redundancy and the offer of a new job in New York.

John asked Rosie if the prospect of living in America was all-bad.

"I have some good American friends and I am sure New York is wonderful to visit but the thought of living there fills me with horror."

"Well perhaps you shouldn't worry until it is a reality."

"Yes you are right I know and worry doesn't help anyone anyway."

"It is early days, it may not happen, Tom may hate America."

"What if he does like it John?"

"If he does like it and if you really don't feel happy about it then surely Tom can't make you go?"

"Do you know of anyone who commutes from here to New York by any chance?" said Rosie ruefully.

John laughed, "Sorry no, how about another orange juice?"

Whilst John went to the bar Rosie looked at the laughing and smiling drinkers around her, perhaps she was being too negative and worrying before she had too, she resolved to be more cheerful and change the subject.

When he returned she cheerily said, "let's not talk any more about me let's talk about the exhibition instead, much more interesting."

They chatted happily about the college exhibition for a while, helping each other decide on which pieces to submit.

At ten Rosie looked at her watch amazed how quickly the time had gone. "I must go John, thank you so much for the drink and chat, it really helps to talk. Oh, by the way how is Daniel? Grace wanted to know."

"He's fine I'll tell him she asked," said John with a wink.

Before they said goodbye John said, "Let me tell you a saying my Grand Mother told me, I have never forgotten it and it always helps. *Don't let one cloud eclipse the sun."*

He said no more just gave her a quick peck on the cheek and left.

Rosie smiled and thought how lucky she was to have him as a friend.

Tom was not at all pleased to find Rosie out when he arrived home with fish and chips and a speech he had been rehearsing all the way home.

"I can't believe she would stay out tonight of all nights, you would think she would want to be here the last night before I go away for a week"

"Does Mum know you are going away tomorrow, she didn't say anything to me about it, and you haven't told me either" said Grace in Rosie's defence.

"I didn't know for sure until this morning, I met Rosie for lunch."

Ben just said, "Yippee more fish and chips for me, I am starving" before tucking in greedily.

Grace laughed, "You are always starving, you eat like horse, and you will get fat."

"I won't get fat I play too much sport to get fat, any way you can talk, you are always eating chocolate bars."

Tom ignored the children's banter and thought for a minute, perhaps he had not mentioned a date at lunch but he had been so preoccupied with everything he could not remember.

"She hardly ever goes for a drink why this evening?"

Grace put her arms on her Dad's shoulders and said

"Its no big deal Dad she'll be back soon."

Tom looked at Grace, her pretty face frowning at him not

understanding why he should be so cross. Tom smiled at her, how wise young people can be.

"You are quite right Grace, she'll be back soon. Let's enjoy these fish and chips while they're still hot."

Ben, seeing his father was now in a better mood said

"Dad do you fancy a game of Canasta, we haven't played for ages, and Mum can join in when she gets home"

Tom who would have preferred to have a quiet read of the paper and then pack for his trip felt duty bound to say yes after his bad tempered start to the evening.

"Okay Ben, but just for half an hour" then added when he really looked at his son.

"You need a shower Ben you are filthy, you should always have a shower after playing football."

Ben made a face and ignored Tom's comment and said, "Are you playing too Gracie?"

Neither Ben nor Tom expected her to say yes, she liked to spend more and more time in her room lately and she often had homework or study to do. She worked hard at school and was normally diligent about homework, unlike Ben, who had to be encouraged, cajoled and finally ordered to do homework.

"Yes count me in, I'll just get us all a drink." The fact was she did not want to be alone this evening as she knew she would only keep thinking of Carl. She would have preferred a long conversation with Jodie; she knew that would not go down well.

Neither Tom nor Ben said anything just raised their eyebrows in surprise at each other. Grace laughed at their surprised faces and felt pleased she had said yes.

When Rosie eventually arrived home at ten thirty, the house was in darkness and everyone appeared to have gone to bed. Strange, Tom was not normally early to bed perhaps he had gone to bed to read. She could not tell from the front of the house whether their bedroom light was on. Their bedroom was at the back of the cottage, it had a lovely view of the garden and then over the trees to the beautiful church spire beyond.

They chose it because of the view; it was one of the largest rooms, it also had character with beautiful beams and the original wooden floor.

Grace had the largest room, which she filled to capacity with all manner of collections. Both Grace and Ben's rooms and her little studio faced the front and had views of the old post office and a row of terraced cottages.

Before she went up she went in to the kitchen to see Charlie and let him out, he was in his basket obviously settled for the night, when she called him he raised one eyebrow then the other and then as she stood with the door open he decided that she obviously meant it and padded outside.

While she was waiting for Charlie she heard a snuffling noise and peering through the gloom she saw a little family of hedgehogs, quickly she put some cat food in a saucer and a bowl of water down for them. With only a slight hesitation the little family trotted over and enjoyed their unexpected feast.

Charlie gave them a wide berth he had picked one up in his mouth once and had obviously not enjoyed the experience.

Having settled Charlie, she was just about to turn off the light when she noticed a note propped up against the jug of flowers on the table and her post, which had not looked interesting enough to open earlier.

The note was from Tom, his writing large and only just legible said

Have gone to bed early as up at 5,
Have to be at Heathrow at 8.

Rosie was shocked; he was going tomorrow, had he told her? Had she not listened, she knew she had been preoccupied just lately and they had not been communicating particularly well.

She could tell from the short and to the point note with no niceties like kisses for instance that he was not happy. She felt guilty for not being here, oh why had she gone for a drink tonight of all nights.

She idly opened the post left on the table for her. Both letters were car insurance advertisements, she was about to throw them in the bin when she spotted the web site address www.affordableinsurance.com. She smiled, it triggered a memory of a particular evening. The children had been away for the weekend staying on the farm with her parents. She and Tom had been out for dinner with friends. They had had classic fm playing in the car on the way home and the presenter was announcing the stations web site www. etc. She had said "everything is www. these days, I don't even know what it stands for"

Tom had replied that it stood for World Wide Web.

After a moment, Rosie said smiling naughtily "Oh no it doesn't it stands for Warm Willing Woman."

Tom had laughed and replied with a wink, "Oh no it doesn't it stands for Wanting Willing Woman."

It had certainly put them in the mood, from the minute they had entered the house they had fallen upon each other and made passionate love.

Those were the days she thought then a small sensation of excitement began to stir within her. She had a quick shower in the downstairs shower room so as not to disturb the children and then naked, tip toed upstairs and quietly opened and closed the bedroom door. Thankfully, her bedside lamp was on as Toms open suitcase was in the middle of the floor. Rosie stifled a giggle as an image of herself naked sprawled over the case with her bottom in the air and a surprised Tom peering at her came to mind. Crossing the room, she slipped in to bed beside her sleeping husband. Gently she wrapped herself around him and whispered in his ear www.

Tom was in that state of half sleep, on hearing Rosie's whispered invitation all thoughts of having a good night sleep ceased to be important.

Groaning gently with arousal he turned towards her, saying nothing, he lifted the sheet from her and looked on that loved familiar body in the soft light of the lamp. Her full breasts still firm despite having breast fed two babies, he ran his hands tenderly over them, circling her erect nipples with his fingers and then with gentle strokes down to the soft mound of her stomach, and then further down until he felt between her open thighs, moist and welcoming. With a feather like touch, he massaged her until Rosie moaned with desire and reached out for him. Joined as one, they moved in rhythm, both knowing how to please the other, until they came together and still entwined fell contentedly asleep.

THREE

om's alarm went at five, groaning he reached to turn it off without opening his eyes. He lay there as usual until the snooze bell rang. He picked up the clock shaped like a tennis ball and with great satisfaction tossed it towards the door. The novelty clock was a Christmas present from the children. He was surprised to hear a yelp as Rosie appeared bearing tea and laughingly said

"You missed."

"Oh sorry I hadn't realised you were up I'm still half asleep. Thank you for getting tea you did not have to darling. Now put that tray down and get in for a last cuddle," said Tom smiling at her.

Rosie did as she was asked "Tom, you say that as if you are going for ever" she cuddled up close. She could not shake off the feeling of foreboding that she had woken up with, and gave an involuntary shudder.

"Are you cold?"

"No I just have a feeling of trepidation Tom, silly I know."

"Rosie, what ever we decide about the US job we'll be together okay? Oh by the way I mentioned to Grace and Ben last night that we might have an opportunity to go to the States."

Shocked Rosie said, "Whatever did they say, and I thought we had agreed not to unsettle them until we were sure that it was a choice we wanted to make."

"Rosie stop worrying, I didn't give them any details; I just wanted to test their reaction."

"And?"

"They were very pleased, excited even." Tom gave her a kiss then went to have a shower and shave, leaving Rosie puzzled.

She suddenly realised what Tom had done, he had mentioned going to the States, not living there. They had probably thought he meant a holiday, she knew that she was bound to get a barrage· of questions.

She got out of bed knowing she wouldn't be able to sleep any more. Looking out of the window, she could see the sun already rising. It was going to be a lovely day. She watched the sunrise; the spire of St Dominic's Church silhouetted against the deep orange sun. The beauty of it moved her to tears. She closed her eyes and prayed, "Dear God help me to accept what ever the decision is with love."

At that moment Tom appeared wrapped in a towel.

Turning to him she chokingly she said, "I love you so much my darling."

Tom was concentrating on getting ready and with just a hint of irritation said

"I know you do and I love you, I must get ready and go Rosie."

Taking a deep breath and putting on a bright smile she said, "Have you got everything you need?" she looked in the case, seeing the shirts she'd ironed yesterday, so glad that she had done it, she had almost put it off until today. On impulse she took the family picture she kept on her dressing table and tucked it under his shirts, it would be a nice surprise for him when he unpacked.

There was a crunching sound of a car driving over the gravelled drive, Rosie peered out of the landing window and saw a black BMW with two people in it, she recognised Paul, Tom's manager, but not the young woman in the front seat who at that moment got out and got into the back. "Tom, your car's here, there are two people in it"

Tom joined her at the window, "Two?" Looking out he saw Paul and with a gasp of surprise he saw his PA Sally. "Why on earth is she coming to the airport?"

"Perhaps she is coming to America with you?"

"Rosie that's Sally my new PA, she can't come I need her at the office, I gave her piles of work to do."

Looking puzzled and annoyed he picked up his briefcase, kissed Rosie and said, "Bye, I'll ring you."

Rosie followed him downstairs and watched him at the open door while he put his case in the boot.

Both Paul and Sally were looking at her, she waved, feeling very glad that her old dressing gown was in the wash and that she had put on her blue silk wrap. Tom, Paul and Sally waved back at her as the car drove away; she stayed watching until they were out of sight.

Rosie looked at her watch, five past six she would have an hour in the garden and then walk Charlie before having breakfast with the children. She began to feel happier as she dressed in her gardening clothes; time in the garden always gave her a feeling of well being.

Growing up on a farm had made her an early bird. Normally she was up with the lark and walking Charlie across the fields.

When the children had gone to school, she would ring her parents, perhaps they would like her to visit for the weekend.

A visit was long overdue and her mother had sounded tired on the phone last week.

Rosie knew she would miss Tom, but she also knew she would value this time without him to catch up with her parents and have some time with Alice, hopefully. They rarely let more than a month go by without having lunch or an evening out together.

Rosie and Alice had been best friends at school and all these years later still were.

At breakfast both Grace and Ben chatted about the promised holiday in America, Tom had given them a tourist guide of New York, which was crammed full of exciting things to do and see.

"Mum did you know that there are seven million people living in New York?" asked Ben

"No Ben I didn't." replied Rosie, silently thinking that soon there may be seven million and four.

"Guess how many rats live there."

"Rats?" echoed Rosie and Grace

"Eighty million." said Ben with great glee, enjoying the look on both his mother and sister's faces.

"Oh goody, goody I can't wait to go there," said Grace sarcastically

"Ben you are making that up, it can't possibly tell you that in the tourist guide," said Rosie.

"No I saw it on Fact File on TV and apparently they run across the roads and can bite your ankles, especially girl's ankles," laughed Ben. At that point, Grace decided enough was enough and bopped Ben on the head with the tourist guide.

A laughing and screaming chase around the house ensued until Rosie called out "You have three minutes left to catch the school bus, and shall we go to Granny and Gramps for the weekend?" Both children said ok but Ben said his with enthusiasm and Grace with a hint of reluctance. Grace had always loved going to stay at the farm until she reached fifteen and then the very things she used to love ceased to amuse. Rosie's old pony Sparky was too old to ride now and Grace had loved riding.

When the children had left for school Rosie made herself a cup of coffee and took it into the study to drink while she made her phone calls to her parents and then Alice.

The phone rang for several seconds before her mother Louise answered it in a breathless and inpatient voice "Home Farm, if you want eggs we don't have any until tomorrow."

"Sorry Mum, have I interrupted you doing something? I can ring back later if you like."

Louise replied, "Oh it's you and what do you mean am I doing something, of course I am doing something, I am always doing something."

"Mum, are you alright?"

There was no answer. Rosie became alarmed.

"Mum?"

"I am just a bit tired, don't worry." This was so unlike her mother who was always cheerily rushing around.

"Mum the children and I will be down on Friday for the weekend, we can help. Please don't worry about making the beds up, we can do them when we get there and I will bring food with me."

"Thank you dear the beds would be a help and a pudding perhaps, as you know we have plenty of meat and veg."

"Okay I'll make your favourite lemon meringue. Mum if there was something wrong you would tell me wouldn't you?" With a sudden thought, she asked "Is Dad okay?"

"He will be pleased to see you. Bye for now."

Before Rosie had said goodbye, her mother had put the phone down. She thought about her parents, both were in their sixties but that was not old these days.

She knew that her brother Mathew had taken on more of the

heavy work on the farm when Dad reached sixty-five, but perhaps Mum and Dad were still doing too much.

She decided to ring Matt that night; she might not get the opportunity to talk to him at the weekend without either Mum or Dad around.

Deciding not to worry about it any more she rang Alice to arrange an evening out in Norwich, which was an equal distance for them both to travel.

Half an hour later, having had an amusing chat about yet another failed matchmaking attempt Alice's work colleagues had set up, they had arranged to meet in their favourite fish restaurant on Thursday evening. It was good to hear Alice laughing again and looking forward to the future.

For the last two years, she had been in state of grief after her husband had announced one day that he no longer loved her and wanted to be free. Rosie and Tom had spent a lot of time helping her to come to terms with it and regain some self-esteem and confidence.

Rosie and Tom were Godparents to Alice's daughter Ruth, who was just three months older than Grace. Grace and Ruth had always been firm friends. In turn, Alice was Godmother to Ben who loved her. Throughout Ben's childhood Alice had been very good at finding the noisiest, messiest or most gruesome presents for Ben. Accompanying these presents would be a beautiful little book of children's prayers or a bible story.

Rosie had asked Alice if Ruth was free for the weekend to come to the farm with them, Ruth loved coming to the farm, she knew that it would cheer Grace up. Ben was always happily amused helping Matt and his Grandfather. This would enable her to spend some valuable uninterrupted time with her Mother.

Rosie then decided she must put the phone on answer phone and spend the rest of the day painting; she had a commission to paint a picture of the village post office as a present for George, the postman who was retiring next month after fifty years.

The building that housed the post office was four hundred years old with a crooked tiled roof and wisteria covering the front. The wisteria had looked beautiful but had finished flowering now. Rosie had taken several photographs of it so that she could paint it in full bloom. She took her stool, easel and paints into her small front garden where she had a perfect view of the post office.

For a short while, she sat looking at the scene in front of her deciding to paint the post office to the side of the picture in order to paint the village sign and the gently rolling hills beyond.

Rosie had often met George walking his spaniel Scamp when she walked Charlie in the afternoon. They would walk and talk together and George, who knew everyone, would entertain her with tales of the village when he was a lad and the antics that some of the villagers had got up to through the years. George was not a gossip though; everyone in the village trusted him. He often did acts of kindnesses for people like collecting pensions or prescriptions, the odd bit of shopping and delivered them with the post.

He noticed when old Mrs Thomas hadn't taken in the milk as usual, getting no response when he had knocked on the door he had gone round to the back of the house to find her on the ground having fallen whilst hanging out her washing. He had called the ambulance and taken in her old Labrador to look after until she was back on her feet again.

George never talked of the things he did for people, he just did them, and if ever asked he would always make light of it and just say in his broad Norfolk accent "Love thy neighbours as thy self."

Rosie was delighted to have been approached by the chairman of the Norseford Village Community group to paint a picture for him. She would have happily done it as a gift but the committee had insisted on paying her £200, which was her usual fee. Over £1000 had been collected from the villagers, the remaining money they were giving in travel vouchers for George and his wife to spend on a holiday.

Rosie painted for four hours, only stopping for a bite to eat. She had first made a simple but precise pencil drawing of the overall composition. Using masking fluid, she had covered all the flowers, the cherry tree, and the village sign. Wetting the paper all over, she painted the sky leaving the white clouds as clear paper. She chose Prussian blue with a touch of alizarin crimson in places to create the darker clouds. While the paper was still wet, she laid a wash of green going from the hill in the background to the foreground covering the entire area of grass and plants.

Working in her usual loose way slowly the picture emerged as she put in definition to the building and the flowers.

Feeling tired Rosie decided she had painted enough for one day, standing back from her painting she looked at it with a critical eye. More definition was needed and people to bring it alive, she would paint George walking Scamp in the distance and she must put his wife Madge talking to someone outside the post office. Rosie would paint her with a cake tin in hand, for Madge was famous for her cakes not only did she always win the prize for the best Victoria sponge at the produce show, she made cakes for anyone she knew who was unwell, grieving or having a bad time for one reason or another.

Thinking about this made Rosie feel hungry, it was definitely time for a cup of tea and if the children had not eaten them all, a chocolate biscuit. Putting her painting things away Rosie heard the phone ringing and the answer phone click on then a voice, which she could not distinguish from upstairs, leaving a message.

Sitting down at the desk in the study with a cup of tea and a couple of malted milk biscuits, all the chocolate ones had gone, she pressed the play button on the phone. There were three messages, one from Tom in a hurried voice saying he was about to go into the departure lounge and that he was not pleased as Sally was coming to New York too and that he was pretty sure that she was having an affair with Paul and he would ring her ASAP. This deeply saddened Rosie as she liked and respected Paul's wife Jane, she and Rosie got on well when they met at the various firm do's.

One from the dental receptionist reminding her of her appointment tomorrow, she hated going to the dentist even though he was very dishy and always spent a long time concentrating on her mouth.

The last call was from John, asking if he could pop round to see her with some of his paintings, he needed her advice and had left his mobile number.

Rosie rang the number and John answered, "Hi, Rosie I wondered if I could pop by this evening if you are free, I can't decide which paintings to choose." Rosie sensed a hint of embarrassment in his voice, "Of course John it will be nice to see you but I am sure that any you put forward will be chosen."

"Thanks Rosie but I would value your opinion, I will bring a bottle of wine." He rang off before she could reply. Bottle of wine? He was obviously planning to stay so not just popping by then. Rosie groaned, she had been looking forward to a quiet night in with the children and watching the film Dumber and Dumber, Ben's choice. It was something she loved to do with them, they took it in turns to choose the film and they always made wonderful fruit filled ice cream smoothies and shared a box of maltesers. She would have to try and politely say that he could not stay long, since he had not mentioned a time. She rang his mobile again only to hear the voice mail; she left a message asking him to come early.

Hearing voices she realised that they must be home.

"Mum!" yelled Ben as he came in the front door.

"Hello Ben." said Rosie as she emerged from the study and seeing David, Ben's friend said, "Hello David, how are you?"

Impatient at these niceties Ben asked "Mum may David stay for dinner because we want to get our armies ready, we are having a battle at Jim's tonight?"

"David is welcome to stay for dinner of course, but I thought we were having a film night tonight." smiling at David, she looked pointedly at Ben. "I can't tonight and Grace is at Beth's," said Ben producing a crumpled note from Grace.

Rosie read the scribbled note.

Going to Beth's to work on dance routines, sorry about film night
Beth's Dad will bring me home
Grace Xxx.

Hiding her disappointment, she loved their evenings together either playing games or watching their favourite films she said "Oh well never mind, I'll make dinner early if you want to be off."

"Mum, I'm starving now; may we have a milkshake with ice cream please?"

"Yes if you want to make it your selves and remember Ben no milkshakes upstairs." Ben grinned remembering the half empty glass full of flies and mould that Rosie had found under his bed along with a plate of half eaten very stale peanut butter sandwiches that had turned blue.

Rosie left them to it and decided to ring Matt, it was always difficult to get hold of him, he either was out on the farm or out with Eve his wife.

They had only been married for a year; Matt had seemed for years not to be interested in girls giving the excuse that he was either too busy or too hard up to take girls out. The truth was he was shy and being quiet by nature had found it difficult to meet girls.

He had been persuaded to join the young farmers club by a friend and hey presto Eve appeared, within a year they had married.

Rosie was in luck; Matt's deep voice answered the phone. "Hello Matt, I am glad I caught you in."

"Hi there Rosie, I hear from Dad that you are coming home for the weekend, so I'll have that little monster of yours under my feet will I?"

Rosie laughed knowing that Matt was very fond of Ben and was secretly pleased that he liked to spend so much time with him. "Matt I am ringing you because I am really worried about Mum, she was just not herself when I rang this morning, she sounded exhausted and sort of despairing."

"There is something wrong, you're right, it's Dad he's slowed down and he's different somehow, and you know Dad, stubborn as a mule, he won't go to the doctor."

"He's been slowing down for a while hasn't he and he is nearly seventy?"

"It's more than that Rosie; he walks differently and is very stiff, you will see for yourself at the weekend."

Worried Rosie suggested, "Perhaps he has had a mild stroke?"

"Maybe, I'll warn you now he's like a bear with a sore head and that's what's getting Mum down. She's trying to do the things he's not doing and is worried sick about him."

"Why on earth hasn't anybody told me?"

"I mentioned it the other day to both of them and Dad denied there was anything wrong and Mum just said that she didn't want to worry you, but she is pleased that you are coming."

"I should try and come more often."

"You come more than enough for me."

Rosie laughed knowing he didn't mean it, "Thanks Matt I love you too, see you at the weekend, bye."

Rosie hoped that she would be able to persuade Dad to go to the doctors; she knew that if anyone could it would be her. Perhaps she would treat her mother out for lunch on Saturday, a break from the farm would do her good.

While she made dinner she wondered what she would take to cheer up her father. She remembered how much he used to enjoy old-fashioned bread pudding, she would make him one and add crystallized ginger the way he liked it best.

Dinner was ready, as she called the boys down the doorbell rang, "Who on earth could that be?"

John stood on the doorstep looking very smart with a bottle of wine in one hand and a bunch of white lilies in the other. Rosie felt aghast, she had forgotten that John was coming and realised how shabby she must look in her old painting jeans and a loose faded cotton top, her hair tied up in a bun. She hadn't realised but she also had a splodge of hookers green on her nose.

"John, my goodness how kind of you, I am sorry I'm not very organised this evening, I have been painting all day and I haven't even changed. Go through to the garden and I'll pour us some wine."

John laughed, "I can see that, don't worry I'll have a wander yonder."

She rushed upstairs to change and then wondered why she was worrying about what she was wearing, it was only John and he normally saw her in her painting gear. Why was he looking so smart and why had he brought her flowers?

Rosie suddenly began to feel awkward, had John misunderstood when she accepted a drink the other night. She knew that John was lonely at times; his wife had tragically died in a car accident three years ago. John knew Tom well and must know that they were happily married. Perhaps after the heart to heart the other night he thought she was unhappy. She suddenly realised that they would be alone in the house. "I am being silly," she told herself but nevertheless decided to stay casual and changed her jeans for a denim skirt and her top for a white t-shirt. She brushed out her hair quickly and deciding against any make up, hurried down stairs.

John was in the kitchen holding an opened bottle of wine and two glasses "Ben showed me where things were and-" suddenly he looked at Rosie and laughed and said "Rosie, you look enchanting."

Rosie thoroughly enjoyed the evening in John's company they chatted about the exhibition, both helping the other to decide on which paintings to submit for selection. Rosie liked John's work and had bought one of his paintings at the last exhibition. John had bought two of hers, one for himself and one for his mother's seventieth birthday present.

Rosie suggested that John should submit one painting of his old style and one of his new, together they agreed on a pen and ink of Cley windmill with the marshes in the foreground and an atmospheric but simple water colour of a huge oak tree in winter silhouetted against a dramatic winter sky.

From Rosie's paintings, they chose again two very different ones, a loose and watery study of Just Joey roses, the coppery co-lour contrasting with the brilliant green of ladies mantle and the other, the view from Rosie and Tom's bedroom of St Dominic's church spire surrounded with trees of different hues. The spire looked golden as it caught the light of the setting sun.

They were satisfied with their choices and decided it was time for another glass of wine. John poured while Rosie found some cashew nuts and crisps. With two teenagers eating everything in the house, Rosie always had to hide a few odds and ends in case unexpected visitors came.

They talked a little about Tom's desire to move to America but Rosie found it too difficult and decided that she might find herself being disloyal to Tom so changed the subject. Instead, she asked John about his childhood and his work with the National Trust. Rosie realised that night that although she had known John for years, she didn't really know much about him at all. The more she knew of him the more she liked him.

It was nearly ten o clock when Ben crashed noisily through the front door making them both jump. Ben appeared in the sitting room bespattered in paint from painting his Warhammer models. Rosie groaning and grinning at the same time said, "I can see you have had a good time Ben."

"I've had a brilliant time Mum and won the battle with my new lizardmen army."

John watched Rosie and Ben together and thought how hard it must be for his children not to have a mother to come home to. He was looking at his watch and thinking he had better go home when Rosie said, "Well it has been lovely to see you John but I think I had better sort out my son and get organised for tomorrow."

While John collected his paintings and prepared to go Rosie called to Ben as he went upstairs "Ben throw your clothes down, they will have to be washed they are covered in paint and your other school trousers are torn at the knees"

"Yeah, yeah I know, sorry Mum. I forgot I have some maths homework to do."

"Well at least you had fun. I will come up and see how you are getting on in a minute, but Ben if you haven't done it in half an hour you will have to leave it as its getting late."

"Mum could you write a note and say I will do it tomorrow?"

"No Ben I won't, I am afraid if you don't do it you will have to take the consequences."

To John she said, "Sorry John I must sound like an awful nag."

Laughing John said, "No it sounds very familiar, and Rosie you said the right thing, as hard as it is to see our children getting into trouble it's the only way they learn to take responsibility for themselves."

"Yes it is one of the hardest things."

"Oh and by the way, Ben is not the only one who gets covered in paint." Grinning at her, he tapped her gently on the nose. Rosie still oblivious just smiled up at him.

John realised how much he liked her looking at him in that way and longed to take her in his arms. The feeling shook him, he must be badly in need of some female company. Perhaps at last he was getting over Jenny's death, he remembered feeling that he would never want anyone else and yet here he was with a very real desire for Rosie. If he was honest with himself, this was a feeling that had been growing for sometime.

Just as John was leaving, Rosie had a sudden thought she would invite John to dinner and ask Alice, "John would you like to come to dinner one evening, I can't tell you a date as I would need to see what Tom is doing."

Blushing John replied with only a slight hesitation, "Well if you are sure Rosie, I would love to come to dinner or we could go out?"

Naively, not realising that she had given John the wrong idea she said, "No John I would like to cook for you, and if I have my way this might be the beginning of something special."

Encouraged, John leant forward, gave her a kiss on the cheek, and was just about to kiss her more thoroughly when a car turned in the drive, it was Grace arriving home.

As the car door opened Rosie said "Hi darling." With the

sound of the car engine and the chatter from Grace, John thought Rosie had said "Bye Darling." John pleased and surprised winked at Rosie and whispered in her ear "I love you calling me darling." and squeezed her hand.

When he saw the look on Rosie's face, he groaned and realised he had been utterly stupid, as if she would call him darling. "I am sorry Rosie." he didn't say any more as Grace gave him a funny, what are you doing here, look as she passed him on the step but brightly said "Hello John." and to Rosie "Hi Mum, I am shattered, we've danced all night!"

Rosie broke into song "I could have danced all night, I could have danced all night and still-"

"Stop, stop my ears can't take any more!" shouted Grace above the singing and they all laughed. When Grace was out of earshot he said "Rosie I have been crass, forgive me it must be the wine and being alone with you and I really-"

"Please John don't say anything you will regret we are good friends and that is very precious to me," then added, "and anyway many people call everyone they meet darling." she smiled at him.

John knew she was kindly trying to dispel the awkwardness "Trust me to pick someone who doesn't."

Seeing John's discomfort she said "John I am very flattered, in fact you have made my day, and if the truth be known I think you are very gorgeous" and then hurriedly in case he got the wrong idea again "Actually just right for a dear friend of mine who I would like to invite with you for dinner."

Recovering, John laughed and replied, "You mean you would like me to come to dinner to be crass to your friend?"

Rosie laughed, "Most definitely."

As Rosie watched John drive away she thought, why is it that sex always gets in the way? She knew that she was drawn to John it was obvious that he liked her in that way although until tonight she hadn't really noticed it.

Was it true that men and women could just be friends?, she hoped so. If she was honest with herself there was a moment this evening, when John had smiled at her and had gently touched her nose, that she had felt a slight frisson of excitement at being touched by him. She pushed the thought away, and mentally ticked herself off.

She wondered if John had been out with anyone since his wife had died, if not then how much he must need some affection and must miss the intimacy of married life.

Of course, romance hardly came into the equation with men or so it seemed. Perhaps she was just being sexist or too harsh on men. She smiled to herself; she liked men and certainly was not one of those women who thought that men were superfluous to life. Over enthusiastic feminists rather frightened her and over the years had done the cause of women's rights no good at all.

After all God created men and women to love one another and to be equal companions.

Thinking of John as she tidied up the sitting room, putting her paintings back in the study and washing up the glasses, she knew with out a shadow of a doubt that if she were single she would happily accept an offer of a relationship with John.

She found herself wondering what sex would be like with him. Ashamed at herself for thinking it, she forced herself to think of Tom. She wondered how much he missed home and the family or was he having such a wonderful time that he had not even thought of them.

Was he having temptations, were there any single women offering him more than a cup of coffee?

Where were these rogue thoughts coming from, she loved

Tom dearly she must keep focused on him. John had obviously unsettled her.

When Rosie went upstairs, she looked in on Grace who noticed immediately the smudge of green on Rosie's nose. Rosie laughed "Oh no, I have spent the whole evening with a green nose!" and she thought to herself with a laugh well it is amazing what effect hookers green can have on the opposite sex.

Ben was fast asleep with his head on his maths book; Rosie looked at her son and as she watched him sleeping an overwhelming feeling of love swept over her. Ben, Grace and Tom were the most important and precious people in her life, far more important than the house or material things.

For the second time that night she felt ashamed of herself, she had not been fair to Tom. What choice did he have? He had to go to America to look at the job there.

The firm would give him a good redundancy package, which would give him time to find another job.

In addition, she would run some painting classes and perhaps even open an art gallery. She could do some more illustrating too; she had done quite a lot before the children were born.

With all this in mind, she began to feel positive about the future.

She was ready for bed when the phone rang. It was Tom sounding as if he was just next door. Knowing very little about technology it always amazed her how she could talk to someone on the other side of the world so clearly, it seemed like magic.

Feeling a rush of pleasure at hearing Tom's voice she said "Hello darling it's so good to hear your voice, how was the journey?" Tom, sounding rather formal, replied "It was fine, sorry I didn't ring when I got here, there was no time, it was all go from the minute we arrived. There was a welcome meeting, then a look round the offices followed by a prolonged lunch meeting."

Rosie puzzled for a moment realised that of course Tom was several hours behind her time. "Oh don't worry I thought you would be resting, you must be exhausted."

Tom replied, "Yes I am exhausted I will be leaving for the hotel soon hopefully."

"I can hear lots of noise and by the sound of your voice there must be other people near?"

"Yes I am standing in a large open plan office; there are probably about twenty people."

Rosie feeling mischievous said, "Do you know Tom I have just come out of the shower and have not a stitch on, what would you like to do with me?" Tom laughed and clearing his throat said in a businesslike voice "Well that is quite interesting give me a moment and I am sure I could come up with something to please you."

Rosie giggled.

Back to his normal voice Tom said "I haven't got long I am afraid Rosie do you want to know how things are progressing here?"

"Well yes it must be interesting but a bit awkward for you too isn't it?"

"Why should it be awkward?"

"Well knowing that you won't want to work there?"

Tom did not reply to that just said, "Mmm, how is everything at home?"

Rosie told Tom of her painting and her conversation with her mother and Matt but for some reason she could not explain, omitted telling him about John's visit.

"Tom, I am going out with Alice tomorrow evening, and then we are going to the farm on Friday straight from school so it might be a good idea to either ring us there or even better give me a number I can contact you on."

Tom hesitated; he thought it might be a bit awkward if Rosie rang him, he did not want to be disturbed if he was in the middle of an important meeting.

Sensing his reluctance, she said, "Tom, just give me a time when we can conveniently contact you, I hardly ever bother you at work, unless it is important, surely there is a number I could ring in an emergency?"

"Sorry Rosie, of course, I just don't know what they have planned here. I will ring you with the number tomorrow." Changing the subject he told her, "They certainly are going out of their way to make me feel welcome and they are all looking forward to meeting you and the children. I have met two other English colleagues and they and their families are enjoying living here and we have already been invited to visit them."

Rosie replied, sounding appalled, "Tom, you promised me that you wouldn't make a decision but it sounds to me as if you have already."

Sounding exasperated Tom said "You are obviously tired darling, I'll ring you tomorrow, you might have found your sense of reason by then, sleep well." He blew her a kiss and was gone.

"Damn, damn, damn!" What was happening to them she felt suddenly so far apart from Tom and not just in miles. Was she being unreasonable? She hated arguing, they rarely did and never did they go to bed without having cleared the air first. Rosie recalled the piece of advice Tom's mother had given them when they had married "Never go to bed on an argument."

Had they argued or had she just been cross? What she did know was that this wretched job was coming between them and causing friction.

Rosie lay in bed worrying about it, tossing and turning she

thought she would not sleep but after an hour, she did, though fitfully.

She had an awful dream of her mother-in-law lying on their bed , which was in the centre of a large busy office, eating her father's bread and butter pudding and shouting at her and Tom, who was wearing a Stetson hat and nothing else saying, "You can't get into bed." over and over again. Had there been anyone to listen he or she would have heard Rosie whimpering in her sleep.

In New York Tom was feeling exasperated with Rosie, she did not seem to want to understand that he had a lot to do and plan.

Tom remembered when Rosie had left university, she had backpacked around Australia and New Zealand and had insisted on doing it alone. After three months apart, he had missed her so much he had flown out to join her. In a restaurant looking out over Sydney harbour he had asked her to marry him. He had hoped she would return to England with him but although she had said yes to his proposal she had continued her trip as planned.

Where had that adventurous girl gone, had she grown staid and middle aged and he had not realised it. To be fair he did not think so, he still found Rosie fun and she loved to travel on holiday to new places every year. Why then was she so averse to this proposed move to America, others managed it.

He was too tired to think anymore about it. He decided to go back to the hotel, he thought longingly of the large comfortable looking bed awaiting him in his hotel room.

An hour later Tom was fast asleep, awaking the next morning disorientated but refreshed.

It was not until coffee break when he suddenly had an idea, perhaps his mother would be able to talk to Rosie. She had moved many times and he did not remember her making too much fuss.

He had no time to worry about it, there was a meeting to attend to and he could see Polly waving and smiling at him and pointing at her watch. Polly, an intelligent, bright blue-eyed shapely blonde had been given the job of showing Tom the ropes; she was doing a splendid job.

He found himself looking forward to her idea of showing him New York at night and wondered what she had planned.

When Tom spoke to his mother Lillian, before going out that evening, he got a very different response to the one he was expecting.

"Tom, I sympathise with your position but have you truly considered how disruptive this move would be for Rosie and your family. You are right we did move but it was only into the forces accommodation, we kept the family home and I knew that eventually we would come home for good. I enjoyed it at first but once you and James were born I found it very difficult."

"We managed Mum and we had several moves, I am proposing one move that's all for heavens sake."

"Tom, there is no need for that tone with me. If this is the way, you are talking to Rosie no wonder she is feeling belligerent about it. Have you considered looking for a post in England, there must be jobs needing your qualifications and experience?"

"Mum you don't understand I have worked with this company all my working life."

"Well perhaps it is time for a change then. You should ring and really talk to Rosie, I mean talk to not at. I love you dearly Tom but you are very like your father when he sets his mind to something, he becomes very single minded."

"Thankyou Mum you have been very helpful." Tom said sarcastically.

"Sarcasm is the lowest form of wit Tom and I am truly sorry

but I can not persuade Rosie. This is something you will have to sort out together and believe me Tom an interfering mother-in-law will not help at all. What I will do though, if you like, is to ring and see how Rosie is and ask her out to lunch, she may want to talk to me about it."

"Okay Mum, thanks I must go now Polly will be waiting in the bar for me."

"Who is Polly?" asked Lillian rather too sharply.

"She's my assistant here and has been a great help. She is showing me New York tonight. Bye Mum I'll see you soon, love to Dad."

Lillian put down the phone and felt a cold chill run through her and said aloud "Oh, dear God, not history repeating itself."

Rosie was trying to decide what to wear for her evening out with Alice, she was always beautifully dressed in interesting clothes and Rosie often felt country cousin like beside her. Rosie favoured the bohemian style, long skirts and loose tops with chunky jewellery.

She decided to look smart tonight and tried on her brown linen trousers "Oh good they fit." she said happily as she had to be in a slimmer phase to wear them. Choosing a white blouse, which had white embroidered detail around the half sleeves and collar. She loved the quirkiness of the hem, which was long one side and short on the other. Adding a colourful bead necklace and earrings, she looked in the mirror, yes that would do. She brushed her hair vigorously and twisted it up on top of her head then fastened it with a wooden clasp.

Just as she was about to leave the phone rang, it was Lillian, which surprised Rosie as her mother-in-law would normally only ring on Sunday evenings.

"Hello Lilly is everything alright?"

"Yes dear everything is fine, I just thought since Tom is away you might like to come out for lunch with me, how about tomorrow, my treat?"

Rosie was touched, she knew how busy her mother-in-law was with her various charitable works and social activities as well as looking after her lovely home and garden which always looked immaculate. In fact, she made Rosie feel tired just thinking how much she crammed into one day. "Lilly I would love that, I have a painting to finish off in the morning so should be able to meet you at one. I will have to rush off after lunch as I have to pack for the weekend and pick the children up from school in order to get to my parents in time to help Mum with dinner."

"Isn't Louise well?"

"Well I just don't know, she certainly isn't herself and Matt says she is exhausted and also worried about Dad who is not himself either. So I am hoping to see what the matter is and also help a bit."

"Is there anything I can do Rosie, have the children for instance?"

"That is very sweet of you Lily but they want to come and I think Mum would be disappointed if they didn't. They will help with some of the chores and my Goddaughter Ruth is coming too, she loves the chickens and is very helpful and I have not seen her for a while either. Actually Lily I have to dash I am meeting Alice in an hour." They agreed to meet in the vegetarian restaurant at one the next day.

When Rosie entered the restaurant she saw Alice sitting in a candle lit alcove, one of the reasons they liked the restaurant was its intimate seating so you could have a good chat without being overheard.

Alice was looking very stylish; Rosie knew that Alice spent a lot of time and effort to look good. She had lost weight since her divorce and now was enjoying the feeling of buying new clothes in a smaller size.

The betrayal of her ex-husband and the consequent divorce had left Alice feeling unattractive and vulnerable. Although she did not realise it, with her deep brown eyes, wide smile with enviously straight white teeth she was very striking. Lately she had grown her chestnut hair from a neat short crop to a French style bob; it looked softer and suited her.

"You look wonderful Alice," said Rosie as she gave her friend a hug.

"So do you, natural and feminine as usual." smiled Alice.

Looking at Alice and thinking of John, Rosie thought yes I think it just might work.

They had a wonderful evening catching up on each other's news. Alice tried to persuade Rosie that she might enjoy New York and Rosie began to feel excited about a holiday there at least but even Alice knew that Rosie was a country girl and could not imagine her living in any city again, certainly not a metropolis like New York.

Rosie had great pleasure in telling Alice that she had a very attractive mystery man lined up for her. Rosie would not tell Alice anything about him but promised to set a date for dinner as soon as possible. She did not want Alice to form an opinion about him before she met him.

On the way home that night Alice felt that perhaps a new chapter in her life was about to start.

FOUR

Tom felt he deserved a good evening out after the difficult time that both his mother and wife had given him. He was convinced he was doing what was right for his family, it astounded him that they should be so obtuse.

He was determined to forget home and really enjoy whatever Polly had organised. He gave himself a last quick look in the mirror and grinning at himself thought that he looked quite good for forty-one.

Having wondered what to wear, he had decided to be smart casual, wearing a light sports jacket with a white shirt and black chinos. He never took a great deal of bother with clothes but he wanted to make a good impression on this trip and like it or not he knew that people noticed what you were wearing.

Rosie was not a great clothes person either, preferring to look individual, fashion rarely came into it. Grace seemed to need the latest fashion, being artistic though like her mother she added her own adornments to personalise them. Ben on the other hand lived in jeans or sports gear.

Thinking of his children he realised with a pang of conscience that he had not spoken to them yet, he would ring in the morning and hopefully, if he timed it right, catch them when they came home from school, the five-hour time difference made it awkward.

Putting his family out of his mind he made his way downstairs to find Polly. She was waiting for him in the main reception lounge looking very pretty in an olive green knee length swirl skirt, a fitted black lace top and black strapped high-heeled shoes. Her only jewellery was a pair of long dangly earrings, which sparkled in the hotel lights.

As Tom walked to greet her he thought how gorgeous she looked dressed for the evening, it took him by surprise he had not really noticed what she looked like particularly or what she had worn at the office.

Polly who was very self-assured had already ordered a bottle of red wine and two glasses. Smiling she greeted Tom with "I hope you are a red wine drinker most Brits seem to be."

Tom slightly taken aback replied, "Hi Polly, yes quite happy, I hope you put it on my bill?"

"Tom the firm pay for this night out after that it is down to you."

"Really? that is a surprise." Tom was relieved and pleased; he had thought that he would be in for a very expensive evening. Settling down on the deliciously squishy leather sofa beside Polly, he cheerfully said, "So tell me Polly what else do we Brits do?"

Polly laughed, "Well let me see, you get up early, eat early, go to bed early, whereas we do the opposite. Which means that you probably won't get to bed tonight until at least three or four in the morning."

Tom knew she was teasing but it was true, he had not been out that late for years. Not wanting to sound too English and middle aged he just smiled and said, "I am game for anything and quite happy to be out past my bedtime."

Smiling Polly asked, "What kind of food do you like Tom? There is every type of restaurant you could think of here."

"I like most food but I am not so keen on hot Indian. I would really like to eat at a good American restaurant as I do know that contrary to most people's idea of American food it isn't all burgers and fast foods."

"You are so right; well in that case we have to go to the Bridge Café, round the corner from here. It is an eighteenth century building and really worth a look, as I'm sure you know we don't have the type of historic buildings you have in England. We could have an entrée there and then go on to the TriBeCa, I like Bubby's it is cosy and they serve good healthy American food."

"TriBeCa, I don't think I have heard of that before."

"It is short for triangle below canal, it is very trendy and has been transformed from a down market wholesale garment district to an up and coming community. There are many chic eateries, galleries and even recording studios. Every Spring there is the TriBeCa Film festival founded as an artists response to the 9/11 terrorist attacks."

"Sounds like a good place to go for the main course but what about dessert?"

Polly laughed and thought for a moment "Well we are spoilt for choice, but I think for a real treat we must go to Gothams in East Village for dessert, to people watch and be seen. After that, I have some great nightspots to show you. How does that sound to you?"

Tom felt a little alarmed by such a frenetic evening ahead, quickly replaced by a sense of adventure. He was in New York with a beautiful young girl about to have a night on the town at the expense of his company, and he was going to make damn sure to savour every minute.

Goodness knows what state he would be in the morning, he could feel that the wine was already going to his head. He certainly needed to eat. Afraid he might get tipsy before the evening started he tucked into the peanuts and olives that had been served with the wine.

"Wow what an itinerary!" as he said this, a peanut stuck in his throat, he coughed and coughed getting redder and redder until he could hardly breathe. Polly was alarmed and gave him a resounding thud on his back, which resulted in him projecting the peanut out of his mouth like a bullet, it landed with a plop into the coffee of an elderly, expensively dressed, lady sitting opposite. This made her jump so much she spilt her hot coffee over her young companion who in turn let out a cry and jumped up knocking the laden tray out of the hands of the passing waiter. Beer, gin and tonics, ice cubes and slices of lemon shot through the air along with various expletives.

Tom was horrified at the farce- like series of disasters he had set off, apologising to everyone in sight he turned to Polly for help, she was doubled over and shaking. Thinking she must be hurt in some way he bent over her in concern but quickly realised that she was helpless with laughter.

For Tom the tensions of the last few days released like a catalyst within him and in moments, he too was laughing uncontrollably.

Unfortunately the elderly lady was not amused and tutting loudly she shook her ample frame like a disgruntled hen and marched out leaving her poor young charge to scurry after her.

Thankfully, at that moment the receptionist came to tell them that a cab was waiting for them.

Once in the yellow cab Polly was just able to tell the driver to go to Bridge Café before dissolving into giggles again. Tom told the driver what had happened, they both chuckled. "It is good to hear people laughing, after September 11th I thought I would never hear laughter again". He said this as he drove near the sight of the former World Trade Centre. This had the effect of sobering them up very quickly. Tom asked whether rebuilding had started yet, knowing that it had not but felt the need to say something positive.

Polly said that work had started on a new subway hub. "Tonight Tom we are going to have a wonderful evening and we will toast all who died that terrible day, I lost someone very precious to me as did almost every one in New York but we just have to carry on, with them in our hearts."

Tom felt moved by her words, took her hand, and gently squeezed it.

They arrived at the Bridge Café, the driver accepting a generous tip said, "Keep smiling and have a great evening."

The charming eighteenth century café had been painted a striking red and outlined in black; to Tom it looked a little incongruous amongst the modern buildings surrounding it. The smells emanating from its open doorway reminded Tom how hungry he was. He made appreciative noises and invited Polly to lead the way.

Inside was a complete surprise, not interestingly old or quaint as the exterior but actually very trendy and obviously popular.

The waiter showed them to one of the two remaining free tables. Polly explained to the waiter that they would be having an entrée only as they were doing a whistle stop tour of New York. Tom asked if there was anything on the menu that he should not miss. "The lobster cakes are exceptionally good sir, and may I suggest that you try one of our speciality beers?"

"Sounds good to me."

"Me too." said Polly and added with a mischievous grin "But please don't bring us any peanuts will you."

During the evening they chatted about everything from work, their childhoods to which books they liked to read.

The atmosphere of New York at night acted like the very best champagne on Tom. He laughed, ate and finally danced until he almost staggered into bed at four-thirty having had the best night out he could remember.

Thankfully, Polly had informed him that he did not need to be in the office until the lunchtime meeting at twelve after having teased him that they had a breakfast meeting at seven. Tom grinning at the thought fell instantly asleep.

Tom in his exhausted and inebriated state was in blissful ignorance of a note that had been pushed under the door. His phone flashed beside the bed indicating a message from reception which he had also failed to notice.

Polly who had booked herself into the hotel too was unable to get to sleep despite being exhausted with throbbing feet from having danced for hours in her high heels. She knew that this evening, which she had not originally thought she would enjoy, had been a turning point for her. She had laughed and laughed, something she had done little of for the past five years. Tom who she had expected to find stuffy and formal had proved to be good company and fun in a gentlemanly way.

She felt as she lay in those wonderfully smooth crisp white sheets in the unfamiliar bed that tonight she would have liked to share it with someone. If Tom had been unmarried, she knew she would have suggested it. It was not like her, she had never had casual sex. At that moment, though she longed to be held passionately. It struck her then that she was at last coming out of her tunnel of grief. It was a heady feeling, almost more intoxicating than the alcohol that she had consumed. As she drifted off to sleep, she forgot for the first time since that fateful day to say "Good night sweetheart." to her lost fiancé.

FIVE

Rosie having left Alice with a light heart made her way to the multi- storey car park, she hated these places after dark. She hurried up the dimly lit concrete steps to the third floor. She was wondering why they were so smelly and gloomy. The walls covered in graffiti and scrawled obscenities. Perhaps she should contact the Council and ask them to pay for an art project. Perhaps even have a group of disaffected youth to help her do some attractive and interesting graffiti.

Just as she reached the final bend of the stairs, a group of four men sitting on the steps surprised her, it was dark and they gave her quite a shock, they were not talking just sitting there. She had to ask them to move as there wasn't room for her to pass. She asked them politely and they looked at each other before one stood up to let her through. She smelt the sickening smell of alcohol and stale cigarette smoke on them as she passed. Without any real reason she felt the hairs on the back of her neck rise, a feeling of vulnerability hit her and she quickened her pace, longing to be in the relative safety of her car.

She heard her own footsteps clicking on the concrete steps but almost immediately, she heard heavier footsteps running up the stairs behind her. She instantly felt fear surge through her, she too started to run, as she knew instinctively that she was in danger. With her heart pounding and her feet tingling with the adrenaline rush she, panicking, looked around for her car, where had she parked it? In the corner behind another larger one she spotted it, she ran although it felt as if her feet were leaden. As she reached her car panting hard, she heard the heavy footsteps behind her. Two men with hooded tops were almost upon her. With shaking hands, she fumbled with the keys, in her panic, not finding the one she needed she silently prayed please God help me.

Just as she found the correct key, they reached her she screamed and as one of the men roughly pushed her out of the way and grabbed her bag and keys she screamed again so loudly that it made her ears ring.

In those terrifying moments, she knew that if she screamed loud enough at least someone might hear her and come to her aid. She thought of her children and Tom as if everything was in slow motion, she saw them vividly, then hearing a voice somewhere in the distance she screamed help again.

As the man with her keys opened her car door, he yelled "Shut that bitch up!" Rosie swung round to face the other younger man who had been nervously pacing around the car looking from side to side. For a split second, they made eye contact.

Savagely kicked in the stomach, bizarrely Rosie's last thought as the pain overwhelmed her and she fell to the ground, was that the young man looked petrified.

Her head hit the cement pillar and everything went hazy then black, she lost consciousness as the car sped away screeching around the multi-storey bends.

Within minutes, a young couple who had heard her screams came running to help. As they ran the boy yelled to his girlfriend, who was struggling to keep up with his athletic pace, to ring 999. "You need an ambulance and police!"

The first person Rosie saw as she struggled to open her eyes through a haze of drugs and pain, was Matt. She weakly smiled at him and winced as a sharp pain shot through her head. "Oh ow what have I done, Matt?"

Matt told her all he knew. "Rosie you have had a nasty crack on the head and have very impressive bruises. You have been in hospital since you were found last night in the multi- storey car park."

Rosie tried to move but ached all over and as she mentally started to take in what Matt had said, she immediately thought of Grace and Ben. Tearfully she cried out "Matt, Grace and Ben are at home they-"

"Hey shh don't worry they are with Alice and Ruth, they are fine." Relieved she drifted back into the haze but not for long as a nurse came to take her observations. Taking her hand gently in hers she started to speak in a broad lilting Irish accent. "So we are awake are we, well don't you worry yourself now, you are going to be fine. You have had a terrible shock so you have."

Responding to that wonderfully reassuring voice Rosie managed to nod and say "Yes we are awake so we are." Matt chuckled and knew that Rosie would be okay, that sense of humour of hers never far away. His eyes filled with tears, brushing them hastily away he realised how worried he had been and how exhausted he felt having sat up watching her all night.

"Well it's good to hear you making a little joke so it is. Do you feel like talking? The police are here to see if you can remember what happened to you now, but don't you worry they can come back later if you can't manage it at all?"

"I don't think I can, not yet." She tried to remember and only a vague image of her car came to mind.

"Oh I quite understand you are not yourself, no it will be quite a while yet, and don't you bother yourself now. I'll tell them to come back tomorrow so I will."

She nodded then asked, "Has my husband been told? He's in America, I want him to come home." she felt panicky again and waves of nausea swept over her as she tried to lift her head.

Matt had not managed to track Tom down but had left an urgent message with Tom's firm and they had said that they would pass on the message to the hotel where Tom was staying in New York. Matt had asked for the name of the hotel but they had said that it would take them a little time to find the details. Matt had asked to speak to either Tom's secretary or manager but the receptionist had said that both Paul and Sally were in New York too.

Matt had lost his temper at that point and shouted at her "What kind of incompetent company has three of its employees in New York and not know where they are staying, for pities sake woman someone must know!"

Affronted at his manner she had icily replied that they were not lost or mysteriously disappeared she just would need some time to find the details, and it was not her fault, she was new.

Matt had apologised and just asked her to do her best.

To Rosie he said, "A message has been left for him Rosie, so I am sure you will hear soon."

"I am going to be sick." raising herself and crying out with the pain as the world swam around her. The nurse quickly supported her and looking at Matt said kindly "Off with you now, go home and get some rest why don't you?"

Matt knew that he had to go and leave her to rest and he felt exhausted and he knew too that he would have to pop in to see his parents they would be worried sick.

He sighed at the thought of them, this would not help his

mother who was finding the farm and his father's deteriorating health hard to cope with. If his father would not go to see a doctor then the doctor will have to come to him.

He knew his father was frightened at what the doctor might find but none of them could carry on ignoring it any longer. He was proving to be a liability on the farm and was becoming more of a hindrance than a help and that upset the both of them.

He decided he would have a couple of hours rest before coping with his parents; he would ask Eve to ring them and tell them not to worry.

Rather than wait until he got home he stopped in the reception to give Eve a ring

"Hello love it's me I am coming home, yes she has come round but very groggy, could you let the folks know? I am too tired to face them, I will go and see them later. Eve could you ring the doctor and ask him to visit Dad? Don't tell Mum otherwise Dad will blame her, you know what he's like at the moment."

"Yes of course Matt, please don't worry just drive home safely."

"I had hoped that Rosie would be able to do something with him this weekend but that is obviously out of the question now."

Matt felt a sudden overwhelming feeling of vulnerability, how much more was there to cope with, he longed to be home and in the arms of his wife. "Eve I love you very much, I am sorry I don't say it enough."

Without waiting for a reply he put the phone down and headed for home.

When Tom awoke it was almost eleven thirty. He jumped out of bed and swiftly remembered the amount of alcohol he had consumed the night before, groaning he drank the bottle of complementary water beside his bed. There was no time to make a coffee in fact there was only just time to get showered and shaved and he would have to take a cab to the office.

At that moment there was a knock on the door. Hastily wrapping a towel around his waist, he opened it to see Polly standing there beautifully groomed and looking as fresh as a daisy. Suddenly aware of what a sight he must look, he put a hand up to smooth his hair. With one hand on the door handle and one hand smoothing his hair, his towel, so hastily wrapped, slid to the floor.

Horrified he grabbed it up. Polly, without a flicker of embarrassment said, "Well I can see you are determined to make a good impression, shall we go?" She smiled as he apologised.

"I am so sorry, you go on Polly I will catch you up WHEN I am dressed". Closing the door he heard her giggling.

Unfortunately, when Tom had opened the door the note on the carpet had blown under the chair, and rushing around he yet again did not notice the phone flashing.

All thoughts of ringing home to speak to the children had gone from his mind. He must not be late for the meeting he wanted to make the right impression. As he was shaving, he thought of Polly and his unplanned exposure and while laughing cut himself with the razor. "Oh great!" he exclaimed as he dabbed at his bleeding chin with the towel.

He arrived at the office and his secretary Sally handed him the agenda for the meeting and said "Hi Tom, they have just started." Tom thought it didn't take her long to catch on to the informal approach, he preferred it, but had been used to her calling him Mr Holden.

"Hello Sally, thankyou."

With some trepidation, he entered the conference room. Everyone looked up, all smiling broadly. Paul was chairing and said, "Don't worry Tom, we haven't started yet, we are hearing from Polly about your night on the town."

"Oh good, we had a fantastic evening." He smiled at Polly feeling relieved, he didn't mind being laughed at and often made jokes at his own expense but he didn't today want to appear as a figure of fun.

Paul formally opened the meeting and started with the first item on the agenda, -security measures.

Tom opened the folder that Sally had given him, there was a handwritten note stuck to the document inside. It read,

This morning started very well
A sight I saw, I will not tell.

He wanted to laugh but dare not. He took a sidelong look at Polly who had a smile on her face but was looking down at her own papers.

The meeting dragged on and Tom tried hard to concentrate but was ravenous. He was very relieved when there was a knock on the door and a girl arrived pushing a trolley laden with bagels, pastries and much needed coffee.

It was not until he was back in his hotel room that he saw the phone, beside his bed, flashing. He pressed the message button, an agitated voice said. "You must ring this number as soon as you can, your family are trying to get hold of you."

He looked at the number; it wasn't a number he recognised. He looked at his watch; it was six fifteen which meant it would be eleven fifteen in England. He wouldn't get them now as they would all be asleep at the farm. He checked the time of the message, with a shock realised it had been left yesterday.

"Oh hell!"

Feeling a pang of concern he thought at least if he rang home and left a message on the home phone they would know he had rung.

On reflection, he thought that it had probably been Rosie ringing to apologise.

He hoped his mother would at least have helped Rosie come to terms with moving; then again, it might be that she was furious with him for asking his mother to put his side of things.

He then remembered that he hadn't left a contact number she must have rung his office. This made him inwardly curse, why on earth hadn't he found a contact number for her. He wanted to speak to her now but knew better than to ring the farm this late.

When he rang to leave a message on the home phone the annoying BT voice said the messaging service was full.

He rang Rosie's mobile, thinking it would cost him a fortune to ring a mobile from the hotel phone. The phone was switched off, as he feared, she invariably forgot to switch it on or if she did remember, she left it on and then she forgot to charge it up. "Damn, damn, damn!"

Rosie and technology did not mix, and he often found this frustrating. He left a short message, knowing that she probably wouldn't hear it. It was a pity that he hadn't Grace's mobile number with him, she would without a doubt listen to her messages even if she had run out of credit and couldn't ring back.

Well he comforted himself with the knowledge that he had tried. He realised that he was hungry; he would have a walk and see what there was in the local district to eat. He knew that there wasn't a great variety of places to eat in the evening in the Financial District. Many cafés closed after business hours or so Polly had told him last night.

Thinking of Polly made him feel lonely, it wasn't as much fun going out alone, he had expected to see something of Paul in the evenings but he was staying in an other hotel- presumably with Sally.

Tom still felt annoyed that Sally had come to New York and wondered how Paul's PA was coping with Sally's work as well as her own. He suspected that she was none too pleased; he must ring her in the morning.

Walking amongst the tall buildings that New York was so famous for Tom realised that looking up he could hardly see the sky, it appeared so far away.

He felt so small as if he were a midget in a giant's world it somehow had a humbling effect on him and he felt deflated. For the first time since he had arrived in New York he found himself wondering what he was doing there.

L illian sat in the restaurant window so she could see Rosie arrive and watch people as they walked by. She enjoyed people watching, she particularly enjoyed looking at the different fashions and guessing the occupations of the people wearing them.

She was a little early and had already ordered a sparkling elderflower juice with lemon, no ice. When it came the glass was filled with ice. She didn't like to complain but thought, "Why do restaurants put so much ice in their drinks these days? Perhaps it is a cost cutting exercise, the more ice the less drink."

She was fed up with cost cutting exercises. She had heard it all morning, never before had she heard so many excuses from local firms. She was trying to organise a charity auction for the hospice funds and it seemed that everyone was having a cost cutting exercise.

Just thinking about it made her feel miserable, perhaps she was turning into a grumpy old woman, she did not want to be one of those people who were continually saying things are not what they used to be.

Rosie had promised her two paintings for the auction, she

must remember to ask her about it and perhaps some of her students would oblige.

Having finished her drink quickly before the ice dissolved Lily glanced at her watch, it was five past one, why is it that time went so slowly when you are waiting for someone and so quickly when you are with them. She hoped Rosie would be on time today as she only had an hour and a half to spare.

She read the menu all through and then read it again and chose what she would order. She toyed with the idea of ordering for both of them, knowing that Rosie liked most things.

Rosie had taught Tom to be more adventurous with food. He had been a fussy eater as a child and always skinny; it probably had something to do with her cooking which she never had liked doing. On the other hand Rosie was very creative with food not only was it always delicious but beautifully presented with decorative flowers or creatively cut fruits and vegetables.

Lillian thought of her husband Henry, who had a soft spot for Rosie, perhaps if she had been a better cook he would not have had such a roving eye. She knew that wasn't the case, he was more discerning than that.

She hated the ridiculous saying that the best way to a man's heart was through his stomach, revolting thought; she let out an involuntary laugh.

Where was Rosie? Lillian thought when she looked at her watch and found it was half past one. She had not expected Rosie to be exactly on time since Rosie was rarely punctual but never late enough to worry.

She decided to ring her at home, in case she had forgotten or was absorbed in her painting. She was probably very distracted with worrying about Tom's work and her parents.

Using her new mobile phone, which Ben had taught her to use, she rang their number. There was no answer, she tried to leave a message but the tape must have been nearly full as it stopped half way through, she had only managed to say "Hello Rosie I am sit-" not much of a message, short and almost to the point.

Sighing, she decided to order lunch, she had fancied nut loaf but decided against it as one of her fillings had fallen out so she would have to have some more dental work done. She had just been to the dentist and hygienist and that had cost her a fortune. She would have the stuffed mushrooms instead.

She tried to catch the eye of the waiter. She tried a slight lift of her head and a smile when he appeared to be looking in her direction, no joy. She then tried a little wave, still no joy. By this time feeling exasperated she said "Excuse me." when he came near, ignored again she thought "What is the matter with the man is he blind and deaf?"

Invisible, that is what she was, long in the tooth and invisible. She remembered her sister Margaret, who was eight years older than she was, lamenting one day that no one seemed to notice her any more and treated her as if she was incapable.

To her shame Lillian had secretly thought that if Margaret dressed a little more smartly and wore her hair more fashionably then people would notice her.

She suddenly had a thought, I will just get up and leave, I am obviously not worth noticing so perhaps they may notice me if they think I am leaving without paying for my drink. That is exactly what she did, not hurriedly just calmly and quietly, smiling to all around as she went.

Once out on the pavement she glanced through the window into the restaurant. She saw the waiter looking very alert suddenly, seeing her through the window he raised his hand as if to stop her.

She too raised her hand and waved to him smiling, feeling the most delicious and wicked sense of justice.

Now she was turning into a batty old woman behaving very badly she laughed at the thought, well at least she was not turning into one of those ladies who sported a blue rinsed perm and non-iron crimplene dresses.

Just as she was deciding what she should do now her mobile phone rang and vibrated in her pocket, it made her jump, expecting it to be Rosie she answered it with "Hello where are you? I feel as if I have been stood up"

"Lily it's me." replied Henry

"Oh what's the matter Henry? You sound odd and you never ring me on my mobile."

"I have just had a call from Grace."

Lillian giggled it sounded like a fall from grace "So have I" she replied and giggled again.

Ignoring her Henry continued, "Darling listen, she remembered too late that you were meant to be meeting Rosie for lunch."

"Where is Rosie then?"

"In hospital."

Horrified she shouted "In Hospital! Henry for goodness sake tell me what has happened."

"Don't worry she is alright."

"Alright, how can she be alright you have just told me she is in hospital."

Henry had an annoying habit of talking to a mobile as if you could not have a proper conversation.

"She has been attacked and had her car stolen."

"Oh how utterly dreadful! Poor Rosie, I'll go to the hospital straightaway. meet me there Henry."

She switched off the phone before hearing his reply, and then she hurried to her car. Henry would come to the hospital she

knew that without a doubt because he would know that she needed him.

She loved him, from the moment she had seen him playing tennis all those years ago to now and she knew she always would.

She was over the pain of his past indiscretions and the past is
where she firmly left them.

Lillian had always been faithful to Henry but once when she
had grown tired and jaded, fed up with suspicions of another
little fling, she had gone away for two weeks to stay with a friend
in Cornwall. He had not known where she was and to this day,
she had not told him. By way of explanation, she had left a note
saying;

*Henry, I am going away for a while to come to terms with the
pain of betrayal*

I need to trust you and I need you to trust me.

*I will be staying with someone who will show me love and un-
derstanding.*

Your wife, Lily

Lillian had never seriously contemplated leaving Henry but
she had grown bitter and not very pleasant to live with. Everything changed the day he had asked her for forgiveness.

She remembered it vividly, though it was ten years ago, she
had been in hospital recovering from a lumpectomy for suspected
breast cancer.

Henry, seeing Lillian so pale and vulnerable had felt a wave of
protectiveness and was suddenly terrified that he might lose her.

He had gently sat on the bed and had taken her hand in his
and with eyes brimming with tears he had told her that she was
beautiful and that he loved her more than he could say, he then
asked her for forgiveness.

Looking at him, she had seen true remorse and love in his eyes and had said to him "You are my love, my only love and I forgive you."

He had shown nothing but love and devotion ever since and they had grown to deeply love each other.

Tom was surprised when he returned to the Hotel, having caught a cab to Central Park where he had enjoyed a free concert while eating a bagel and doughnuts, to see Polly who was sitting in the lounge facing the door waiting for him. With a worried look on her face she came hurrying to meet him, "Thank God you are back Tom, everyone has been trying to get hold of you."

Puzzled he said, "Who is everyone?"

"Your family Tom, come and sit down and I'll tell you."

Suddenly afraid he said, "I don't want to sit down, what has happened Polly, tell me please?"

"Your wife is in hospital, she has been hurt by a car thief."

"Oh hell no, I must get to her, please don't tell me she has she been run over?" Tom was ashen and walking hurriedly to the reception, he would have to get a flight tonight.

Hurrying beside him, she said, "No Tom, apparently the thief hit her. She isn't badly hurt but she has concussion."

Tom was impatiently glaring at the receptionist who was on the phone.

"Tom, I have booked you a flight, we need to leave in half an hour. I will drive you to the airport."

Tom looked down at Polly, her earnest worried face peering up at him "Thank you Polly, you have been amazing. I must go and pack, are you sure you want to drive to the airport, it is getting late, and I could call a cab?"

"Certainly not Tom I will drive you and then wait with you until you go through." and then looking at him with affection she said, "It is the least I can do after all you have done for me."

Tom knew instinctively that Polly felt something for him, he had seen it in her eyes the night before, but what had he done for her? He could think of nothing.

"What do you mean Polly? I haven't done anything for you."

"Tom last night you set me free, free from a pain I thought I would always bear. You made me laugh more than I have done in five years and you made me feel more than just grief." and she hesitated and then added, "You made me feel desire."

Tom, aware that he had to pack and then check out knew that he did not really have time for a meaningful conversation. Listening to Polly, he also knew he must take time to respond. He owed her that.

"Polly, I am so glad and so sad for you too. Who did you lose?"

My fiancé Jake, he was an emergency worker and when the WTC collapsed he was buried underneath the rubble."

Tom took her in his arms and gave her a hug and then putting her away from him said, "Polly, I had a wonderful evening last night too, one I will always treasure. I wish that I-"

Smiling at him, she interrupted and said, "Tom you go and pack while I settle your account and check out for you, it is nearly time to go."

As Tom hastily threw everything in his suitcase he thought of his feelings for Polly, he had so enjoyed being with her and felt genuinely pleased that he had been an unwitting instrument in her recovery but thinking of Rosie hurt and lying in hospital made every other thing or anybody else seem unimportant. Guiltily he remembered thinking earlier that he would have liked to be with Polly this evening, what might have happened if they had spent the evening together he would never know.

He hurried downstairs and went to the reception to hand in

his key card noticing for the first time a cabinet, with jewellery displayed, on the wall.

"Thankyou Mr Holden, Miss Chilters asked me to tell you that she has just gone to fetch the car."

"Thankyou, I would like you to leave a message for me at Norwich City hospital in England. It is urgent I need my wife to know that I am on my way to her. I have jotted down the details here, would you be able to do this for me do you think?" As he said this, a lump came into his throat and he swallowed trying to stop the emotion from spilling over.

"Yes of course Mr Holden straight away," sensing his distress she added, "I am sure all will be well try not to worry."

Tom felt touched by her kind words of comfort.

Then looking at the jewellery cabinet more closely he made up his mind to buy something to take home for Rosie but all he could see was a mass of sparkle, feeling too agitated to look properly he said to the receptionist.

"Can you tell me, which piece of jewellery in the cabinet do you like best?"

Taken aback the receptionist looked in the cabinet, and with only a slight hesitation said, "Well I like the dragonfly brooch and the silver poppy necklace best I think, but everything in the cabinet is beautiful. They are all made by a local silversmith."

Rosie loved dragonflies, she often pointed them out to him flying around their garden admiring the beautiful iridescent blue of their wings.

A poppy for remembrance it was perfect for Polly. He felt a sudden emotional feeling of thankfulness, what a wonderful co-incidence. To the receptionist he said, "Thank you a great choice, I will have them both but quickly please."

Wrapping up the gifts the receptionist thought that Tom was the perfect man, he hadn't even asked the price, just bought them. Being inquisitive she asked. "Are these for your wife?"

"One is for my wife, the other for someone who needs a special thank you."

She smiled and with a sigh said, "Oh I wish my husband bought me jewellery, I am afraid he isn't the romantic type."

Smiling back Tom gave her his visa card for payment and impulsively said, "Could you charge for three pieces and keep your third favourite piece for yourself."

Shocked and embarrassed she replied, "Oh Mr Holden, I couldn't possibly and you don't know how much they are."

Reading the receptionist's name on her lapel, he said, "Do you know Cheryl when your wife could have been killed but is alive and you have met a wonderful person you may never see again money is not important."

Seeing her hesitate not knowing whether she should accept or not he leant over and took the first piece out of the cabinet and said "This is the one for you" it was a silver butterfly. "There just right, life is too short to hesitate."

Cheryl took it out and pinned it to her jacket and with tears in her eyes said "Thank you so much, I love it." then leaning forward gave Tom a kiss on his cheek.

At that moment Polly appeared. Quickly Tom took the two little jewellery boxes putting one in his pocket and one in his suitcase.

"Goodbye Mr Holden, have a safe journey and I will make that call for you now."

"Goodbye Cheryl and thankyou," smiling at her and picking up his briefcase and suitcase he went to join Polly.

"I am glad you are ready, we should make it to JFK with time to spare if the traffic isn't too bad. Have you managed to ring home Tom?"

"Cheryl the receptionist is doing it for me I gave her all the details, I just want to get to the airport and on to that plane. Polly at times like this I wish I could just say beam me up Scotty and within seconds find myself transported to where I want to be."

"I know Tom; I fear the journey will seem awfully long," she laughed and added, "You will feel as if you are trekking through the universe."

The journey to JFK took an hour and they chatted about sights they saw on the way and a little about work, both of them avoiding anything too personal. When they arrived Polly was about to turn into the car park when Tom stopped her. "Polly, would you just pull over into the lay-by please." Glancing at him, she did as he had asked and enquired, "Are you alright Tom?"

He didn't reply to her question as he didn't think he was alright, he just said "I hope you won't be hurt if I ask you not to come in with me but say our goodbyes here, I hate goodbyes and the airports are always so difficult because they just prolong the agony."

Choked, Polly said a tearful "Okay." She did not know why she felt so bereft at the thought of saying goodbye.

"Is it goodbye Tom, aren't you coming back?"

"Polly I just don't know but everything is upside down at the moment and I can't make a decision right now. What I do know is that in such a short time I feel as if you have become special and I have a feeling, a deep feeling of sadness, if this is goodbye."

With a sudden realisation, he understood what he had just said and why he had said it, he would not be coming to America to work.

Polly rested her head on his shoulder not trusting herself to speak.

Tom took the little box out of his pocket and handed it to her. She looked up at him and saw him smiling down at her. As she lifted the lid he saw a dragonfly glinting in the light of the car. Before he could say anything Polly exclaimed in delight "Oh Tom how did you know I was passionate about dragonflies, I have loved them since I was a girl, I will treasure it always."

Tom could only marvel at his luck, bent to kiss her, and said, "I think it must have been meant for you Polly."

"Tom, I have something for you too but please don't open it until you take off and look out of the window, promise me." She handed him a slim flat parcel and he took it, slipping it into the side pocket of his briefcase.

"I promise Polly," kissing her again, he got out of the car and retrieved his suitcase from the boot.

Polly got out too and came round the car to where Tom was standing miserably not wanting to go and yet desperate to leave and be on his way. She reached up and gave Tom a fleeting kiss barely touching his lips "A dragonfly kiss." She said nothing more but got in the car and watched Tom as he walked towards the terminal. He turned once and waved. Neither had said goodbye.

When Tom was sitting in the plane beside the window, he took the parcel that Polly had given him and true to his word, he did not open it until the plane had left the runway. He removed the outer wrapping of the parcel and with delight found inside an enlarged copy of the photograph of Brooklyn Bridge that she had taken on their night out. It was a stunning photo; the bridge had been lit up dramatically against the night sky. It would be a special memento of their time together.

Tom remembered that it was on the bridge she had said that she had felt so happy and thanked him for a wonderful evening. He looked out of the window and there it was beneath him lit up and in miniature amongst a million other lights of Brooklyn, it was a marvellous sight and one he knew he would never forget.

SEVEN

Cheryl had taken a while to compose the sort of message that she thought she would like to receive if she was in hospital miles away from her husband. Being starved of romance herself, she poured great sentiment into the message.

Once she was happy with her chosen words, she had rung the hospital.

It was only after hearing the English nurse's response to the message that she wondered whether she had been too romantic. Cross with herself she remembered too late the famous British reserve, but glancing at the brooch Tom had given her, she comforted herself with the thought that there are exceptions.

Rosie felt a huge sense of relief on receiving the news, through the bathroom door, that at last they had reached Tom and that he had sent a special message. She had been in the bath when it had arrived and so the nurse had kindly written it down for her.

Feeling refreshed and with her bruises soothed by the warm water she sat on her bed, leaving the curtains pulled around her, and in the relative privacy picked up the note, she read it presuming that these had been Tom's very words.

My darling precious wife, I am coming home to you as fast as I can, every minute I am away from you is agony. I never want to be so far away from you again.

I have a very special present for you, a treasure for my treasure.

I love you with all my heart, keep safe until I am there to take care of you and envelop you in my arms.

Rosie could hardly believe it, she blushed, just thinking about the nurse who had received it and giggled at the thought. Then she felt tears pricking her eyes, it seemed sad that it should take a disaster to make Tom realise how much he loved her and use words that he had never felt moved to use before.

She thought, this has obviously made Tom decide to turn down the American post, why else would he say that he wouldn't ever want to be so far away again.

A feeling of relief swept over her, they would not have to face the huge upheaval.

Her emotions seemed so heightened now, everything so vivid she knew that it was a result of having a terrifying experience and the relief of surviving it, perhaps it was her bruised mind getting things into proportion.

Trying to calm herself by taking deep breaths, as the victim support worker advised her, she at last gained control.

Rosie had said that she was ready to speak to the Police today, if Tom could be here with her she knew that she would cope with it better.

She silently prayed for his safe return.

The curtains pushed quietly aside by Doctor Philips who stood there smiling down at her. When she looked up at him he saw tears in her eyes, he wondered whether the hospital Chaplain had visited Rosie yet.

He said with uncharacteristic jollity, "Well Rosie how are you feeling today?"

Rosie lay back on her pillows; they were hard, unlike the soft and welcoming feather pillows at home. They made her feel hot because of the plastic covers beneath the pillowcases. She was cross with herself for feeling so weak and tearful, she had thought of herself as strong and capable not silly and pathetic.

Unable to hold back the tears she told him she was feeling ridiculously tearful and that it was very unlike her.

Drawing up the chair beside the bed Dr. Philips sat down and passing her a tissue from the box on her bedside table said, "Well it's very reassuring to hear that you are normal, you have experienced shock and trauma, and you must give yourself time. I have come to give you your test results and perhaps no one has told you how severe concussion can affect you and shock too for that matter."

Rosie looked at the kind elderly doctor and felt instantly reassured.

Wiping her eyes and blowing her nose she smiled weakly at him and replied, "I have had a victim support worker who has helped and my husband is coming soon, and I am sure once I am home I will feel better."

Dr. Philips nodded and opening the file of her hospital notes proceeded to tell her the x-ray results. "You have had a very nasty blow to the head and sustained a fractured skull which has caused bruising to the brain tissue beneath. I hear that you are still experiencing headaches and nausea?"

Rosie answered, "Yes I seem to have a dull headache and sometimes shooting pains if I move quickly also nausea most of the time, oh and also a continuous buzzing in my ears."

"Ah well that would be tinnitus which can be caused by head

injury. That may well only be temporary but I'll get our ENT chap to have a look at you. Are you experiencing any dizziness?"

"Yes I did feel dizzy after my bath just now," replied Rosie feeling a little sheepish as she had been told not to have a bath without the help of a nurse but she had just wanted to have some privacy and she hadn't wanted to be a nuisance when the nurses seemed rushed off their feet.

"Aha and what about your memory, do you remember much about the incident?" asked Dr. Philips as he wrote.

"Well it is becoming clearer, I am being questioned by the police today so I am hoping that details will return but it all seems very hazy at the moment."

Dr. Philips rose from the chair and again smiling at her said "Rosie, sometimes the exact details never return whether there is a head injury or not, shock can give people amnesia, a mental defence. In my mind, it can be an advantage. Who wants to remember a difficult event? You may experience flashbacks in the future."

Rosie nodded as Dr. Philips continued, "In the light of what you have told me I think it would be advisable for you to have a CT scan which will tell us if there has been any bleeding, this is nothing for you to worry about it is just a precaution. You say your husband is back in England, that is good, and what about your children, have they visited you yet?"

"No, Sister thought it wasn't very wise," at the mention of her children tears came again "Oh I am sorry, how stupid."

Dr. Philips patted her hand and said, "Well a visit from them, in my opinion, is the best thing possible for you and for them, I will personally get the wheels in motion."

Gratefully she smiled at him "Thank you so much."

"Rest now if you can, I know it isn't easy in a busy ward" he waved as he went, leaving the curtains around her.

Dr. Philips asked the Sister on duty to organise a visit from

Rosie's children, the hospital Chaplain and to book a CT scan immediately. Looking at the pretty, efficient nurse in front of him and seeing the ring on her finger he asked her if she had children.

Surprised at his question she replied "No Dr. Philips not yet but I am planning to one day."

"Well, Sister take it from me they are expensive and a pain in the proverbial at times but no loving parent wants to be away from the little devils for long. Children are more resilient then you might imagine and very often wise, caring and believe me Sister the best thing to bring a smile to a traumatised mother."

Smiling broadly, he then strode away; realising as his bleeper went that he was late yet again for his outpatient's clinic.

Rosie tried to rest and free her mind from anxiety.

The kind victim support worker had helped her to come to terms with her ordeal but it was the concerns for her family too that made her feel so helpless.

Her parents had been expecting her this weekend, she had hoped to help, and now she had only added to her mother's distress. Even knowing that it had not been her fault, she still felt guilty at all the extra work and worry she was causing everyone.

Matt had been a great support and had thankfully organised a doctor to visit Dad. Matt had suggested that it was time to ignore Dad's insistence that he was fine, as he obviously was not.

She had gratefully left him to do what he had felt right.

The weird thing was she felt somehow detached from it all as if she was in another world. She had to drag herself back into the world she was supposed to be in and away from the fog that was continually trying to engulf her.

She looked around her, mentally taking note of every detail of her surroundings. The curtains, still pulled, obscured her view of the patient to her side but allowed one of the patients in the two beds opposite her. One, who had been admitted early that morning, looked grey, pinched, and periodically moaned in pain. The other a very old lady called Maud, who every now and then would cry in a frail voice, "Help, help me!"

Rosie several times had rung the alarm bell for her but had been told not to do so as Maud was very confused. She cried out again while Rosie watched her, in response Rosie called over, "Don't worry Maud, someone will be here in a minute."

On the table over the foot of her bed were the beautiful white roses that Tom's parents had left for her with a card propped up against the vase.

Rosie leant forward and picked up the card to read it again, she had glanced at it previously but her eyes had seen things through a mist and she could not remember what it had said.

Lillian had written it, she recognised the slightly spidery handwriting, and the familiarity of it was somehow comforting.

Darling Rosie,
So sorry that you have had such a wretched experience, rest and get better soon. Please do not worry everything and everyone is fine, we will look after things until you are able.
All our love, Lillian and Henry

Rosie had been having an x-ray when they had visited yesterday and they thoughtfully had not waited to tire her further. She felt grateful to them, as she hadn't felt like talking much yesterday.

Matt had told her Alice had sweetly taken the children to stay with her and she was sure both Grace and Ben would have been happy with that. Alice had rung the ward to send love from them all and said that all was ok and again not to worry.

Rosie said to herself I must not worry I must trust and then a sudden thought came to her. "What about Charlie and Sammy?" Rosie felt panic rise in her again, no one had mentioned the animals.

Rosie pushed her call button and when a nurse popped her head around the curtains, she told her of her concern for the animals.

Just as the nurse was about to answer, John arrived bearing a bottle of grape juice, a bunch of freesias and a box of Belgian chocolates. "I didn't know what to bring you but as the reverse of stressed is desserts I thought that some chocolate indulgence might be welcome." Rosie was delighted to see him and gave him as broad a smile as she could muster.

"To answer your question, I am looking after Charlie and the lady at the post office is looking after Sammy."

The nurse smiling was relieved, she was far too busy to chase up carers for animals. Briskly she said, "All is well then, I will open the curtains fully so that you don't feel cut off from everyone else." She proceded to do that and Rosie was glad, perhaps seeing others and watching the comings and goings of the busy ward might help her ground herself in reality.

"John, all these gifts thank you so much. How on earth did you know I was here?"

"I called round and found your parents-in-law, watering the pots in the garden, and they told me what had happened to you. I offered to take Charlie, it will be fun to have him taking me for walks." John smiled at Rosie but was horrified to see how bruised her face was and the left side of her head shaved revealing a neat row of stitches in her scalp.

Rosie laughed and winced at the same time "Thank you John, he does love his walks and his tummy rubbed."

"And what about you Rosie?" said John in a concerned tone.

"Well I am not sure that I'm up to a tummy rub at the moment," replied Rosie finding humour from somewhere.

"It is good to see the thugs didn't take your sense of humour as well as the car."

Rosie smiled "I feel very odd actually, as if I am not really here but I am nowhere else either. The police are coming later today to take a statement and I am not sure what I can remember, it is all a bit hazy. I am hoping Tom arrives in time to be with me, he sent a message and is on his way."

"I expect the shock has made you forget, perhaps in time you will remember more detail. Though it might be better for you not to remember everything, after all it must have been terrifying."

"I think you are right but I feel I ought to try so that the police have a better chance of finding the culprits, I would hate to think of them doing this to others." As she said this Rosie yawned, and John seeing it decided he must leave her to rest.

"Rosie you are tired I am leaving you so that you can rest, it is the best way to recover. I have picked up your paintings and will submit them for you on Tuesday. Take care and see you soon."

He bent down and gently kissed her on the good side of her head. Rosie did not ask him to stay any longer, he was right she did feel dreadfully tired and ached all over. She just said, "Thank you John, you are a dear friend."

Maud called again, "Help, someone help me!"

John looked over to her concerned and Rosie told him about her. She then had an idea "John it is so kind of you to bring me all these things but would you mind if we gave the flowers to Maud, she hasn't any and I would still be able to see them from here."

"Of course not, I will ask someone to put them in a vase for her. I will go now and leave you to rest."

With that, he smiled and gave a small wave as he went. Rosie closed her eyes and despite all the noise of the ward fell sound asleep.

Matt had played down the extent of Rosie's ordeal to his parents and hoped that by the time they saw her she would look less bruised and battered. He walked into the old welcoming farmhouse kitchen to see how his father had coped with the doctor and to have his usual tea and cake with them.

He had never known a time when his mother had not had cake ready on the table for tea and today was no exception. Sometimes she bought one from the Women's Institute stall at the market if she had been too busy to make one. She always had to have some cake in the house for, "The hard working men."

Matt was relieved to see his mother looking happier, in fact she was humming while she put the old kettle on the Aga.

"The doctors' visit went well I assume Mum?"

Louise turned to smile at her son "Thank you Matt, yes it did thank heavens. He is referring him to a specialist but he suspects it may be Parkinson's disease."

Shocked Matt replied, "That isn't good surely?"

"Well no of course not but at least the doctor has seen him and has started some medication, your Dad seemed relieved to at last talk about it and admits that there is something wrong. Matt he has been very difficult lately, as you know."

"Where is he now, he must be feeling shattered at the idea of Parkinson's?"

"He has gone for a walk, you know he always does when he has something to think about, he will be in the top meadow I expect."

Matt got up from his chair to go and find him "Sit down Matt, your Dad needs to have some time to himself to think things through and you haven't started your tea."

Matt was puzzled at his mothers attitude "You seem very calm about it Mum, you seem cheerful even."

Louise came and sat down at the table opposite Matt and with a big sigh said,

"Matt, I know now your Dad thought he had a brain tumour and so did I, he wouldn't talk about it and made me promise not to tell anyone. I can't tell you what it has been like, it has been a nightmare."

"Yes I know Mum I have watched you, and Dad has been like a bear with a sore head and frankly more of a menace on the farm than a help. How do you know it is Parkinson's? I don't know anything about it."

"The doctor has told us a bit about Parkinson's but until it is confirmed we can't be sure. Some of the symptoms he described are just like the ones your Dad has been experiencing. If it is that then we know what we have to cope with. It won't be easy Matt and one thing is for certain you are going to need some more help on the farm."

Louise looked at the tired face of her son, put out her hand, and covered his. "It has been a strain on you too, I know that, I am so sorry, I should have gone to the Doctor." She smiled at Matt who sat quietly thinking.

Louise marvelled at how different Matt was from Rosie, Matt so quiet and Rosie so talkative and then with a feeling of horror and shame suddenly realised that she had not rung the hospital to ask about Rosie.

"Matt I must ring the hospital, I know you said it is nothing to worry about but I must find out what is happening. I just wish I could go and see her, perhaps they are allowing visitors now?" She got up to go to the phone. Matt stood up and putting both hands on her shoulders steered her back to her chair and said, "Mum, I have got to tell you something before you ring the hospital."

"You are worrying me now Matt, what is it, what has happened?"

"Mum I told you that Rosie had a slight accident with the car, well there is a bit more to it than that."

"Oh heavens! Matt what is it?"

"Rosie was attacked by car thieves, she was knocked to the ground and we think she must have hit her head when she fell. They took her car and left her there, thankfully she was found quickly and taken to hospital."

Louise was horrified, and crossly said "Oh my poor girl, why didn't you tell me Matt, why keep things from me? I am not a complete fool!"

Defensively Matt replied "Mum you had enough on your plate coping with Dad's illness, to be honest I thought you were heading for some kind of breakdown. I am not the only one who has been worried you know. Rosie has been worried about you too. One of the reasons she was coming this weekend was to help you with the house and to try to sort Dad out. I just thought you could do without more stress."

"Well I can tell you it is very insulting to be protected from things as if I were a child or senile."

"Ok sorry Mum but I can only do what feels right."

"I know, I am grateful for your concern but I have coped with quite a lot in my life so try not to keep things from me." She patted his hand "Now I do want to see her, could you go and see your Dad and tell him, he might want to come too." Sighing deeply, she added, "They say things come in threes, what ever will happen next?"

"Do you want Dad now or shall I just tell him about it?"

"I want to go as soon as possible or perhaps I had better ring Tom and ask if he and the children are visiting."

"Tom isn't home from the States yet, it has been difficult tracking him down."

Horrified, Louise said, "What about the children? Who's looking after them?!"

"Alice has Grace and Ben, I thought that was best and she offered to have them until Tom came home. Eve will be home, she will give you Alice's number if you want to ring the children, and

Eve would take you to the hospital too I expect. She mentioned that she would be going into the hospital with some odds and ends that Rosie will need." Before Louise could respond, Matt added hastily with a wink and a grin.

"I do know you are perfectly able to drive yourself of course."

Louise laughed, "Absolutely right but if Eve has the time I would be pleased to be taken and it will be good to see her. I have to admit I am tired, tired of being afraid." She gave Matt a smile and went to ring Eve.

Matt found his father, not in the top meadow as expected but to his surprise in the paddock with the ponies Mischief and the new young foal Whisper.

Matt leant on the gate for a moment and watched his father stroking Whisper; he could see that he was talking to her.

Matt had been looking forward to Grace and Ben coming this weekend since Whisper was a surprise for them. Mischief was getting too old to be ridden. Matt had bought Whisper at an auction a month ago.

He hoped that one day soon, he and Eve would have children and Whisper would be just the right size for youngsters to learn to ride.

He hadn't discussed buying another pony with his parents as it had been a vague thought and ultimately an impulse buy. His father Norman had been furious and insisted that he would have nothing to do with the pony.

Matt knew that his father had been increasingly resentful of the decisions that Matt made for the farm since he had taken over the main responsibility of managing it. He had made every effort to run things by him and valued his father's knowledge and experience but just lately Norman had become intolerant of any of Matt's ideas.

Matt saw his father gently handling the foal, giving it a thorough check whilst quietly murmuring to keep her calm.

Looking across the meadow Matt watched the tall willows rustling in the breeze and beyond them to the cows contentedly grazing in the pasture. He felt a sense of peace, this was where he belonged.

Matt had studied business and management at college and had toyed with the idea of going into retail of farm machinery. When he had left college, like Rosie, he had travelled around the world for a year. On his return home he had fully intended to tell his parents that he didn't want to be a farmer, but the feeling of relief and pleasure he got when he saw the farm took him completely by surprise and made him realise that farming was for him after all.

Norman spotted Matt and called over to him, "Come and hold her for me while I check her feet."

Grinning Matt happily obliged, without saying a word he dutifully held her whilst Norman with a shaky hand lifted each hoof in turn.

"Well Dad what do you think of her?"

"She'll do."

Norman gave her a final pat and then turning to Matt he said, "I expect your Mum has told you what the doctor said?" Not giving Matt time to respond he went on to say, "Well we are going to have to take on full-time help Matt so you had better look around and see who's willing, young Sam perhaps. Mind you I am not about to give up lending a hand, it might be shaky but apparently I not going to push up the daisies quite yet."

Matt laughed, "I am glad to hear it Dad!"

Without preamble, Matt said, "Rosie is in hospital, she didn't have a minor car accident Dad, she was hit by car thieves who stole her car."

"Dear God, whatever next?! Does your mother know?"

"Yes, she's preparing to go to the hospital now."

Despite his slowing gait, Norman was indoors within minutes. He agitatedly called Louise, who was upstairs changing, to hurry up.

Ten minutes later Matt watched Eve and his parents drive out of the farm gate, he fervently prayed that they would find Rosie in a better state than he had left her.

When Tom breathlessly arrived on the ward having run from the car park and up the stairs, he asked at the nurse's station where Rosie was. He assumed that she must be in a single room as he had peered in to all four of the four-bedded rooms and not been able to find her.

The nurse showed him the way; he was very shocked when he realised that he had simply not recognised her, Rosie was asleep and had therefore not seen him.

He stood looking down at her battered face and felt a rush of protectiveness; he was wondering whether he should wake her when, sensing his presence, she woke.

Through gentle hugs and tears, he learnt the details of her ordeal. When she had told him all that she could remember and still holding his hand tightly she thanked him for his message and told him how much his words had meant to her.

"It made so much difference Tom," and smiling, painfully reached out for the note on her bedside table.

Seeing her wince, Tom anxiously said, "My poor darling, are you in a lot of pain? Shouldn't you have pain relief, I'll call a nurse?"

"Tom, it's ok, I am having pain relief, and if you had a peek under this glamorous hospital nightie you will see that I have just had a round with Frank Bruno."

Passing the note to Tom, she smiled up at him and said, "I

want to hear you read this to me." She lay back on the pillows to listen.

Taking the note Tom started to read the message to her.

"My darling precious wife, I am coming home to you as fast as I can, every minute I am away from you-" and then he let out a roar of laughter and turning to Rosie to share the joke he said "I should have told-" then saw the look on her face, a look of questioning hurt.

"You didn't send that message did you Tom and if you didn't, who did?"

Tom read the whole note before answering and trying not to laugh he defensively said, "Rosie I just wanted to get home to you as fast as I could, I am sorry." Then unable to stop himself, he laughed again. "It was the hotel receptionist, surely you didn't think-"

Rosie interrupted, "Yes Tom I did, I was surprised because you aren't normally romantic but," and through tears she said, "I thought this had made you realise." She could not go on; she just closed her eyes whilst tears trickled down her cheeks.

Upset Tom took her hand, which lay limply in his "You can't doubt that I love you Rosie, please don't cry. I am so sorry you couldn't get hold of me. You know that I would have been here sooner if I had known."

Rosie smiled a weak smile "Yes I know Tom and I have to admit it did make me giggle at the thought of the nurse receiving it."

Suddenly he remembered the present and reaching in his pocket, he said glancing at the note, "I have a treasure for my treasure."

Rosie opened her eyes and saw Tom holding out a green velvet box, his dark brown eyes willing her to like it. He remembered Polly opening the box and revealing the dragonfly, he had been so pleased that she had been delighted with it but at this moment wished there was a dragonfly in this one too.

Rosie took the box and opened it, knowing that she should look delighted with what ever was inside, and seeing the silver poppy glittering at her, smiled with genuine pleasure. "Tom it is beautiful, thankyou for remembering how special poppies are to me, how clever of you."

Tom smiled back, relieved but also desperately trying to remember why poppies were so special to her. He would have to ask Grace, she would know.

"I am so glad you like it darling."

At that moment, Christine, Rosie's chief nurse for that day came to take her observations. Seeing Tom, she laughingly said, "You must be the romantic everyone is talking about, do you have any single brothers by any chance?"

Tom looking suitably embarrassed replied, "I do actually but I am afraid he is a biologist and buries himself in his laboratory."

"Ooh! I like a bit of human biology myself!" This made both Rosie and Tom laugh.

Tom was touched that Rosie hadn't felt the need to disillusion her and decided to be honest "I am afraid I have a confession to make I actually had quite a bit of help in writing that message, in fact the receptionist at my hotel sent it on my behalf."

Rosie took Tom's hand and said "Sorry, you can tell everyone from me that he is a perfectly normal unromantic male but he did bring me home a beautiful necklace, here have a look."

Christine opened the box and said, "It is very lovely; I still think I would like to meet your brother."

"Tell Christine why poppies are so special to us, Tom." Rosie was beginning to have some fun at Tom's expense, she had noticed his expression when she had said how clever he was at remembering, it was obvious that he hadn't a clue.

Tom did not have to think of an answer, because at that moment Sister Edwards came to say that there were two police constables waiting to speak with Rosie.

Tom stood up, stretched and said, "I will go then Rosie and I'll be back as soon as I can."

Rosie looked alarmed, "Tom please stay, I could do with some moral support."

"Rosie, I won't be much use will I, I feel exhausted, I'll have to have a sleep or I'll be asking you to move over. I have also been in these same clothes for more hours than I care to think, they will be walking off on their own." He laughed not realising how vulnerable she was feeling.

Rosie did not trust herself to reply but could see that he did look tired and she had to admit that he certainly needed a shower.

"I will go home and check on everything, have a sleep and a shower and the next time I will see you I'll be clean and better company."

She didn't want to be selfish and was aware that the officers were waiting for her. "Ok Tom I know you must be jet lagged I'll see you later."

Tom hoped that she did not mean for him to come back again today, the thought of driving back into Norwich was not something that he relished. He cheerily said, "You might look pretty beaten up but you are alive to tell the tale Rosie, that is all that matters. You are probably tired too perhaps it would be better if I collected the children later then we can all come in together tomorrow."

Rosie looked at Tom and thought tiredly, he has no idea, no real understanding. Fed up with feeling so sorry for herself, she thought, he is right, she was alive to tell the tale if only she could remember it. "Go then Tom but ring the children first, they may want to stay with Alice until tomorrow. " and turning away from him she called out to the Sister who was just leaving the ward that she was ready to speak to the police.

Then turning back to Tom, she said "Thank you for coming all this way as soon as you heard and thank you for the necklace." She heard herself and through the fog that was her mind, she sounded so formal but Tom did not appear to notice.

He bent down to kiss her, squeezed her hand and said quietly "Be brave." and then he went.

Rosie saw the police officers walking towards her, one tall giant of a man and one slim young police officer, both were smiling at her as they approached. Their smiles gave her courage. She took a deep breath and said to herself, as a shooting pain shot through her head and a wave of nausea engulfed her, I can handle this.

EIGHT

Feeling dog tired, Tom was glad to get away, he hated hospitals and seeing Rosie so bruised and in pain made him feel helpless and guilty somehow.

He strode down the endless corridors to the exit, stopping occasionally to look more closely at some of the paintings that adorned the walls. The paintings were by local artists and were for sale, some for quite large sums of money.

Tom thought, not for the first time, that he wished Rosie had more business sense. Her paintings were just as good as these were; she could make a lot more money if she tried. Tom decided that once she was home and back to painting, he would suggest a business plan, perhaps her work would sell well in the States.

Just thinking of the States made him think of Polly and he smiled to himself, how kind and caring she had been and admirably efficient. With a shock of realisation, he knew at that moment that he had begun to fall in love with her. Was it love or was it purely that he was flattered by her obvious attraction to him.

For the first time in his marriage, he felt uncertain about his commitment to Rosie, no wonder he felt guilty.

There in the hospital corridor he stood still while people passed by, some looking at him oddly. He didn't recognise himself and thought, "What kind of man thinks of another woman while his wife is in hospital?"

He had always thought of himself as a decent, honest, faithful sort of guy and had even taken pride in the fact that he had never felt tempted by another woman, admired but not tempted. It was only a few days ago, that he had righteously condemned Paul for having an affair with Sally.

He had a sudden longing to speak to the children, they would ground him surely. He would ring them as soon as he got home; he began to stride towards the exit.

As he reached the reception area, he saw Louise, Norman and Eve at the desk, presumably asking the way to Rosie's ward.

Tom hesitated for a moment then quickly turned into the small shop, he didn't feel up to having a chat with his in-laws but Eve had seen him look in their direction and had noticed him hesitate.

Eve was about to call after him but he dived into the shop as if he was trying to avoid them.

Eve did not say anything to Louise or Norman but was surprised and then intuitively felt that Tom must be guilty of something to behave like that.

Then as soon as she had thought it, she dismissed the idea as fanciful; Tom had always been friendly and welcoming. He probably hadn't seen them at all.

Grace, Ben and Ruth were having fun designing cards for Rosie; they were sitting at Alice's dining table which was strewn with an assortment of coloured card, paints, pens of varying colours and a wonderful mix of craft materials.

Ben knew that both Grace and Ruth, being artistic, would

produce cards which were beautiful and creative; he would have to think of something different. Having perused Alice's and Ruth's bookshelves he had found a book of fascinating facts and a book of jokes, he would make a card to amuse his mother.

Yesterday Ben had been upset and angry at not being allowed to visit his mother, in his imagination her injuries had grown to be so horrific that he had convinced himself she would die or at the very least be severely disabled. He also felt angry with Dad, where was he, and why hadn't he rung to speak to them?

He had looked up head injury in Alice's family health book and read that in severe cases of head injury amnesia may occur, in some cases brain damage and paralysis. That was bad enough but it went on to say that, more severe head injuries may result in unconsciousness, which then may be fatal.

It was not until Ben had knocked on Alice's bedroom door at three in the morning, and asked her in a broken voice whether if Mum died would it be an accident or murder, that Alice realised how worried he must be.

She had jumped out of bed and putting her arm around Ben had tried to reassure him as best she could. Guiltily she realised in trying to protect him she had in fact inadvertently worried him more. Grace had, though upset, taken the news quite calmly and had been very practical in dealing with it. Ben had been very quiet and so Alice had decided just to answer any questions if or when he asked.

Alice had merely told them that Rosie had suffered a head injury and concussion because of a fall, when the thieves stole her car.

She did not know all the details yet herself but Matt had told her that Rosie was alert but feeling shocked and dizzy. Cross with herself she felt responsible for not telling Ben this and consequently allowing Ben to fret without putting him fully in the picture.

Alice took Ben into the kitchen and while she made him a

mug of hot chocolate, apologised and told him all she knew. Alice answered all the questions that Ben put to her as best she could, and then suggested that they ring the hospital in the morning to find out more. Ben went back to bed a little reassured, but he still felt angry with his father for being away and out of touch.

The next morning Alice suggested they ring the ward after breakfast so that they could speak to the day staff. They had been eating breakfast when the phone went, there were smiles all round when they received the news that they could visit later that afternoon.

It was Ruth's idea that they make cards for Rosie and they had all agreed that it was a good one. Smiling at Alice, Ben had stated that his card was going to be far superior to the girls', which had caused guffaws and much friendly banter between them all.

Alice left them to it and decided to pop out and buy Rosie something special.

Perhaps a new nightdress, something pretty and alluring. Perfume would be helpful in masking the hospital smells but she could not remember which one was Rosie's favourite.

Alice then remembered Rosie treating her to a pamper day when she had been at rock bottom after her divorce. She would return the favour, flowers for now and the promise of a wonderful relaxing and pampering day to look forward to.

After half an hour of browsing Alice found a beautiful hand painted card in Exquisite, her favourite craft shop, and then hurried to the florist and bought a cream orchid already in a small vase with water.

Pleased with her purchases she wondered what she should make for dinner, thankfully neither Grace nor Ben were fussy eaters but neither had eaten much yesterday and she wanted to tempt them with something delicious. Then with sudden inspiration decided on a picnic, fresh air should give them an appetite and Ruth loved evening picnics in the park. Warming to the idea she decided they should take some games too, perhaps the tennis rackets and she must buy a football, Ben would like that and they could all have fun mucking about with it.

She knew she must also prepare the children for their visit to Rosie, Matt had said that she was very bruised and had some of her head shaved.

It was an hour and a half before she had completed her shopping and laden with good things for the picnic returned home. When she stepped in the door, she heard shouts of laughter and a perceptible change in atmosphere than the one she had left.

Grace, smiling came to greet her and offered to help bring in the shopping and in an excited voice said without taking a breath, "Uncle Matt rang; Mum's doctor has said that we can visit Mum for a short while. Grandpa and Granny are visiting this afternoon so we will have to go in this evening. Dad has rung too, he is home and has been to see Mum and she is going to be ok but looks the pits all black and blue. Alice if it is ok with you he would like to take us all out for lunch tomorrow and then we will go and visit Mum in hospital again with him before going home, which means we can stay here tonight."

Laughing Alice replied, "Goodness Grace could you say that again a little more slowly and with a full stop or two!"

When all the shopping was unpacked, Alice went into her elegant dining room to see a chaos of paper and art materials. They showed her the cards they had made.

Grace had cut hers into an irregular shape and had made a collage of blues and greens with various pieces of silk and wool. Inside she had simply put *with love from me to you.*

Ruth had painted hers, a tree with an owl sitting on the branch and a caption above saying "Toooo wwish you wwell."

Ben's was huge and covered in splatters of paint of different colours and written on top in large capitals BE PREPARED TO

LAUGH AND BE AMAZED, inside were various facts and jokes.

Alice thought that they were all good in their own very individual way.

"They are wonderful, just like you, all very different and all very special I am sure Rosie will love them." she smiled at their pleased faces.

"I have bought a picnic which we can have for lunch instead of the dinner I had planned. Lets take it to the park so we can play football and tennis then later we will go and visit Rosie."

When the Police had eventually left, Rosie she was exhausted but relieved the ordeal was over, they had been very kind and patient with her.

Prompted to remember in various ways she found the reliving of it painful.

They had said that the couple who had rung for the emergency services had caught a glimpse of the culprits and had thought they had heard one of them call the other Carl, but Rosie had not been able to confirm that.

She was worried that her house keys were on the same key ring as her car keys and could not remember whether there was anything in the car with her address on it, she did not think so but could not be sure.

Rosie did not care about the car, to her it was just a means of transport, however she remembered the picture she had painted and had just picked up from the framers had been in the boot, she had painted it for Matt's birthday.

Eve had asked her to do it; it was a painting of the view behind the farmhouse. It was a lovely far-reaching view of the meadows and gentle hills and you could just see the roof of Matt and Eve's cottage nestling amongst the trees. She had painted the old gate in the foreground and had spent ages painting in fine detail the lichen on the old wood. Matt's birthday was next week; there was no way that she would be able to paint another in time.

Again, tears threatened, she took a deep breath. Her mouth felt dry and her tongue furred, she drank a little water but her throat constricted with emotion and she had difficulty swallowing. To make matters worse she badly needed the loo and it was so damned painful to walk.

She was just struggling out of bed to go to the bathroom when her parents and Eve arrived, she could see them coming along the corridor towards her.

Their dear familiar faces bought instant comfort and she felt a sense of relief that both her parents had felt well enough to visit.

She could see, in just the few moments it took for them to reach her, that her father was walking not in his old usual stride but with an awkward gait, slightly stooped and with slow short steps. It saddened her to watch him, then she saw him spot her. A look of anguish came over his face and she moved towards him and accepted a warm embrace. Although painful, she loved the comfort of those familiar strong arms gently holding her. "Oh Rosie, my little Rosie what have they done to you?"

Trying to relieve his concern, she jokingly said, "Well I never was very good at contact sports."

Her mother with tears in her eyes took her hand and went to lead her back to bed and at the same time murmuring words of comfort as if she was a small child again.

"Mum it is so good to see you, please don't worry, I am going to be ok. I am so glad you came; I was just going to the bathroom and could do with an arm to lean on. The nurses are so busy I don't like to call them."

Eve said, "I will take her Louise, it has been a long walk from the car park, you sit down." She could see that it had been quite an effort for Norman to walk so far without support. She remembered that just recently she had been surprised to see him using a stick to walk about the farm, it was a rough stick he had made himself from a branch from an oak tree, perhaps he hadn't thought to bring it.

Rosie gratefully took Eve's arm, and when they were out of her Parents' hearing said, "Do I look so awful Eve? I haven't seen myself yet. Dad's face looked shocked when he saw me and I felt shocked when I saw him, he looks so much older away from the farm."

Eve considered for a moment, she too had been surprised at the extent of Rosie's bruises and the swollen eye and ear and the shaved head and stitches had given her a battered look. "Well I have seen you look better but I am sure in a few days everything will calm down, is it very painful?"

"At times when I have to move but they are giving me painkillers which help. It isn't the pain but the weird way I feel which has been hard and I feel so tired." They had reached the bathroom door and Rosie asked if Eve would wait outside for her and assured Eve that she would call if she needed help.

While Rosie was in the bathroom the hospital Chaplain arrived to see her, on seeing that her bed was empty and that visitors were obviously waiting for her he simply handed a card to Norman and asked them to tell Rosie that he would visit again soon.

The card had the list of Chapel services and warmly welcomed all to them.

Underneath the list of times were the words;

I sought the Lord and he heard me,
Yea he delivered me out of all my fear. Psalm 34

Norman read the text and quietly said to Louise, "I have been afraid."

And Louise took Norman's hand and said "I know love, me too."

Her parents and Eve had stayed until supper had arrived, it had been wonderful to see them but she felt tired at the effort of communication.

After her supper of soup and ice cream, Rosie painfully had changed into the clean nightdress. Brushed what hair she could and put on a little splash of the perfume that Eve had thoughtfully brought in for her.

Eve had put in a sponge bag various cosmetic items and a small lipstick mirror. It was with this she had nervously looked at herself, it was not her at all but some grotesque half-woman half-monster, no wonder both Dad and Tom had recoiled at the sight of her. One side of her face was looking normal, the other was so swollen her eye was hiding behind a misshapen mass of various shades of purple flesh.

When the nurse came to her to ask if she needed any pain relief she gratefully accepted, she wished that there were something she could take that would switch off the continuous ringing in her ears.

Thankfully when Eve arrived with Grace and Ben the throbbing in her head had eased, when she saw their anxious faces peering round the ward door she was able to wave without wincing and smiled as broadly as she could.

Eve let Grace and Ben have a few minutes alone with Rosie before she and Ruth joined them.

After an initial hesitation, the children were asking all sorts of questions and gave Rosie the cards that they had made.

When Eve and Ruth joined them, Rosie was reading the jokes and facts from Ben's card.

A man came rushing into the Doctors surgery shouting
"Doctor, Doctor I think I am shrinking!"
The doctor, who was busy, replied,
"Well you will just have to be a little patient."

Laughing Rosie said, "Very appropriate."
Ben pleased that he had made Rosie laugh said proudly, "Now for some facts."

Did you know that a giant Atlantic squid has eyes almost twice as large as footballs; it is the largest eye of any animal that has ever lived?

"Ugh!" said Grace, making Ben grin.
Rosie continued to read.

Did you know that an adult heart pumps 13,000 litres of blood per day and beats 40 million beats a year?

"Goodness Ben that makes me feel tired just thinking about it, where did you find these facts?"
"From my fantastic brain of course."
"Oh ha ha." Grace pulled a funny face at Ben, "That is the best joke ever!"
Rosie smiled at their familiar banter and said, "Why don't you read them to me, Ben?" Glancing up she saw Eve and Ruth, "Hang on, here are Eve and Ruth you can read them to us all." She smiled at Ben, "It was a wonderful idea Ben, and Grace your card is quite lovely, I will treasure them both."
She held both her arms wide, "Bundle of love."

Both children moved close and awkwardly with the bed in the way accepted willingly her embrace. It felt so good to have them in her arms.

Releasing them, she felt very touched by how gently they had held her and the effort that they had both put into the cards for her. She longed to be home with them and with Tom and to feel normal again. "I love you so much, Dr. Philips was right you are the very best medicine."

They grinned as both Eve and Ruth gave Rosie a gentle kiss. "Are you feeling a bit better?" asked Ruth handing her the card she had made.

"Just seeing you all makes me feel better." smiled Rosie

Ben announced, "I am going to read you one joke now and you can read the others after we have gone Mum, so you can amuse yourself when you feel bored."

Eve handed Rosie her orchid and card said "Open this when we have gone too, it is something to look forward to Rosie when you are up and about."

Rosie felt emotion welling up again, rapidly replaced with laughter when she heard the beginning of Ben's joke.

"Doctor, doctor I am obsessed with breasts."

Grace giving Ben a friendly thump said, "Ben you can't!"

At that moment, a large rose shrub appeared carried by a grinning Tom. He had decided to visit again after all, home had felt very empty without his family.

"Hi there, I called into the garden centre to buy some flowers and spotted this, it is called Paws and comes with love from Charlie and Sammy, and I will take it home with me and plant it if you tell me where."

"Oh Tom, thank you darling, what a lovely idea, I wish you could take me home with you and plant me in my bed."

Tom putting down the rose smiled and hugged Grace and Ben "Am I glad to see you, it is strange at home without you all."

He smiled at Rosie then turned to Alice and said "Thank you for coming to the rescue Alice, I hope you will join us for Sunday lunch tomorrow?"

"We would love to Tom and now I think it is time for us to go and leave you two together."

They all turned to say goodbye to Rosie and saw that she had closed her eyes and drifted off to sleep. Quietly they left.

When Rosie next opened her eyes Tom was there sitting in the chair beside her, reading a newspaper. She reached out and touched his arm, he looked at her, smiled and said "Hello sleepy head."

"Have they all gone Tom? I just closed my eyes for a moment."

"Rosie, you have been asleep for nearly an hour, it is almost eight," seeing Rosie's eyes fill with tears he took her hand and gently said, "They will be here again tomorrow, you have had a lot of visitors today and it has probably all been too much for you."

Rosie nodded, it had been exhausting, "I am not sleeping very well, and for the last two nights they have checked my observations every hour but they are doing it less frequently today."

Tom smiled at her and said, "Well you will soon be home; they won't keep you here any longer than necessary. The police called just after I arrived back, they have been observing the house in case we had any unwanted visitors. They advised us to change the locks, which I have organised for tomorrow."

"Oh Tom, do you think they will be able to trace the house? I don't think that we had anything in the car to identify us, I did have a painting in the boot with my name on but that is all, as far as I can remember."

"You only sign your pictures with Rosie H anyway don't you?"

"Well I actually signed this one Posy, it was for Matt and he always called me that. My full name might have been on the wrapping, I had just picked it up from the framers. I feel really fed up about it; Eve had commissioned it for Matt's birthday next week."

Tom dismissively said, "Rosie, that is the least of our worries, you can paint another one. That reminds me, there are paintings on the walls of the hospital corridors, all as good as yours and for sale for quite large amounts of money. You should churn out a few more and sell them in a variety of places." He refrained from saying anymore when he saw the look on Rosie's face.

Rosie felt angry and hurt at his lack of understanding and icily replied "If I were a factory then perhaps I would churn out more as you so kindly put it, I do have other things to do other than painting. In fact I would love to do more but taking my art classes, running the house, caring for our two children and the garden does take up quite a lot of time."

Tom felt annoyed with himself for mentioning it, "I am sorry, I know you have a lot to do. I just thought that you might consider being a little more business like."

A sudden thought hit her, "Oh Tom, would you inform my students that I won't be there? There is a list of names and numbers on the pin board in the study, all you have to do is ring the first number, and they will ring each other. The hospice too, they will wonder where I am."

"What do you want me to say?"

"Well you can suggest that the classes meet back in September, we normally break for the summer any way but to the hospice say I will be back after our holiday Tom."

"I will do that tomorrow morning." Reaching for her hand, he gave it a gentle squeeze, "You must be exhausted I will leave you now and I do love you, you know that surely?"

Rosie replied, "I know Tom, I am irrationally emotional and

I feel so odd, weirdly unconnected." Looking up at him she said, "Kiss me Tom, let me feel your lips on mine."

So Tom kissed her just as the bell rang for the end of visiting.

NINE

Rosie was determined to go to the Art exhibition; she had been discharged from hospital two weeks ago and was thoroughly bored with being quiet and resting. She was still experiencing headaches and occasion dizzy spells but not as often and they were lessening in severity.

Everyone had been so kind, friends and neighbours had rallied round to help. She had felt so blessed by the love they had shown her.

As she walked around the garden, a sense of wellbeing crept over her, and made her tingle. The sun was shining and the garden was full of summer flowers, she bent to pick a sprig of rosemary, and crushing it between her fingers she smelt the wonderful pungent perfume and felt truly happy. Today she was going to break out, rebel, leave the restraints of pain and fatigue behind her. The feeling was quite heady like the effect of a good champagne. "Yes, on with my life!" she shouted, much to the surprise of Charlie who was padding around the garden with her. He looked at her quizzically, and responded with a sharp bark. Sammy who had been lying languidly soaking up the sun meowed in protest. Rosie laughed, "It is all right you two, I am just returning to normal, whatever that is."

Today was the first day of the exhibition and she had decided to go, she knew that she would not have coped with the crowds of the preview day.

John had offered to go with her yesterday but she had declined, thankfully, as he had rung last night and told her the college was packed. The local press had been there and TV cameras had been filming for Look East. John urged her to go though as he said that there were some good pieces of sculpture as well as pieces of art from other art classes well worth seeing.

She decided she would call a taxi and hang the expense; she was still without a car and could not face the bus journey.

An hour later feeling as if she had emerged from an enforced hibernation, she was walking through the doors of the community arts centre, aware of the familiar sense of excitement and expectation she always felt at art shows and live theatre.

To her shock and delight, on the poster advertising the show was a print of one of the paintings she had submitted, the one with the view from her bedroom window.

She began to wander around the exhibits taking time to study each piece. Thoroughly absorbed she jumped when she heard her name being called. Turning she saw Jo, one of her fellow students coming towards her, smiling she said, "Hello Jo isn't it marvellous?"

"Hello Rosie, so good to see you, we have all been worried about you. Have you noticed your paintings yet?"

"No I have only just started looking, I am savouring every moment as it is my first time out and I feel like an escapee."

"I have been round a couple of times so I will leave you to enjoy it but come over and find me when you have finished and I will treat you to coffee, I am on duty at the sales desk for another half an hour."

"Thank you Jo, I'd like that."

"I was going to ring you later as it happens as I have a surprise for you Rosie; I'll tell you when we have coffee."

Rosie had an enjoyable half hour and was delighted to see a red sticker on both her paintings, she had no idea what they had sold for, as she had not priced them herself. She had left it for John to decide.

She noticed that John had also sold both of his paintings and Jo had sold one of hers too.

Rosie found Jo sitting at the sales desk, "Well done Jo, you have sold one of your paintings and I am delighted to see red stickers on mine. I didn't take a leaflet so don't know the prices put on them."

Jo handed her the list and watched Rosie find her name and felt delighted to see her face when she saw how much they had sold for, "£400 pounds each! I don't believe it Jo, that is more than twice the usual price I put on them for the shows."

"Well the pricing was done by the panel this time, I have two cheques for you here, and you might recognise one of the names."

Rosie took the cheques and looked at the names, Giles Barton, and a Mr O Read, she did not recognise either of them. "I don't know either name."

"Rosie you goon, Giles Barton is one of the news readers on Look East. He left his card and wanted you to get in touch with him. Exciting isn't it?"

"Goodness, I wonder what he wants to speak to me about?"

"Well ring and find out, use my mobile and call now. He might want to commission you to do another painting," said Jo excitedly, infecting Rosie with her enthusiasm.

"Okay I will ring now, may I sit down though? My back is beginning to nag a bit."

She dialled the number on the card and was disappointed to

hear an answer phone so she left a message and her own mobile number. Handing Jo back her phone she said, "If I don't hear today, I will try again tomorrow and will let you know, shall we go for that coffee?"

Jo's replacement arrived and they headed for the canteen when Rosie heard her phone ring with a screeching parrot ring tone.

"What on earth is that?" laughed Jo.

Rosie fumbled for her phone, which always managed to get lost in the depths of her capacious bag.

With a chuckle Rosie told her that Ben had chosen the ring tone; she answered it just in time.

"Oh hello, yes speaking." A pause, "Well thank you I am glad you are pleased with it." Rosie winked at Jo. Jo was wishing that she could hear both sides of the conversation. Rosie listened for several minutes and only uttered the words "really" and "me" Jo watching was amused to see a variety of expressions crossing Rosie's face.

"Well yes I would love to," another pause. "Next Wednesday at ten, at the Tudor Hotel, yes that is fine for me, thank you; I'll look forward to it."

Giles had obviously made a joke as Rosie laughed then said "Well I should hope so, goodbye Giles."

Rosie laughing did a little jump for joy then yelped in pain.

"Oh gosh are you ok Rosie?" said Jo looking concerned.

"It's okay, I have some bruised bones and which apparently will take ages to heal. Anyway never mind bruises they are boring in the extreme, much more interestingly I have been made an offer which sounds rather exciting."

"Oh Rosie tell me all about it over coffee, you find a seat and I will get the coffee and something indulgent to celebrate."

Rosie found a seat by the window, which had an uninteresting view of the car park and a small patch of grass where several students had congregated.

Rosie watched them and realised that they were all smoking. Why do young people want to poison their beautiful young healthy bodies, she thought. They must know the harm they are doing to themselves, it is in large print on every packet they buy.

She remembered hearing a comedian say that the warning labels had become so big he expected to hear people asking for a packet of 'Smoking Kills'.

She felt thankful that both Grace and Ben had promised not to smoke, and she remembered Tom's father, on the day his brother died of lung cancer, telling them that if neither of them smoked he would help support them through university.

Jo arrived bearing a tray with coffee and two plates with huge pieces of sticky chocolate cake on them, saying, "I hope chocolate is one of your vices."

Rosie laughed and said, "It certainly is, mmm it looks very yummy, very good for my waistline and perfect timing as I was watching those students all smoking and feeling far too righteous."

"Oh good, a big slice of over indulgence will do you the power of good then. Now tell me all about Giles, I am all agog!"

Five hours later Rosie was preparing dinner, she had told the children that they were going to have a celebratory meal tonight but refused to tell them the reason, she wanted to tell them all together and see the expressions on their faces.

She had laid the table earlier with their best china and cutlery, the white linen napkins and the beautiful glasses that they had bought in Prague last year.

She had put a bottle of sparkling wine in the fridge to cool. At the market earlier, she had bought four pieces of sea bass, which they all liked but rarely had as it was so expensive, two bundles of asparagus and strawberries. She put some new potatoes in hot olive oil, sprinkled them with sea salt and rosemary and popped them in the oven to roast.

Feeling tired but happy she went into the garden to pick some flowers for the table, she chose some bright green Ladies Mantle, three of the white Macmillan roses, three pink Elizabeth roses and some soft grey leafed Senecio. Then filling her rose bowl with water she arranged the flowers and placed them in the centre of the table, she stood back to look and was pleased.

Then she called up to Grace and Ben "Grace would you walk Charlie please, and Ben would you please run to the shop and buy some double cream and some shortbread biscuits."

She heard groans from them both, sighing she climbed the stairs and popped her head round Grace's bedroom door, Grace appeared to be writing *I luv Carl* all over an exercise book.

"Are you meant to be scribbling on your exercise book, and I thought you didn't like Carl or is he back in favour now?"

"Kelly finished with him and is going out with Steve now. She lived too far from Carl so they hardly ever saw each other and Steve lives near her so it is perfect."

Rosie looked at her daughter who was growing up so fast and hoped she was not heading for heartache.

"Carl said he and JJ would cycle out to see Trudy and me on Saturday, so may Trudy come to stay Mum?"

"Yes I think so as long as you get plenty of studying done and if you give Charlie a quick walk before dinner. You haven't told me how your geography exam went to-day how was it?"

"Okay I think. It wasn't as bad as I thought it would be. It's science tomorrow and I am dreading it, I hope you are not expecting me to pass it. It was so ridiculous that I had to take a subject for GCSE that I hate when I could have taken history which I love. Why do they think that they can turn an artist into a scientist?"

Rosie came and sat beside Grace and gave her a hug.

"Oh darling, I simply expect you to do your best and if you do that you may well be pleasantly surprised. Perhaps one day the powers that be will take individualism more seriously."

"One day will be too late for me though."

"How about doing a couple of hours study after dinner, I will help you. Then get an early night so that you are refreshed for tomorrow."

"Will do and hopefully have wonderful dreams of Carl." Grace jumped up and gave Rosie a grin and a kiss on her cheek and ran downstairs to walk an excited Charlie who always seemed to know when a walk was imminent.

Rosie smiled, then went to see Ben who was sprawled on his bed doing what looked like his maths homework, "Why don't you sit at your desk to work Ben?"

"There isn't any room Mum I have got my models on there drying. Do I have to go to the shop I am doing homework?"

Rosie laughed, knowing full well that if his models were wet then he obviously had not been doing his homework.

"Ben it won't take a minute, dinner will be ready in half an hour and there will be plenty of time afterwards. I have left three pounds on the kitchen table, double cream and shortbread biscuits please." Ruffling his hair she went out of the room stepping on something that crunched beneath her feet "Oh dear, sorry Ben."

Ben looked at what had been broken, relieved he said, "It doesn't matter, it's a biro, it ran out of ink yonks ago."

"Ben, you do have a waste paper basket."

"I know but an empty biro isn't waste paper." Rosie laughed, Ben laughed too.

Twenty minutes later Tom turned into the drive almost running into Ben who came to greet him. "Hi Dad, Mum has made a special dinner because she has got a surprise, and she is back to normal I think."

Tom grinned at his son and his choice of words, "Ben you should come to work with me and chair our meetings, I could do with someone who gets straight to the point."

Rosie who had taken the opportunity to lie down for a few minutes heard Tom arrive home, she quickly got up and brushed her hair twisting it up and fastening it with her favourite mother of pearl clasp. She sprayed on some of her best perfume and went to greet him, with a mounting feeling of excitement at the thought of sharing her news. She would have liked to skip merrily down the stairs instead of stiffly taking one-step at a time. Seeing Tom looking up at her she said, "Hello darling, why don't you go and pour us a glass of wine, I have some good news."

"Okay and that makes two of us." Tom smiled up at Rosie, he knew she was trying hard to appear better.

The news that he had was going to turn their lives upside down, whatever decision they made, but for him there really was only one choice.

Just as they began their meal Tom said "Well it seems we both have some good news to share so Rosie you tell us yours first?"

Grace and Ben exchanged a look; they could sense that the special meal and Dad's rather formal announcement meant that both pieces of news must be important.

Suddenly Rosie felt nervous at telling Tom her news. She presumed that Tom's news would be about America and if that were the case then would her news affect his decision. She knew that he had deliberately mentioned little about it while she was recovering but what he had said had unsettled her. He had obviously enjoyed his visit even if it had been too brief; he even had a framed photograph of New York on his desk in the study.

Simultaneously Grace and Ben said "Come on Mum!" Rosie unable to stop grinning from ear to ear said, "Okay, well I went to the college today." Tom interrupted "How did you get there?"

"I took a taxi."

"A taxi, how ever much did that cost?"

Rosie gave Tom a withering look and replied, "A lot less than I would have spent over the last three weeks on petrol."

Tom looked abashed "Sorry, carry on."

"Well both my paintings sold, one of them to a man called Giles Barton who is one of the news readers on Look East"

Everyone together made noises of congratulation. Rosie enjoying the moment, continued, "That was pleasing but the best bit is he has asked me if I would like to take part in a series of six programmes he is planning for Anglia TV."

This time the family's comments were "Wow, doing what" from Ben, "Are you actually going to be on TV?" from Grace.

Tom looking worried said, "Don't get too excited before you know the details, if it is still in the planning stage it might never happen."

Rosie laughed at Tom "For ever my doubting Thomas, it will happen but they are only doing six programmes initially. If they go down well then there will be more."

"What are they going to be about Mum?" asked Grace.

"The programme will be about a different part of East Anglia each week. He has been looking for a local artist to paint the places they visit, they will then have a competition and ask the viewers to ring in with their answers and the winner will win my painting. That is all I know, I am going to meet him next week and find out more."

Tom pouring some more wine said smiling proudly at Rosie, "This deserves a toast. To my talented wife, I always thought that your paintings were good enough for a wider audience." He gave

Rosie a hug and realised that his news would have to wait, he could not spoil the excitement.

Grace and Ben joined in "To Mum!" and Ben added, "To fame, lots of money, and new football boots." Everyone laughed.

"What is your news Tom?" smiled Rosie warmed by her family's enthusiasm.

"I can't compete with that, it can wait."

Later when Rosie and Tom were in bed, Rosie snuggled up to Tom and said, "It was a good evening wasn't it? And nothing can take that away from us Tom."

"That's a funny thing to say," replied Tom warily.

Rosie did not reply for a moment but she wanted to be fair to Tom, she was aware that his support was important to her and she felt grateful to him for withholding his news tonight.

"Tom, I love you and I know that my resistance to America has been difficult for you. I don't feel any different about moving but you are my husband, my good hard working loyal husband and I realise I should be supporting you and I am sorry."

Tom did not say anything but turning towards her he gently kissed her, he had been afraid to hurt her. Now he caressed her, conscious that her bruises were still painful but feeling her respond, he was encouraged, she welcomed him to her and tenderly they made love.

Afterwards they lay entwined and Tom said to her "Tomorrow we will talk."

Rosie already almost asleep just mumbled something that was indecipherable.

Tom lay there thinking, he felt encouraged by Rosie's declaration of support but had an overwhelming feeling that whichever way he put it to her she would find it difficult to agree.

The next morning Tom decided to use flexi time, and take the morning off. He had insisted that Rosie stay in bed and had got up, woken Grace and organised Ben. Rosie surprised, luxuriated in a rare lie in.

Once Ben and Grace had left for school he then prepared tea and toast and took it back to bed.

They talked, Rosie was alarmed at hearing that Tom had only one month to decide whether to take the offer of a post and promotion in America or face redundancy. Either way the packages offered were generous but Tom talked enthusiastically about the job and it was obvious to Rosie that Tom had made up his mind. What he did not tell her was the feeling of restlessness he had felt since his return. He had only been there for a short time but it had left a deep impression on him.

In an unenthusiastic voice Rosie asked, "Tom, you said that the company would pay for the family to have a trip out there if we were considering relocation, presumably that still stands?"

"Absolutely, I will need to book a hotel and flights as soon as possible then we can have a holiday and look into housing, schools etc."

Rosie looked directly into Tom's eyes and taking his face in her hands said in a tender voice, "Tom, in no way have I said yes but I am prepared to go and see. Why are you so keen to go Tom? I thought that we were happy here and with the redundancy package we would be fine until you found another job."

Tom did not answer immediately, he did not truly know why himself. Was it Polly or was it the thought of a new challenge. He knew that he could have a new challenge here.

He remembered his last night there and feeling claustrophobic when he walked between the high rise buildings and thinking that perhaps New York wasn't for him, so why?

Sighing he looked at Rosie and said perfectly truthfully, "I don't know Rosie, I just have a gut feeling about it. I am drawn back to it."

"Will you tell the children that you have an opportunity to work and move to America?"

"Yes I must tell them the whole truth I think, that way they can look at New York in the right way, it is only fair."

"We agree on that at least, when shall we go?"

"Next week I hope."

Rosie looked at Tom with an incredulous expression "Tom, you can't have forgotten Grace's exams, her GSCEs no less."

"Oh of course well the following week then, Grace will have finished her exams and Ben will just have to have a week off school."

Rosie grinned and said in a mock superior voice "I have a meeting next week with Giles Barton and obviously I need to work round my filming schedule."

Smiling indulgently Tom replied, "It is very unlikely for anything to happen immediately, if at all, you said that this programme was in the planning stage. Don't get too excited."

"Yes I know, I am aware of that but I do want to take up this opportunity if it is given to me. It gives me a buzz just thinking about it."

"Well that is how I feel about New York, I liked it there; I liked the buzz of something new."

"I feel as if part of you is still there. You seem different, we seem different." Rosie looked at Tom who looked away before answering.

The trouble was she was right, he felt somehow detached as if he was just going through the motions. He loved his family there was no doubt, but her intuition was right, he could not wait to get back to the States.

He turned to look at Rosie who was already looking hurt before he had even said anything. Sighing he said, "I love you and the children you know that, I just want things settled that's all, I need to go back as soon as I can."

"Then you go next week Tom, we can come out to join you as soon as we can." Not waiting for a reply she got up and went into the bathroom for a shower.

Tom sensed that she was irritated but he was obviously wrong for just as he was getting up Rosie popped her head round the door and said with a grin on her face, "Thank you for breakfast, how about joining me in the shower?"

Tom grinned back and said, "You bet."

He followed, willing himself to want to.

Later Rosie was looking through her cookery books, she had asked Ruth and John for dinner on Saturday to thank them for all that they had done for her and of course to hopefully get them together.

Today the new car, arranged by her insurance company, was arriving. Her doctor had advised her not to drive for a fortnight and she had not felt at all like driving but today she felt differently and thought she would drive as far as the farm shop; it was only three miles and the very best place to buy local organic produce. They also sold crafts, made again by local people; she could buy her mother a birthday present and a belated one for Matt.

Although her Mother's birthday was not for a fortnight, they were going to the farm for Sunday lunch. Eve had rung to suggest a joint birthday celebration. Both Grace and Ben were looking forward to it; Matt had told them that there was a surprise awaiting them.

Rosie wondered what Eve had bought for Matt in the end, she had asked her but Eve had simply said that she had found some thing original.

Rosie heard the sound of a car on the gravel drive, looking out of the window she saw a blue ford fiesta arrive, and a young man in mechanics overalls got out and came towards the house.

Rosie felt a small sense of excitement at the prospect of seeing her new car, well new to her anyway; it was two years old but apparently in very good condition and with low mileage for its age.

The Police had found her stolen car at the old clay pits, they suspected it had been used for two burglaries, based on eyewitness accounts, but they had not yet found the culprits. The Police informed her that she would have to do an identity parade when they had any potential suspects in custody. She was dreading that and did not think that she would be able to identify them as she had only a very vague memory of their faces, especially the older one.

Having signed the appropriate paperwork the car was hers, waiting until the driver had gone she went to have a look at it. She would like a sporty car like Alice's one day but for now, she could only afford to be practical. She allowed herself to hope that if Giles offered her the position of artist on the programme he was presenting she would have more money to make choices.

The car, recently valeted, had that fresh new smell. She sat in the driver's seat and breathed in deeply, and enjoyed it knowing that it would not last long.

She always meant to keep the car clean and immaculate but before long she knew it would accumulate various odds and ends of hers and the children's, crumbs from hastily eaten sandwiches, sweet wrappers etc. She promised herself that she would try to get into a routine, perhaps Ben would like to clean it regularly for some pocket money.

Suddenly there was a knock on the car window making Rosie jump. Mrs Jenkins, the secretary of the PCC stood there smiling. "Hello Rosie, sorry did I startle you? I have come to collect the painting for George if it is ready."

"Hello Mary, I was miles away and didn't hear you coming. I finished the painting before I went into hospital, thankfully. My friend John framed it for me, I hope you like it."

Rosie led the way indoors and went to fetch it from the study leaving Charlie to give Mary his usual exuberant welcome.

As soon as she entered the study she noticed that on Tom's desk was another photograph beside the New York at night one that he had there. The photo of she and the children tobogganing in France, which usually sat on his desk, was now on the window-sill. She had not moved it so Tom must have; it was odd, as Tom never moved things around.

Forgetting Mary, she picked up this new photo to look at it closely. It was in an identical frame to the other one and looked expensive. The photograph was of an old building painted red and in front of the door was a young woman, above her a sign saying Bridge Café. Rosie presumed that it was somewhere in New York, but who was she and why did Tom have a photo of her. Tom took many photos but never put them in albums or framed them, it was something that they both thought they ought to do and never got round to. Someone else obviously did, perhaps the woman in the photo gave these to Tom. Rosie with a sense of foreboding, turned over the frame and undid the back of it and taking the photo out saw, as somehow she knew she would, a message written on the back.

> *Tom,*
> *Hoping to bridge the gap between us.*
> *Polly x*

With her heart racing, she picked up the other photo but before she could undo it, she heard her name called and turning saw Mary in the doorway looking embarrassed and puzzled.

"Oh Mary I am so sorry, I forgot you."

"Are you all right Rosie? I can see you look upset." Mary stepped forward and put her arms around her and hugged her tight.

Rosie hugged her in return. Mary released her and said in a businesslike way "I am going to make you a cup of tea, just show me the way."

Rosie took a deep breath and smiled weakly at Mary and replied that she had a better idea "Have you got time to come to the farm shop with me in my new car, we can have tea there?"

Mary who had planned to go shopping herself to the supermarket and then on to see her elderly mother said, "I would love to come, I keep meaning to go there more often, I just need to pop home for my purse and make a quick phone call. I'll be back in ten minutes."

"Thank you Mary, you must take the painting with you." Picking up the painting, which was propped against the wall, she handed it to Mary.

A genuine smile of appreciation spread across her face as she looked at the painting "It is wonderful, just what I had wanted, Oh and there is George with Scamp going for a walk and Madge with her cake tin, how clever you are!"

"Madge has made us two delicious cakes since I came out of hospital, and George took Charlie for several walks until I felt up to it. Little did I know when I painted them we would be so soon on the receiving end of their kindness."

Mary noticed that Rosie's eyes were again brimming with tears said, "Just thinking about her cakes makes me hungry, lets go and have that tea."

Turning round she went back into the hall and out of the front door calling as she went "Ten minutes and I'll be back."

Rosie watched her go, her ample figure not made for quickness hurried down the drive and Rosie laughed. Charlie came and stood beside her with his tail wagging, his greying whiskery face looking lovingly up at her. Rosie bent to give Charlie a cuddle and thought, what faithful devoted love dogs give us, a lesson to us all.

TEN

Wonderful smells of baking greeted Tom when he came home. Calling out "Hello, I'm home!" He went to put his brief-case in the study as usual and saw his photographs lying down on the desk, one out of its frame. "What the heck?" He picked up the loose photograph and saw the message written on the back, he had not thought to take the photo out of its frame to look for one.

A mixed sensation of pleasure and horror swept over him, he felt excited and ashamed.

Sitting at his desk, he put the photo back in its frame and sat and thought, why was he feeling guilty, what had he done wrong?

Obviously Rosie had found it, would she imagine the worse or just think that it was a present from someone in the American office, which it was of course although he also knew that it could be so much more.

Placing both photographs back in their positions he decided to be honest with Rosie, explain why Polly had given him the photos, and assure her he had no idea that there was a message on the back.

The trouble was he knew that though he and Polly's relationship, if that is what it was, was innocent, both of them wished for more. There was no doubt they had connected, she made him feel young, desirable and needed.

At that moment, Rosie appeared in the doorway and said in a matter of fact voice, "Have you something to tell me Tom?"

Tom stood up and smiling held out his arms to her, "Come here darling, there is very little to tell you."

Rosie stayed where she was with her arms crossed as if to protect herself against what she feared he might tell her.

"There is something then?" She couldn't look at him for fear of what she might see in his eyes, instead she stared at the Turkish rug on the floor absurdly noticing the pattern and tracing with her eyes the furl of leaves around the edge.

Dropping his arms by his side, he sighed, "Let's go and sit in the garden and talk about this and please don't look so angry, you seem to have hung drawn and quartered me before you have heard what I have to say. Whatever happened to innocent until proven guilty?"

Rosie, stonyfaced said nothing but turned, went into the sitting room and out of the open French doors. She walked over the newly cut grass, the smell delicious in evening air, and sat on the seat beneath the old apple tree.

This was her favourite place in the garden, as Tom joined her she got up and said abruptly, "I am not sitting here, I love this spot and I don't want anything to spoil it."

Tom followed her as she strode across the lawn, "Where are we going then?"

Rosie did not reply but went through the side garden gate and stood by the dustbins, "You can have the rubbish bin I'll have the recycle bin."

Tom laughed, "Rosie you are being just a bit melodramatic don't you think?"

"I don't think I am Tom, I would like to think that what I am about to be told can be put in the rubbish bin, taken away and forgotten about," Rosie looked up at Tom still with her arms crossed. Tom saw in her eyes a look of pain and apprehension.

Putting his hands on her arms, he unfolded them, "You don't need to protect yourself from me Rosie, I promise you."

"What do you promise me Tom? Do you promise to love and cherish me forsaking all others for as long we both shall live?"

"Rosie it is my utmost desire to do that, but I am going to be honest. I have been tempted and what I do promise you is that temptation is all it is."

"Tom you can't put *have* and *is* in the same sentence and expect me to be happy with that, obviously you are still tempted as you put it?"

Tom knowing that she was right did not know what to say.

"Who is she Tom? Something must have occurred for her to be sending you pictures and romantic messages?"

"Her name is Polly and she was given the task of taking me out to see New York, at the Company's expense I might add."

"Oh pretty Polly is a hired escort, charming."

Tom felt furious suddenly and hotly defensive on Polly's behalf "Don't be ridiculous Rosie, she does a similar job to me and is a lovely girl who is shattered because she lost her fiancé in the collapse of the World Trade Centre."

Rosie, seeing Tom's expression of compassion, began to understand. Tom obviously felt protective of her.

More calmly she said, "I am so sorry for her, I can't imagine how dreadful it must be Tom, but you have to leave someone else to help her. You already have a family to love and protect."

Tom saw that Rosie's conclusion that he felt protective of Polly was right, he remembered wanting to hold her tight when she had told him. If only it were that simple though, he knew without any doubt that he felt more than protectiveness towards Polly.

"Look Rosie you are right, I do, I mean did, feel protective of her." Taking her by the hand he said encouragingly, "Come on lets go in and eat whatever it was that was smelling so wonderful when I came home."

"That's the parmesan tart case for tomorrows dinner party Tom," then with horror she realised it was still in the oven. "Oh hell, it could be burnt!" She rushed away.

Tom, relieved that the discussion had ended for now, followed.

When Rosie arrived in the kitchen she was relieved to see the tart case sitting on the slate beside the oven a perfect pale biscuit colour. Grace leaning beside it munching an apple, "There you are Mum, I couldn't find you or Dad and the bell on the cooker rang so I figured I had better take whatever it is out of the oven."

"Thank you darling, I had forgotten it. It looks good doesn't it?"

Grace looked "It looks empty but smells good, what's going in it?"

"Asparagus and salmon, it's the starter for tomorrow night."

"Oh yes the match-making dinner, I bet it won't work, they probably won't fancy each other."

"It isn't just a match-making dinner it is a thank you too, and I think they will get on really well."

"I don't think John is very good-looking he has a big nose and a crooked smile."

"Oh Grace, John is good-looking in a charming way, and I like his crooked smile."

"I suppose you will be having really yummy food and we will be having pizza and begging for leftovers?"

Rosie laughed, "Well I did ask you both if you wanted to join us and you groaned and said no."

Grace grinned, "I know but Trudy is coming and she is a veggie."

"I have a good idea Grace, why don't you, Trudy and Ben go over to the Half a Sixpence, if you order before seven they do two courses for eight pounds. I have a feeling that Dad will treat you all if you ask him nicely."

"That is a great idea, thanks Mum."

Ben arrived at that moment, "What's for dinner? I'm starving!"

Grace retorted, "So what's new, you are always starving. Do you want to come over to the Half Sixpence for dinner tomorrow with Trudy and me?"

"What on our own without the olds?" Rosie gave Ben a pretend clip round the ear. "Yes, before six thirty though so you will have to be back from football in good time."

"I get back at six normally unless Jack and I kick around."

Grace made a face and said, "I bet he won't wash Mum and we will have to go out to dinner with him covered in sweat and mud."

Ben decided after that comment that he would rather stay at Jack's than go out with a pair of silly girls who would expect him to look clean and well dressed.

"I am going to stay at Jack's anyway so you will have to do without my charming and witty company."

Rosie knowing full well that Ben hadn't asked whether he could stay at Jack's yet laughed at the pair of them and said, "Perhaps you should give him a quick ring Ben?"

"Okay but what's for dinner? I'll die of starvation in a minute."

Grace teasingly said, "Oh good, don't give him anything Mum."

Tom coming in to the kitchen said, "Would you like me to go and get some fish and chips?"

Rosie looked at Tom and said, "No thank you Tom, I am doing fresh pasta and it will be ready in five minutes, Ben set the table and Grace would you get the drinks please?"

"Can I do anything?" asked Tom.

"Yes, you can come with me please?" Rosie took Tom into the utility room and shut the door and looking up at him she said, "You have a wife and family who love you very much please don't decide to throw us away for someone you hardly know."

Tom gave her an incredulous look, "For heavens sake Rosie, throw you away? One kiss and you have got me divorcing you, which I have no intention of doing."

Rosie interrupted, "Oh you did kiss her then?"

Tom sighed and remembering it felt guilty as the pleasure of it returned to him. "Yes I did kiss her; it seemed the natural thing to do at that moment. It wasn't in any way premeditated I promise you." Tom looked down at Rosie; the sun was shining through the window and lighting up her red hair. "Your hair looks like spun gold." and he reached out and stroked it.

With a sob, Rosie moved towards him and he enfolded her with his arms. Still resting her head on his chest, she mumbled, "Promise me you will remember our love when you see her next?"

For a moment Tom thought of Polly and knew that Rosie was right; he could decide to allow himself to fall in love with her or he could be strong and keep Rosie in mind. "I promise you Rosie you are more important to me than anyone else, and I aim to keep it that way," and at that moment he meant it.

A cry of, "Mum I am starving where are you?!" made them laugh and the door opened to Ben, "Oh there you are I'm-"

Both Rosie and Tom chorused, "Starving!"

"I have put the garlic bread in the oven for ten minutes to crisp up, it should be ready Ben, have you set the table?"

The next day Rosie got up at six to make the desserts, peach wine jelly with a peach puree and chocolate and hazelnut roulade, which she was serving with fresh strawberries. She liked to cook in the early morning before anyone else was about to disturb her. She knew that on Saturday mornings she was safe until ten when Ben would need a lift to football.

She had not decided what she was going to serve for the dinner until her visit to the farm shop then, spoilt for choice with all the wonderful fresh and local produce, she had taken quite a while to decide. It had been Mary who had suggested the peach wine jellies, "Do a Delia and make peach wine jellies, they are light and delicious and they sell fruit wines here."

Having decided, they had enjoyed tea out in the farm shop's pretty country garden with chickens pecking about them and with Mary's gentle manner and dry sense of humour, she had returned home feeling restored.

Rosie let Charlie out into the garden, promising him a walk once she had finished, and picked some fresh rosemary for the lamb from the herb garden.

When she had made the jelly and put the roulade in the oven she took the lamb from the fridge and poked rosemary and garlic under the skin. By the time she had finished the roulade was cooked and smelt delicious, it was her favourite pudding and one of the easiest to make.

Feeling pleased with her efforts she decided to take Charlie for his walk before doing anything else.

It was a beautiful morning; the sun was already warm and drying up the rain which had fallen overnight. The rain had made everything smell fresh and earthy. The birds were singing and no doubt working hard to feed their young. Rosie crossed the green and headed to the fields beyond the village. She did not meet anyone but saw signs of the village awakening. She let Charlie off the lead when she reached the fields to have a run and rabbit hunt.

She loved being out early when no one else was about, it made her feel free as if she could run, dance and sing unselfconsciously. She suddenly had an urge to do just that, spreading her arms wide she ran and skipped and sang as loud as she could, "Oh what a beautiful morning, oh what a beautiful day!".

Enjoying herself Rosie hadn't noticed a Springer spaniel rush towards her from the hedge. As he reached her he barked, making Rosie jump, she swung round quickly and losing her balance, fell backwards landing on her back with her legs in the air. A man she vaguely recognised appeared above her, obviously trying hard not to laugh, he held out his hand to help her up and said, "Are you happy down there or would you like some help?"

Rosie laughingly took his hand and replied, "I am just experimenting with a new kind of greeting, do you like it?"

"Quite charming, it is so nice to see people from different perspectives."

Still holding his hand Rosie rather stiffly got up, "I was rather hoping no one was about."

"Sorry, I disturbed you, I know exactly how you feel; when you are out in the elements on your own you can feel free to do anything that takes your fancy. Unfortunately, unlike you, I am never brave enough to do it, I always imagine that I might be spotted by a lovely young lady," smiling at her he said, "I'm Charles by the way and if I'm not mistaken you are soon to be our famous artist Rosemary Holden?"

Surprised, Rosie laughed, "Goodness no, I am just hoping to be a resident artist on a local programme which might or might not take off. How on earth did you know about it?"

"I am Mary's husband; she is very excited about it on your behalf, understandably."

"Of course Charles, I am sorry, I knew I recognised you but couldn't think from where."

"Please don't apologise, I am afraid I don't get to Church as much as I would like and my work has tended to dominate my life, so I haven't had the chance to get involved in village life as much as Mary has."

"You are a journalist I hear, a foreign correspondent?"

"Yes that's right, but very soon an ex-journalist, I am retiring and I can't wait."

Charlie came bounding up at that moment and enthusiastically took a very personal interest in Charles's Springer spaniel much to her indignation.

"Stop it Charlie," admonished Rosie.

"Oh don't worry, Merry will stand up for herself."

"Well I think I must head back now, I have a dinner party to prepare. You and Mary must come for dinner with us, once you are retired Charles."

"We would love to," with that he smiled, waved, and calling to Merry strode on.

When Rosie and Charlie arrived home, Tom was just returning from the shop with the Saturday papers and the croissants, their regular Saturday treat. Giving Rosie a quick kiss he said, "I see you have been busy already this morning, how about sitting down with the papers and I will warm the croissants and make the coffee."

Smiling Rosie replied "Wonderful," she went and sat on one of the pretty, high back wicker chairs by the French doors in the sitting room. The sun was pouring through, resting her head back Rosie sighed with pleasure and quoting Toad said, "Oh bliss, oh rapture oh poop poop."

When Tom arrived with the coffee Rosie was peacefully sleeping with the papers unopened on her lap, he watched her for a moment. She always looked younger when she was asleep, her face free from expression. Rosie was always laughing and had several quite deep laughter lines but just lately he had noticed her frowning more and he knew that was partly due to him, and of course the car snatch.

He put the tray down and gently kissed her on her forehead and she woke. "Goodness I went fast asleep, mmm the croissants smell delicious."

"Good, let's eat them while they are still hot. I have just rung my parents and they would like to take us out to lunch tomorrow, I said a provisional yes, is that ok?"

"Well I would like to very much but Grace might not as she has her friend Trudy staying tonight so she might have plans for tomorrow, and Ben might be playing football but if not I am sure he would like to go. Why don't you ask them after breakfast, the time has gone when we could decide for them."

Smiling she picked up the review section of the paper and settled down to eat and read.

That simple comment, innocently spoken made Tom realise that it was going to be very difficult to persuade Grace and Ben to move to America. Suddenly this whole idea seemed pointless, he felt deeply alone at that moment and he knew the lunch with his parents would not help from the tone his mother used when he had told her that he was going back to America next week.

He thought of Rosie's parents and how they might react especially now that Norman was unwell. Throwing the unread paper to the floor, he said crossly, "Oh hell!" startling Rosie.

"What is the matter Tom?"

"Nothing is the matter, I need to clear my head I'll take Charlie out again, and a good walk will do me good."

Tom returned an hour later in a better frame of mind, having made the decision to insist that Grace and Ben come to lunch with his parents whatever their plans and then have a family discussion about it in the pub. He had also decided to book the tickets for them all to go on holiday; they would spend one week in

New York and one in Florida taking in Disney World. He would tell them tomorrow.

He shut himself in the study to browse through the internet and find what he wanted. The Company was paying for the airfares and the week in New York. He just hoped that this holiday would impress Rosie and the children enough for them to consider moving otherwise it could be embarrassing for him, as it would look as if he was just trying to get a free holiday before leaving. He knew that he had given the New York office the impression that he was very keen and had hinted that his family were too.

While on his walk he had decided that if either Rosie or the children were stubborn he would insist and that was that but he fervently hoped it would not come to that.

Having booked the flights and hotels, he more cheerfully went out to mow the lawn.

Grace was in a state of excitement and nervousness; she had appeared three times in different outfits for Rosie's approval. Rosie found it impossible to please, when she had said Grace had looked pretty and feminine in a little white skirt and pink top Grace had said, "Oh Yuk!" and flounced off. She next appeared in black combat trousers with a grey and black striped t-shirt, Rosie had said, "You look very smart."

Grace had not liked that either and had shouted, "I am not going for an interview!" and had run upstairs and slammed the door.

When Rosie heard Grace coming downstairs for the third time she took a deep breath and prayed that she chose the right words. Grace appeared in light blue jeans, a white sleeveless t-shirt and leather belt with a sparkly butterfly buckle and at her neck the pretty shell necklace that Trudy had given her for her birthday. Grace looked casual but still pretty and feminine, Rosie did not say anything but looked her up and down then smiled and nodded, thankfully, it worked and Grace smiled back. They both jumped then as the doorbell rang, "I'll get it Mum, it will be Trudy."

It was Carl, Rosie could tell, for if it had been Trudy there would have been sounds of excited giggles and chatter. Instead she heard her say in a very grown up manner. "Would you like to come in or shall we go in the garden and I'll get us some drinks and bring them out?"

He must have chosen the garden because she heard Grace bringing him round the side, their footsteps on the gravel and the side gate opening with its usual squeak. Rosie was intrigued to find out what sort of boy Grace had chosen, would he be fair, dark, short, tall. Rosie stood at the sink; the window above afforded her a perfect view as they came past, which they did at that moment.

Rosie looked out as Carl looked in, for a second they made eye contact. Rosie felt herself reel backwards a feeling of fear and nausea swept over her; she gripped the edge of the sink to stop herself falling.

When Tom walked into the kitchen a moment later he found Rosie white faced and shaking. Taking hold of her, he said, "What's happened, you look terrified?"

In a shaky voice, she replied, "It's him Tom I know it!"

Puzzled Tom said as he led Rosie to a chair, "Him, what do you mean him?"

"The boy who kicked me, the one who took the car Tom, I know it, I remember those eyes. Tom, what can we do, he is in the garden with Grace!"

"If you are sure then I would like to beat the living daylights out of the young bastard, but I suppose we had better call the police."

Thinking quickly Rosie said, "Tom, I would like to speak to him first, I need-"

"Speak to him, are you mad? He might kick you again or

worse, that sort of yob is likely to carry a knife. If he thought you were onto him he could kill you."

Rosie was determined, "I won't put myself at risk. I'll be careful I promise, I need to make sure. Tom will you put his bike in the garage and then call in Grace to make drinks and delay her somehow. I will go out of the French doors when I see Grace coming in. Then if I am right, and I fear I am then we can ring the police."

Tom was not happy about it one bit, "What are you going to say to him, because he won't just come out and admit it will he. If he suspects you suspect him, he will just either deny it or do a runner."

"Do a runner as you put it is all he will be able to do as we will have his bike. Tom, there must be good in the boy, Grace likes him and you know Tom he was frightened that night, it was why I remember those piercing blue eyes, he had looked straight at me like a frightened rabbit."

"Then he kicked you so hard he nearly ruptured your spleen and fractured your skull and good as left you for dead!"

"Tom I know, but he was under orders. Tom, please do this for me and we must be quick as Trudy will be dropped off in a minute and if it is Sally dropping her she is bound to pop in for a chat, she always does and I like to see her of course but I want to have time to do this Tom."

"Ok, ok." Looking unhappy he kissed her lightly on the head and said, "Take care." and left.

Rosie watched him put Carl's bike in the Garage and when Carl went into the back garden she took her little wooden hand-held cross, and quietly opened the French doors. She watched as Tom strode over to the pair sitting closely on the seat together, he talked briefly to Carl and then said something to Grace who got up and presumably asked Carl what he wanted to drink. For a moment, it looked as if it was not going to work as Grace sat down again. Tom said something else and Grace got up, giving what looked like a glare to Tom and started to walk to the house.

As soon as she was out of sight Rosie stepped into the garden, Tom came towards her and as he passed her he said quietly, "Shout if you need me."

Rosie smiled at Carl as she approached him and held out her hand, "Hello Carl I'm Rosie, Grace's mother."

He looked shy and slightly embarrassed as he smiled back and held his hand out too, after shaking hands Rosie sat, slowly and obviously stiffly, down beside him.

Rosie looked at the young man, he was quite tall, with dark hair spiked up with gel and those bright blue eyes.

She had no doubt he was her attacker. Surprisingly she felt calm but overwhelmingly sad.

She wished that she were mistaken; she wished too that she could just say something that would have an effect on him. Feeling the comfort of her smooth wooden cross in her left hand, she prayed that she would use the right words.

She knew that she did not have time for small chat so said, "I have to sit down as I can't stand for long, I am trying to recover from being attacked and having my car stolen, I can't tell you how painful it has been. Have you ever had anything like that happen to you Carl?"

Carl did not look at her but shifted in his seat and looking down at his feet said simply, "Oh er no."

Rosie saw Tom standing at the French doors, he had the phone in his hand, and she nodded at him.

In as bright and cheery a voice as Rosie could muster she said, "It is a lovely day for a cycle ride, Grace has packed up a picnic for you all. Do you and your parents live far from here Carl?"

Carl replied still not looking at her, "I live with my Dad near Diss."

Carl looked at his watch and shifted awkwardly in his seat.

Rosie heard Tom say loudly, "I'll take the tray Grace you go and welcome Trudy."

Rosie would have liked more time but in a quiet and calm way she stood up and said, "Carl?"

Carl looked up and Rosie continued, "You know I would really love to meet the young frightened lad who attacked me and his father or whoever was with him. I would like to ask why? When I had tried to understand I would hold out my hand and say, "I forgive you."

Carl jumped up with his hands in his pockets and stepped from one foot to the other nervously, which again reminded Rosie of that dreadful night.

"Look I just remembered I've got to be somewhere, tell Grace sorry and I'll see her around." He then hurriedly made for the gate.

Tom was standing there talking to Sally. As soon as Tom saw Carl he moved aside, "Are you going Carl? You will be needing your bike then. I put it in the garage, you never know who is around to take it."

Tom, taking his time, made a bit of a fuss opening the garage door.

"You know Carl in the future if you ever feel like doing us a favour I have plenty of good honest jobs you can help me with."

Carl shot him a look of incredulity, "Er right thanks."

Carl jumped on his bike and was just going out of the drive when the police car arrived; he swerved round it as the police car door opened knocking him off his bike. Within seconds, two police officers had picked up Carl, who looked startled and defeated. They cautioned him and put him in the back of the car and one officer got in with him.

Tom went to speak to the other. Rosie saw Carl look through the car window towards her, feeling utterly wretched she tearfully turned away and Sally taking her arm went to lead her indoors.

Suddenly Rosie thought and releasing herself from Sally's arm rushed to the police car, surprising Tom and the police officer.

"Sorry but I have something I must give to Carl."

Simultaneously the officer and Tom said, "What is it?"

Rosie held out her hand, revealing the wooden cross in her palm. The officer having looked at the cross said, "Are you aware madam that all personal items may well be taken away from him should he be kept in custody?"

"Yes."

The officer held out his hand to take the cross, "I will give it to him."

Rosie stepped back and in a shaky voice said, "No I need to give it to him myself."

Giving her a rather exasperated look he said resignedly, "Very well."

They both walked to the car with Tom watching and thinking cynically that Rosie was being very optimistic if she thought that it would mean anything to Carl.

The officer opened the back door nearest to Carl and said something to the other officer, which Rosie could not hear, and then stood aside for her.

Squatting down so that she was level with the passengers, she held out her hand with the cross in it and said to Carl, who had the same wide-eyed expression on his face that she recognised, "This is very precious to me and I would like you to have it."

Looking puzzled and cautious he took it from her and held it open palmed. Rosie stood up not waiting for any response and saying nothing more walked head bent back to the house.

Officer Barns sitting next to Carl said in a quiet voice, "That, young man is the most important gift you will ever be given."

When Tom joined Rosie and Sally indoors, a very emotional scene greeted him. Both Grace and Trudy, whom Tom had told to stay indoors, were in tears. They had watched from the window and both girls turned their tear stained faces towards him. Grace rushed towards him hysterically screaming. "How could you? I hate you! I hate you!" She crumpled into a heap on the floor and dissolved into racking sobs.

Tom tried to put his arms around her but she angrily shrugged him off. When Rosie had come in, she had gone to the girls and told them that she was sure that Carl was her attacker. As she had predicted they had not wanted to believe her.

She wished that she had warned Grace but would she have listened and would she have been able to stop her from going out with him? She knew that she would have been worried sick if Grace had gone off for the day with him.

Sally went to comfort Trudy, who was visibly shaken, and Rosie sat on the floor beside Grace and held her hand, then looking up at Tom indicated to him to join her.

Grace turned to Rosie and in a much calmer voice said, "What if you are wrong Mum, he will never forgive me and I love him so much," again she dissolved into quiet sobs.

Tom tried again to put his arms around Grace, this time she allowed him to hold her and in a small halting voice, "Will I ever see him again?"

Rosie remembered Carl's last words to her and felt duty bound to tell Grace.

"Grace, Carl asked me to say that he was sorry and that he will see you around."

Renewed tears followed, "But when?"

Tom and Rosie looked at each other over Grace's head. They both knew they would not want her to see him again, but what should they say.

Tom answered, "In all honesty Grace you will have to understand that although you liked him you didn't really know him very well, and knowing what he has done and may have done before, you might decide you won't want to see him."

Grace looked up at Rosie with her red swollen eyes and tear stained face. "Mum are you really sure and if you are, I'm so sorry he hurt you."

Rosie looked at her daughter hating to see her so distressed, "I know you are my darling and I am so sorry too that it was him."

Sally not wanting to intrude but beginning to feel uncomfortable at still being there said, "I think we ought to be going and leave you alone."

Grace looked pleadingly at Trudy, "Please don't go!"

"Can I stay Mum?"

Rosie hoped Sally would say yes, "She is very welcome to stay Sally and I know it would help Grace."

Sally hesitated ignoring Trudy's pleading face, she wasn't too sure if she wanted Trudy to stay, what if Rosie was wrong, there could be some awful repercussions from this. "Why doesn't Grace come and stay with us instead, this has all been such a shock for you all."

Grace standing up said, "Say yes Mum, please!"

"Yes of course you may." Rosie said as she got up from the floor with Tom helping her. "Thank you Sally it is kind of you and probably for the best."

Grace was interrupted by the front door slamming and Ben bursting into the room with an outraged look on his face, "Why has Dad been arrested?" on seeing Tom he looked puzzled and said, "Mrs Baker told old nosy parker that she had seen you being arrested!"

There were various looks of horror and consternation until Tom laughed, and then everyone with a release of tension laughed too.

"I think I had better take a stroll over to the post office and offer to buy Mrs Baker a new pair of specs."

ELEVEN

Half an hour before Alice and John were due to arrive Rosie was still doing the finishing touches to the table; she enjoyed arranging flowers for the centre but tonight she wanted the evening to be relaxed and informal so had decided to make the table look simple and unfussy. Earlier she had picked some wild honeysuckle from the hedge at the bottom of the garden and had put it in an old ironstone jug, she placed the jug in the centre and stood back to look, perfect, natural and rustic, the smell was heavenly. Then she wound variegated ivy around each white linen napkin and tucked a small posy of oxeye daisies beneath, they contrasted beautifully with the white china and the fine frosted wine glasses that Tom had bought her in Vienna. Placing two wooden candlesticks either side of the jug in the centre, she chose two pale green candles from her candle box.

She had decided against a table cloth; earlier she had asked Ben to polish the old oak table, a job he enjoyed and had done with gusto, it shone beautifully. Rosie stood back to admire the overall look and was pleased, it looked simple and summery.

Checking her watch for time, she gasped with horror, only

twenty minutes left to shower, dry her hair and dress. She never
left enough time for beautifying herself. She popped her head
around the kitchen door where Tom was making the summer
cocktail with elderflower cordial and sparkling wine to serve in
the garden. In a slightly panicky voice, Rosie said, "I'm just going
to get ready Tom they will be here in a few minutes!"

"Okay but I don't expect Alice will be here on time and I'll
amuse John with some gruesome tales of Alice. Oh by the way do
you want me to put some fruit in the cocktail?"

"Yes please, could you pick some of the tiny wild strawberries
and some small mint leaves." She smiled at him and went. Tom
groaned he had been thinking along the lines of a few pieces of
lemon. He was not in the mood for a dinner party but they had
decided earlier to try to put the events of the day behind them at
least for tonight. He knew there would be difficult times ahead
with police interviews, possibly court cases to attend, and wondered whether it was fair of him to go to America on Monday but
he was looking forward to being there for two weeks before the
family arrived.

He walked into the garden, it was still very warm and as he
bent to pick the tiny red berries he began to relax and feel a little
of what Rosie described as her garden therapy.

Rosie, still damp from the shower was looking through her
wardrobe not liking what she saw. There was not anything new,
just old favourites and impulse mistakes. There was no time left
for trying on and discarding so she picked out a sun dress she had
bought in Italy at least five years ago, it had been worn on all the
summer holidays since, it was a beautiful delphinium blue in a
very fine cotton. She liked its scalloped neckline with tiny mother
of pearl beads sewn along the edge and was low enough to show
a little cleavage without being too revealing. She decided against
jewellery but twisted her hair into a French pleat, which covered
the now hardly visible scar, and fastened it with a mother of pearl

clasp. Quickly she applied mascara, a must with her fair eyelashes, and slipped into a pair of high-heeled white strappy sandals.

Hearing the sound of a car on the gravel she hurried down stairs and out of the open French doors and plucked a half opened pink rose bud, it was one of her favourites called Blessings and had a sweet delicate smell, she put it between the twist of her hair and the clasp.

She heard Tom greet John, as he had predicted the first to arrive, and take him into the sitting room. Rosie decided to check the lamb in the oven before joining them.

It was doing well; she glanced round the kitchen checking that everything was as it needed to be. The tart and bread were ready, she would warm them for starters, the new potatoes scrubbed, and the mange- touts and baby carrots sitting in the steamer ready. She had mixed red current jelly with the zest of an orange and put it in to the tiny filo pastry cups she had made, the jellies were in the fridge and the roulade in the larder. Satisfied that all was ready she went into the sitting room to meet John, he stood up and came towards her, "Hello John, how smart you look."

Giving her a kiss he stepped back appraisingly and said in a surprised voice "Rosie you look absolutely stunning!"

Rosie laughed, "Well thank you John but you don't need to sound quite so surprised."

"Remember you looked very different the last time I saw you, you were sporting a style which was a cross between gothic and punk with a bit of Frank Bruno thrown in."

They all laughed but Tom quickly sobered and said, "We have decided that tonight we won't talk about it, you are right though John she does look stunning." In a proprietorial sort of way he went over and slipped his arm round Rosie's waist. Rosie regarded Tom and felt pleased at his open show of affection, which was rare; perhaps he too was surprised at how good she looked. What was different about her tonight, perhaps it was the dress; she had not been making much effort lately and had worn only trousers and t-shirts for comfort. Either way it did not matter, she was enjoying the attention.

Tom asked if John and Rosie would like to go out into the garden and he would bring drinks. They did as he asked and Tom watched them animatedly talking together as they walked around the garden, Rosie stooping to smell a rose or behead a dead one. Just as the doorbell rang he saw Rosie stumble, the heel of one of her shoes obviously sinking in the grass too deeply, John caught her and they laughed together. They looked so at ease with each other.

Tom felt a twinge of what could only be jealousy, did he and Rosie laugh like that anymore, he remembered laughing a lot with Polly. Why was he thinking and feeling differently towards Rosie, what had happened to change things? He knew what had happened, Polly had happened.

The doorbell rang again and he reluctantly went to answer it, he wished he could watch them for longer, but why? Perhaps he wanted some evidence that Rosie was guilty of flirting with John to make himself feel better.

Alice stood on the doorstep armed with lilies and wine. Tom smiled welcomingly and said, "Sorry Alice, come in, I was busy with drinks and John and Rosie are in the garden, you are looking lovely as usual," and he gave her a kiss on both cheeks.

"Thank you, I'm feeling ridiculously nervous Tom, Rosie seems to have high hopes that John and I will fall hopelessly in love and be happy ever after."

Tom laughed, "Well I can't help you there I don't fancy him myself but seriously he is a decent chap." Then added "Rosie gets on very well with him." Alice looked at Tom, she thought there was an edge to his voice, but he was smiling so perhaps she was imagining it.

"Come and have a quick drink for Dutch courage and then we can join them in the garden."

Alice followed Tom into the kitchen and watched as he poured her a cocktail, taking it she said "Mmm looks delicious."

"It is a pity you and John are driving I could make you both very merry with a few of my cocktails."

"Rosie had asked me to stay actually Tom and I had said no, but Ruth is staying with a friend now so I could, if that is still okay, and the thought of getting a little merry on one of your cocktails is very inviting."

"Good, I am sure it is fine. Cheers."

"Cheers."

"Alice before you join them, we have had a bit of a difficult day, poor Rosie has had to face the chap who might have attacked her the other day. Obviously, it has been traumatic for her, so we have decided not to talk about it tonight. I expect she will tell you all about it tomorrow."

"Oh how awful, poor Rosie, I won't mention it I promise."

"Go through the French doors in the dining room Alice and I'll follow with drinks. If you finish that quickly I will bring you a fresh one." Tom winked at her. She happily obliged and gave him back the glass, and as Tom took it from her he smiled and said reassuringly, "You will be fine Alice, he would be mad not to fall for you."

Alice smiled in return "Thank you Tom," and taking a deep breath went out to join them, saying to herself "Just enjoy it, it doesn't matter if he doesn't like me." As she stepped out into the garden and glanced across to where John and Rosie sat, she changed her mind and under her breath, she said, "Oh please let him like me."

John and Rosie saw Alice coming out of the French doors and Rosie with a quick aside to John. "Here is Alice, she is so lovely

John I do hope you like her." John stood up and did not have time to answer before Alice was in hearing distance.

Rosie thought she looked even lovelier than usual, in pale green chiffon sleeveless dress, which fell to just below her knees and billowed slightly in the gentle breeze.

Rosie went to greet her and kissing her warmly whispered, "You look absolutely beautiful."

With a slight blush, Alice looked up at John who was holding out his hand to her, as she took it he bent and gave her a kiss on her cheek. "Well it is good to meet you at last Alice; I have heard so much about you, I am sure that none of it is true."

Laughing they all sat down as Tom arrived with the drinks, "I have decided you should either stay the night John, or call a taxi so that you can enjoy a drink or two, we can always run your car back in the morning."

John hesitated, he rarely stayed away from home and when he did, he worried about whether the children had locked the house, left the cooker on, or needed him in any way. Since his wife died, he had sole responsibility for everything and even though the children were old enough to cope, he felt neglectful and consequently guilty if he was not there.

"Good idea Tom, I'll call a taxi," and taking a drink from the tray said "Cheers!"

Alice did the same, already the first drink was having an effect on her empty stomach and she smiled broadly at Rosie who she could see was looking at her trying to gauge her reaction to John. "This is my second and I am already beginning to feel a little woozy or perhaps it's just that sitting here in your pretty garden on a balmy evening with dear old friends and new is intoxicating."

Tom laughed and said, "What a romantic thought Alice but I think you will find it is the alcohol."

They all laughed and John looking straight at Alice said, "I think this is the beginning of a perfect evening."

The ice was broken and they all chatted for a while until Rosie decided it was time to eat.

Standing up she said, "I am just going in to warm the starter." Then realising that if Tom came in with her it would give Alice and John a time on their own to get to know each other better, she added, "Tom would you come and help with opening the wine please?"

As soon as she and Tom were indoors, Rosie turned to Tom and said, "What do you think, do they fancy one another?"

Suddenly feeling churlish Tom answered, "I don't know about Alice but it is obvious that you fancy, as you so intelligently put it, John."

Rosie felt as if she had been slapped in the face and angrily retorted, "How dare you Tom! John is a very old friend. In case you have forgotten I have arranged this evening with the particular intention of bringing two lonely, very dear friends together."

"I wonder Rosie whether you are being honest with yourself? Perhaps in reality you are hoping to live out your own sexual fantasies through Alice."

With sudden realisation Rosie understood what Tom was doing, he was trying to find a way of making her guilty in order to assuage his own concience.

"Tom you had better keep your warped psychological theories to yourself, this is supposed to be a special evening, I can't believe you thinking that never mind saying it." She strode off into the kitchen where Tom heard her angrily banging things about.

Rosie felt outraged at Tom's suggestion and yet abashed too, she did like John very much and she supposed that she had always enjoyed the fact that John had liked her although it was not until the other day that he showed her how much. She also knew that John had not seriously considered her anything other than a painting companion and friend; it was just that he was now ready to find a new partner.

Rosie put the salmon and asparagus tart in the oven to warm and took the lamb out, it smelt delicious. Tom came into the kitchen with two bottles of red wine, he put them down on the table and came over to Rosie and resting his hands on her shoulders, he turned her round to face him.

"I am sorry Rosie I don't know why I said it. I watched you with him earlier before Alice arrived and you were laughing with him and it struck me that it was a long while since we had laughed like that together." He wrapped his arms around her and although she felt rigid at first he felt her gradually relax and be held.

Resting her head on his chest Rosie said, "I know you are right in a way Tom, I feel more relaxed with friends than I do with you at the moment, something is different between us and I don't like it."

"Neither do I, it feels as if everything is unravelling like a ball of wool and I can't stop it." Rosie looked up at Tom and with a look of desperation said "Surely we can stop it Tom?"

Still holding her Tom said, "Do you remember me telling you about a signed Norwich City football I had for my tenth birthday. When they gave it to me my parents stressed it was a ball to keep, not for playing with. One day to impress some boys, I had just changed schools and needed to impress, I took my signed football out to play. We were playing on the park near a busy main road, one of the lads kicked it over the fence on to the road and although I ran as fast as I could I couldn't get to it, the traffic was heavy and all I could do was watch it get squashed beneath the wheels of a damn great lorry. Rosie it was precious, I had not taken enough care of it, and finally I was helpless to save it. The feeling was hell and it is how I am feeling now."

Rosie felt a wave of compassion for Tom as a little boy and now as a grown man. Looking up at him, she disengaged herself but holding his hand said,

"Oh Tom, I promise you I am not squashed yet and unlike your football I am determined to find a safe place, but it has to be with your help Tom." Smiling up at him, she said, "We will talk later, the tart will be done and we have some match-making to do."

"Yes we have and I will open this wine and call them in, is Ben eating with us?"

"Ben is next door with Jack playing Warhammer battles and making their own homemade pizzas apparently."

Tom laughed, "If they turn out like the one he made the other day at school he will come home hungry!"

It was about one thirty when John left. After waving him off Rosie shut the door and returned to Alice, who was helping Tom collect up the wine glasses and coffee cups, and said in a reveal all sort of voice. "Well?"

Alice laughed, "He is just what you said he was charming and funny and all round decent."

"I can feel a but coming on."

Alice shrugged and shook her head, "I am afraid that we won't be seeing each other again for a very long time."

Rosie looked utterly crestfallen and surprised, she was sure that they liked each other by the way they were so attentive when the other spoke and laughed heartily at the smallest amusement.

Tom winked at Alice and said, "I think this is my cue to go to bed, goodnight Alice," he touched Rosie on the shoulder, smiled and said softly to her "It was a good evening," and went to bed.

Rosie smiled at him and said, "I won't be long" and as she watched Tom go turned to Alice and said, "I felt so sure, what a pity"

Alice came and sat next to Rosie on the settee "I haven't yet thanked you for a wonderful evening Rosie and for going to such trouble, I know without a doubt that both John and I will never forget it."

"I did hope that you would like one another, wasn't the magic there?"

Alice laughed, "Well I can tell you this that if John had stayed the night I wouldn't be able to sleep a wink."

Rosie looked indignant, "Why?"

"Because I would have spent the night longing to join him."

It took a moment for Rosie to realise what Alice was meaning and then with a wide grin, "Really?"

"Yes really, you were right, I knew it the moment he smiled at me with that lopsided smile, I was hooked!"

"You absolute beast!" Rosie picked up the cushion beside her and hit Alice playfully with it.

Laughing Alice said, "I am sorry I couldn't resist teasing you."

"Well what happens now, I have done my bit?"

"John asked me to go out for the day next Sunday, for a walk on the beach and lunch."

"Oh what a good idea, where will you go? Do you know?"

"Well he suggested Southwold, but I have too many memories there so I suggested Dunwich, we can have wonderful fish and chips and a walk and also I haven't been there for years and years."

"Oh Alice that is fantastic, we are free, we can come with you." The look on Alice's face was priceless until she realised that Rosie was teasing and laughing said, "Touché."

When Rosie eventually went to bed, Tom was fast asleep, their talk would have to wait until the morning, and looking at her watch she found it was already three. As she lay there thinking of the evening the irony of it hit her, was her marriage falling apart as they were being instrumental in bringing Alice and John together?

She thought of tomorrow and lunch with her in-laws. Would Louise intuitively sense discord, how would Grace be tomorrow? Then fatigue took over and she slept until Tom brought her a cup of tea at eight.

"Good morning sleepy head."

Yawning and stretching Rosie squinted as Tom opened the curtains allowing the morning sun to pour in. "Whatever is the time Tom? You are up and dressed."

"It is only eight; I thought I might just beat everyone else in the village to the croissants if I get to the shop early."

"Goodness Tom croissants two mornings in a row we are being indulgent."

"Well Alice might like them."

"Oh Alice, of course, I had forgotten, I am not awake yet we didn't get to bed until three. She was on cloud nine last night she probably didn't sleep at all."

"Well she was awake when I took her in a cup of tea, and grinning from ear to ear."

"Tom I am sorry we didn't talk last night, why don't you come back to bed and we can talk now?"

Tom walked to the window and looked out and sighing said, "Rosie I told you I am going to get the croissants and papers then I need to drop Ben at football."

"Tom, Ben doesn't need to be at football until nine-thirty. I'll get up and when you come back from the shop we can walk Charlie together for half an hour and talk in the fresh air."

"Rosie, we do have a guest here remember anyway I am sure Alice would enjoy a walk."

Rosie looked at Tom's back, he was still looking out of the window, he had his hands in his pockets and his shoulders hunched. "Tom, it feels as if you are avoiding me, you will be gone tomorrow and then when will we have the chance to talk?"

Tom came and sat on the bed. "Ouch you are sitting on my foot!"

He got up again "Sorry, we will talk later, I need to go into the office for an hour this morning and then we will have to leave for lunch with my parents. Have you reminded Ben and Grace I really want-"

Rosie interrupted him, "Go to the office on a Sunday, whatever for?"

"I know, I know but I will be away for a month remember and there are a couple of things I didn't get round to doing on Friday"

"A *month*?!" shouted Rosie.

Tom cursed himself for his stupidity, "Oh hell, it was meant to be a surprise I was going to tell everyone at lunch today, you don't need to look so shocked for heavens sake."

Rosie sat speechless for a moment, "Are you serious? You are going away for a month and were going to tell me as a surprise in front of your parents. How thoughtful of you Tom."

"Oh don't be ridiculous, I am at work for a fortnight then you all come and join me and we have a holiday. I have booked it all. Don't glare at me like that, it isn't a total surprise, we have been talking about it."

"We hadn't decided on a date and what about Ben? He won't have finished school by then. I also need to spend some time with my parents now I am fit enough to help them."

"I have spoken to Ben's school already and in the circumstances they have agreed to allow him to have the time off."

Tom was back at the window not wanting to look at the expression on Rosie's face, he knew that he was railroading her but he had to know her decision on America as soon as possible and if he was honest he hadn't trusted Rosie to get organised in time.

Rosie was incredulous, Tom always left holiday planning up to her and she enjoyed doing it. She heard herself sound sulky and petulant, "I always organise our holidays and now suddenly you have taken over and are sorting us all out as if you don't trust me to cope with it."

"You have been through quite a trauma recently remember?"

"Will you stop being so patronising and saying *if you remember* all the time as if I am going senile?"

Alice was aware of raised voices in the next room although the walls were thick enough for her not to hear the details. She decided to get up quietly and take Charlie for a walk in the hope that when she returned all would be calm. Pulling on blue shorts and a green t-shirt, she quietly tiptoed downstairs with her shoes in her hand so as not to make too much noise.

Both Charlie and Sammy came to greet her, Charlie immediately rolled on his back for a tummy rub and Sammy brushed herself against her leg obviously hoping for food. "Sorry Sammy I don't know where your food is kept," she whispered giving her a stroke.

Walking through to the kitchen Alice saw Charlie's lead hanging on the hooks with various keys by the back door. She did not have to call Charlie as he knew instinctively and was there beside her with his tail wagging furiously and thudding on the cupboard door beside him. "Ssh Charlie."

She then let herself out of the back door quietly closing it behind her. All was well as she rounded the house but when she met the gravel drive she tried to walk quietly but the stones seemed to make a terrible din and Charlie was skittishly jumping up and down and barking excitedly. As Alice glanced back she heard Rosie call, "Wait for me!" from the bathroom window.

"You don't have too Rosie I am quite happy."

"No Alice I need a walk, I will be down in a sec."

Alice sat on the rather wobbly bench seat by the lilac tree and enjoyed the feel of the morning sun on her face and looking across the green she watched the village come to life.

"It is another lovely day." Tom made her jump.

"Oh hello Tom, I was miles away enjoying watching the birds darting about and seeing the early comings and goings of the village."

"Have you seen the baker's van by any chance?"

"No I don't think so."

"Oh well it must have been and gone, you can watch me now try and beat the rest of the village to the croissants." With that he strode out of the drive.

Alice watched him walk with long strides towards the village shop noticing him waving to someone but not stopping. Rosie then appeared with two apples in her hand and a bonio for Charlie. "Something for us to munch while we walk." She handed the bonio to Alice.

Alice laughed, "Very funny."

"Sorry to leave you waiting but I really wanted a walk."

"I have had a very pleasant time sitting near your lilac tree and watching the world go by and Charlie has been only mildly sulking beside me. I love the rose you have planted to ramble amongst the branches, what is it?"

"It is lovely isn't it, its called wedding day. I think we have a blackbird's nest in that tree, did you hear the young?"

"I'm not sure; I certainly heard a cacophony of bird's song."

"Let's go shall we?"

They walked in companionable silence for a short while until Rosie stopped and turning to Alice said with a look of unhappiness, "I love it here Alice."

"Oh Rosie I know you do and I can see why."

They started to walk again, "I can't get near to Tom at the moment and I know he is unhappy too, he started to really talk to me yesterday and I felt near to him but he has shut down again today and it feels as if there is this great chasm between us."

"Have you said that to him?"

"I have tried, I know it sounds ridiculous but opportunities are few and far between with all the busyness of life. It seems as if we are walking two different paths side by side sometimes we converge and it is good. Then our paths veer away from each other." Rosie sighed deeply, "I expect it is my fault Alice if I was prepared to tip everything upside down and go to America he would be happy I suppose and we wouldn't be so far apart."

"Does Tom really want to go to America?"

"Well that is what bothers me Alice I don't know, I think he has worked for the same firm for so long and worries about change. The strange thing is because of all the moves he had to make as a child he has always said that he wanted our children to have a stable school life."

They walked single file over the wooden footbridge, which led over the little stream to the fields, where Rosie let Charlie off the lead. As Rosie bent down her top came loose from her trousers and Alice caught a glimpse of now yellowing bruises across her lower back. She felt a surge of compassion for her friend who seemed to have had so much to cope with and obviously more troubles ahead.

Not knowing how to help she simply said, "Life has so many twists and turns Rosie, nothing ever seems to stay the same for long."

Rosie looked at Alice and smiled, warmed by her obvious concern then said, "You are right there, Tom said the other day that he was relishing the idea of a new challenge and to be truly honest I fear that the new challenge he talks about is not the job but the woman he met in America."

Alice was genuinely shocked, she had always thought of Tom and Rosie as being rock solid and had envied them their relationship, hoping one day to find the same. "Oh no Rosie I can hardly believe it, are you sure?"

Rosie told Alice all she knew, by this time they had turned round and were making their way back towards the village.

When Rosie had finished Alice asked, "What are you going to do?"

Rosie was quiet for a moment and shrugging said, "At this moment Alice I have no idea what I can do, all I do know is that I can pray. Will you come into the church with me, there isn't a service until six tonight but it will be open."

"Of course."

They made their way back through the village, with Charlie who had been chasing rabbits panting beside them, up the gentle hill to the church. The sun lit up the old porch with its flint stones glinting and the flagstone floor worn down by all the centuries of worshippers.

The heavy oak door was open wide, as they entered the welcoming coolness they heard the organ begin to play. Alice and Rosie slipped into a pew at the back to listen. Charlie as if feeling quite at home lay down in the aisle beside them. Rosie knelt to pray while Alice sat quietly as the sound of a pure and clear voice began to sing softly at first but soon filled the church with the hymn O Lord my God!.

Alice breathed in deeply enjoying the smell of beeswax on the obviously recently polished pew. She let the sound of organ music and singing wash over her as she looked around and studied the stained glass in the huge stone arched windows. One she particularly liked and suspected was of a later period than the others. It had subtle colours rather than the vivid reds and blues so often used in early stain glass, and was of a more simple design. It depicted a smiling Jesus holding out his hands as if reaching out in welcome and Alice found herself smiling back.

As the music stopped she turned to Rosie and was horrified to see silent tears falling unchecked down her cheeks, "Oh Rosie what is it?"

"It is my favourite hymn and Be sang it so beautifully." Rosie closed her eyes and said nothing more in explanation.

Alice not knowing what to say felt concerned and reached in her pocket for the tissue she had thankfully put there, she handed it to Rosie who took it and smiled at her in gratitude.

Alice watched an attractive, smartly dressed lady, who she presumed was the organist, come down the aisle towards them and Rosie, now composed, said as she reached them, "Be that was beautiful thank you."

"Well thank you Rosie, I don't know why I came in to play it, I just felt moved to do so," and saying no more bent down to stroke Charlie then she smiled and walked out of the church.

Turning to Alice, Rosie said, "That felt like a precious gift, come on Alice I think it is time for breakfast, suddenly I feel ravenous."

TWELVE

A lice and Rosie arrived home to find that Tom had already left but had obviously made the coffee as the smell greeted them as they entered the kitchen. "Mmm the smell of freshly ground coffee," said Alice appreciatively.

Rosie saw six croissants on a plate by the Aga and propped up beside them a note.

Rosie,

As you can see, I managed to beat the hordes to the croissants but only just! I am afraid there is a disgruntled Mrs Pringle about, so be warned!

Grace is home and only talking in monosyllables, perhaps Alice can work her magic.

I have taken Ben with me so that I can pick him up from football and there then will be time for him to wash, unlike the last time we met my parents!

We will need to leave at twelve thirty if we are going to be at the Hotel by one fifteen.

Say goodbye to Alice for me.

Tom x

Rosie read the note and laughed, Mrs Pringle was formidable at the best of times, as they had found out on the first Sunday they had attended church in the village. She had wondered why several people were smiling very broadly at them until a very plump woman in tweed had come up to them and said in a very imperious manner, "*You are sitting in my pew!*". Rosie apologising had started to stand up, intending to move, but Tom had held her down and said "So kind of you to tell us, we will remember that in future."

She remembered very clearly the frosty look that Mrs Pringle had given them as she huffed and puffed her way down the aisle to another pew, so different from the warm welcome that the others had given them that day.

"What are you laughing at, and what are you cross about and promise me you will never play poker?" laughed Alice as she watched the changing expressions on Rosie's face, pleased to see that Rosie had found something to amuse her and then sorry that it so quickly turned to annoyance.

Rosie showed Alice Tom's note, "Here you can read it; it sums up our relationship exactly. Happy and considerate one minute and then superior and belittling the next."

Alice read it and felt embarrassed; she could understand Rosie not liking the inference that she would be able to help Grace rather than her. "Perhaps he meant to say that sometimes the one closest isn't always the best person to help, I know that Ruth quite often gets angry with me about something and yet doesn't with others."

Rosie looked at Alice who was obviously feeling uncomfortable, "I know, you are right Alice and I would appreciate you having a word with her but as I told you she was desperately upset and understandably. I think I ought to ring the Police and ask them what is happening."

"Good idea they might not tell you much though. Is Tom just making a joke about Ben and washing?"

"Partly I think but he was not amused at the time, unfortunately it was only when we were sitting at the table that Grace, who was sitting opposite Ben, had unkindly pointed out how filthy Ben's neck was. Ben furious at Grace had kicked her hard under the table and a row ensued. Tom blamed me but Louise sweetly came to my rescue and said that she had given up nagging Tom and his brother James to wash when they were young and that a little bit of dirt did not hurt anyone.

They both laughed and Rosie explained, "Ben is too old to be supervised in the bathroom but like a lot of boys seems to be allergic to washing, I just forgot to check that day."

Alice laughed "Oh, I don't have that problem; Ruth spends hours in the bathroom."

"Grace too," said Rosie smiling. "Alice, let's have breakfast and talk about something exciting like the prospect of you and John. I am being over sensitive I expect and an absolute bore," and she screwed up the note and flung it in the bin.

"Alice, would you mind putting the croissants in the oven and pouring the coffee, I want to just pop up and see Grace for a minute, and ask her to join us"

Alice did as she was asked and then cleared away what looked like the remains of Ben's breakfast, there were cocoa pops scattered all over the kitchen table and milk splashed too, making muddy pools on the scrubbed pine.

She went to the larder where she found the butter dish and various jams and honey, which she put on the table and then found the plates, cutlery and mugs. Having laid the table she looked around her at the old farmhouse style kitchen.

Alice liked Rosie's house and it's frayed at the edges look. Always full of life, there were various plants on the windowsills and jars with what looked like cuttings rooting. Adorning the walls were several colourful paintings, obviously done by Grace and Ben at different ages. On the wall behind the table was a large pin board which had a beautifully hand painted frame, it was full of leaflets on everything from swimming pool info to theatre programmes, photos, school letters, recipes and right in the middle a piece of verse in large bold print

There is so much in God's world for us all
If we only have eyes to see it,
And the heart to love it,
And the hand to gather it to ourselves.

"That's true," said Alice out loud, thinking of John.

"What's true Aunty Alice?"

Alice jumped "Oh Hello Grace, you know you don't have to call me Aunty now you are nearly grown up"

"I know but it makes you sound cuddly."

Alice laughed, "How about a cuddle right now." Alice opened her arms wide and Grace went into them gratefully. After a minute or two, Alice released her and said, "I think our croissants are ready, I am glad you are joining us for breakfast."

"Well I am not very hungry," and then when Alice took them out of the oven and Grace said, "Well maybe just one with some honey." Alice knew that she would be okay. "Where is Rosie, Grace?"

"She is phoning the police, she said to start without her." At that moment Rosie appeared.

"I'm here."

"What did they say Mum, what is happening, have they arrested him, is he in prison?"

"Hey Grace give me time, he didn't tell me much only that Carl had admitted the crime but had been released on bail and they were following further lines of enquiry. They have asked me to come into the station to answer some questions, which I am doing tomorrow."

"I can't believe he did that to you Mum, I am so sorry."

"Did he ever give you any signs that he was doing anything illegal?"

"Not to me, he was so cool Mum and great to be with. It does not seem possible that he could do that."

Rosie put her arm around her and gently said, "Well Grace he has been led into crime, we don't know why. I should think that his home life is difficult or he mixes in the wrong crowd, it was certainly someone a lot older who was with him that night. Perhaps he takes drugs Grace?"

Grace looked down at her feet, she knew that he did, she also knew who sold them to him. "Yes Mum but he never offered them to me, I swear."

"Why didn't you tell me?"

"Oh come off it Mum, You know you wouldn't have let me see him if you knew."

"Grace, drugs make people do things they might otherwise not do. If you know from whom he is getting them then you have a duty to inform the police. Drug dealers are in effect murderers Grace, you could save lives."

"I think I do know who he gets them from but I don't know his name," said Grace miserably.

"Do you know who might know?"

I am going to ring Jane, she lives near him, she might know about his family and also she is friends with the girl who goes out with a guy who sells them."

"Be careful Grace, it might be better not to say too much to anyone else yet for his sake and for yours."

"Do you think he will be at school on Monday?"

"I don't know Grace, I rather suspect not."

"I am going to text him."

"Let's all have breakfast first and take time to think about it."

Alice said, "Good idea, I am starving," and picking up the plate of croissants she put them on the kitchen table and sat down.

Rosie seeing the table laid said, "Oh you have got everything ready, thank you Alice."

"Well you worked very hard yesterday on that wonderful meal and refused to let me lift a finger to help clear up, so laying the table for breakfast is the least I can do."

While Rosie fetched the coffee pot Alice turned to Grace, Alice ached for her and putting her hand on Grace's she said, "Grace we all make mistakes of different kinds and it is great when we have friends to support us when we are living through the consequences of those mistakes. What you have to remember is to never compromise your own integrity."

Rosie returning with the coffee looked at her friend and smiled, Tom was right Alice does have a gentle wisdom, which she could see was working its magic on Grace.

Tom unlocked his office door and sat at his desk, he had planned to ring Polly, something he felt he could do from the office and not from home. He needed to keep her separate, to himself.

He had planned to thank her for the photograph and apologise for not seeing her note earlier but he realised that she might ask what prompted him to look for the note and he would have to admit to Rosie finding it.

No, he would simply ring and say that he was coming over tomorrow but of course, she would know that already. He wanted to let her know that he was looking forward to seeing her; he wanted to give her some sort of signal without committing himself, committing himself to what? An affair, a quick fling no strings attached. Was there such a thing?

What he did know was that already they had crossed the

threshold of working colleague to friends, now what was an unknown territory for him was whether he was capable of keeping the friendship on a purely platonic level.

Who was he kidding? No one and certainly not himself, just thinking about it aroused him.

He lifted up the phone and dialled her mobile, the only number he had for her other than her office one, he heard it ringing and then an infuriating voice asking him to leave a message. He hesitated for a minute then said, "It's me, I am coming to bridge the gap," and then he put the phone down.

He had been cryptic but he was sure she would read into that what she wanted to and he just hoped he would be able to judge her feelings, something he knew was not his strong point.

They would have two weeks together before Rosie and the children came out, he was pleased he had booked a different hotel for the holiday so as not to have any embarrassing mix ups.

He felt excited at the prospect and longed to be on his way to her, only today to get through.

He was not particularly looking forward to seeing his mother but he knew he could rely on Dad to understand his desire to move with the firm. He will help him explain to the children that a man has to provide for the family and if that means moving abroad then so be it.

He was glad he had booked the holiday week as well as the New York visit. He would make sure that they had a fantastic time and make them see that America would offer them a much more exciting life than sleepy old Norfolk could.

Feeling positive, he took the brochures on the holiday out of his filing cabinet. He then wrote a note for Debbie, his new secretary, with all his contact numbers and put it on her desk. Sally had transferred to the New York office and according to the reliable office gossip, was Paul's mistress when he was over there. He wondered whether Jane, Paul's wife, suspected Paul was being unfaithful. He thought of Jane who was a hard working GP and mother to Paul's two sons and in Tom's eyes attractive and good company. He felt a loss of respect for Paul and then suddenly Polly came into his mind and he understood how easy it is to be tempted. Would he be able to resist? The thought was too uncomfortable and he dismissed it.

Before closing his office door Tom glanced around his office and smiled, enjoying the thought that he would not be there for a month.

Tom arrived at the football pitch just in time to see Ben saving a goal before the whistle went. Tom watched as Ben and his team were cheering and whooping. He tried not to look at the defeated team as they made their way gloomily off the pitch. He felt for them, remembering only too clearly the feeling of defeat.

Ben was busy chatting about the match and had not seen Tom who was trying to get Ben's attention by waving at him, when Ben eventually saw him he just waved back and carried on chatting. Tom exasperated then shouted, "Ben, hurry up!" It had the desired effect as Ben started to walk towards him but stopped when a team mate kicked a ball at him, Ben unable to resist kicked it back and Tom was astounded to see Ben running off in the opposite direction. Tom looked at his watch; it said ten past twelve, and then angrily bellowed, "Ben!"

"Keep your hair on mate," said a chap nearby who was also waiting. "You'll give yourself a heart attack."

Tom in defence said, "We have actually got to be in Holt for lunch at one fifteen and we will obviously be late."

"Well you won't make it at all if you burst a blood vessel, I'll give them a whistle," and he put two fingers in his mouth and blew an impressive whistle.

Tom had remembered trying to do that as a lad and had never

succeeded. To his chagrin, all the boys stopped playing and Ben came trotting towards him. He mumbled thanks and not waiting for Ben turned round and started to stride towards the car. He heard the expert whistler say to Ben, "Well done lad, you are man of the match."

Ben caught Tom up as he reached the car, "We won Dad nine to two, I was goalie and I'm man of the match!" Ben looked so pleased with himself Tom did not have the heart to give him the telling off he had intended. Trying to be calm, he simply said, "Well done Ben, now we must hurry."

Ben gave Tom a blow-by-blow account of the match on the way home; surprisingly it put Tom in a better mood. Tom felt genuinely proud of Ben, and pleased that he was proving to be a good team member.

When they turned in the drive Tom said, "Right David Beckham the second, you have three minutes to get washed and changed, and I mean washed."

"Okay, Okay." Tom ran indoors yelling. "We won!" and when he couldn't find anyone downstairs bounded upstairs still yelling. "We won!"

Rosie and Grace were upstairs changing; Alice had only just left so Rosie had to race around.

Rosie called, "Well done Ben!" through the bedroom door, then quickly opened it, and called to Ben. "Don't forget to wash your neck."

"If anyone else tells me to wash I'll roll in the dung heap like Charlie."

Grace hearing this knocked on Ben's door and said, "Ben, I hope you are going to wash!"

Downstairs, Tom, who was getting agitated, heard lots of shouts, laughter and banging doors and then a scream from Grace. More shouts, laughter and banging doors.

He called up as loudly as he could, "We are going now, do you hear me NOW!"

Rosie called, "Be down in a minute!" in an infuriatingly re-laxed, we have all the time in the world sort of voice.

Grace came hurtling down the stairs shrieking with Ben following her wielding what looked like a soaking wet flannel and shouting, "I'll get you back!" Tom grabbed Ben as he went past and said "Have you washed?"

Ben swung the wet flannel round and it splattered against Tom's face.

"Aarh, yuk!" Both Ben and Grace fell about laughing.

They arrived at the Holt Arms at one twenty five, he had told the family one fifteen in the hope that they would be there by one thirty.

Lillian and Henry had just arrived and ordered drinks, on seeing Tom and Rosie, Lillian exclaimed, "My goodness you are nice and early."

Henry held his arms wide open for Ben and Grace, who from an early age had loved their Grandfather dearly. Both Ben and Grace simultaneously looked around to see as if any one was watching and both, despite a busy hotel, went into his arms for a hug. Henry had seen the furtive looks and inwardly sighed, how quickly they had grown, and he gave them an extra strong hug and a kiss on each head.

Lillian greeted them all warmly but more formally, "How lovely it is to see you all, we have ordered your usual drinks and our table is by the window in the dining room," turning to Rosie she said, "I have a surprise for you."

"Oh really, how exciting!"

"I think you will be pleased."

Rosie looked at her parents-in-law, how different they were

from her own parents. Lillian so immaculately dressed in a classic summer suit in navy linen with a simple yellow cotton blouse beneath, navy shoes to match. Henry in a smart sports jacket and white shirt and the ever-present bow tie, looked very dashing. He loved to be flamboyant and his bow ties were a source of amusement, todays choice was obviously in honour of Ben as it was red with black and white footballs all over it.

"Wicked bow tie Gramps!"

"Well done Ben you have noticed, how very observant of you. I am glad you like it, I had it made especially."

Grace asked him what would be the design if he had made one with her in mind. "Ah now that is a very good question Grace, and the answer is you will have to wait and see."

Tom began to relax as they made their way into the dining room; his parents seemed to be in very good spirits.

"Tom, would you wait a moment, let the others find their seats. I have something for you, I am hoping you might find it of interest." Tom turned round to look at his father who had an envelope in his hands.

"Yes of course, what is it Dad?"

"Well before I show you, I don't want you thinking that I am interfering in any way."

Tom was intrigued, "You never have Dad, I'm sure you won't start now."

"Good, good, well here you are then, I've done the same thing for your brother before now." Hearing that Tom assumed his father was about to give him some money, although why the large brown envelope? Tom opened it and took out its contents, he was wrong it wasn't money but several employment advertisements that had been cut out of what looked like various papers. Tom felt annoyed but looking at his father he said, "Why Dad, what are you trying to tell me?"

"I want you to see that there are many opportunities here in the UK and you will see when you get home and have time to look at them properly that all of these are asking for your qualifications and you have plenty of experience to offer."

Coldly Tom replied, "In case you have forgotten I have a perfectly good job waiting for me in the States."

"I am well aware of that Tom but I am also aware that you have been telling me for at least three years that it 'bored you but paid the mortgage.' Your very words I might add."

"Exactly Dad that is why I want this new challenge."

"Tom, believe me when I say that the same job just different geography won't change anything and what is more you will have shipped your unfortunate family over to America for what?"

Tom felt annoyed, how dare his father question his decision. "I am sorry Dad but you have stepped over the mark. You really do not expect me take that from you. We moved homes when James and I were young so frequently it wasn't worth unpacking."

"Tom that is an exaggeration and you know it but the fact was that we were able to keep the family home and we stopped moving once you reached a critical time in your education"

"Family home, that's rich you were never there Dad. I have to say I thought you of all people would support me in this."

"I can't Tom I am sorry. What you don't know, and I am very ashamed of the fact, is that your mother and I nearly divorced over my inability to put the family first."

Tom was unmoved. "But you didn't Dad, and at the risk of being rude, yours and Mum's life is not mine. I intend to be there for my family."

Henry looked at Tom and saw himself at Tom's age feeling bored and restless, not with his work but with his wife. He didn't know if this was the case but he suspected as much and at the risk of annoying his son further said, "Tom like it or not you are like me and I remember how it felt to want new experiences and I am not talking work here. Rose (He was the only one who called her that) is a wonderful woman, what you have with your wife and family is the most important thing, I ask you to remember that." He walked away towards the dining room leaving Tom both annoyed and abashed. How did he know, had Rosie said anything to him, surely not.

Tom felt even more determined to say what he had planned and to surprise Rosie and the children with the holiday arrangements.

He bought another pint at the bar and carried it through to the dining room where, to his absolute horror, sat his parents-in-law. They were obviously the surprise his mother had mentioned. He swore under his breath and greeted them as warmly as he could. He was shocked at the sight of Norman who looked somehow diminished but it was not long before Norman was holding forth about some new Government scheme that irritated him.

"Political hogwash that's all it is, some upstart probably never farmed in his life thinks he can pull the wool over our eyes. Popularity vote that's what that is, won't work with me."

Rosie, sitting opposite Tom caught his eye and grinned, Tom grinned back "Glad to see you are in good form Norman," said Tom

"Oh sorry Tom didn't see you come in, I was getting on my soap box again I expect." He looked straight at Tom. "I am glad you are home looking after my daughter, I don't want her wandering around on her own at night any more."

Tom did not have the time to answer before Rosie spoke, "Dad, I was meeting Alice and having a girl's night out, it wasn't Tom's fault."

"You should meet during the day, much safer."

Tom decided that now was as good a time as any to tell them about the holiday and his possible plans. He cleared his throat loudly and looking straight at Norman made his announcement.

"Well I have booked a fortnights holiday in New York and Florida so we can all go away and recover from the ordeal."

Ben said excitedly, "Great when?"

"In two weeks after Grace's exams, Ben you will have the end of term off school, I have cleared it with the head."

Norman, who understandably thought the *all* included him, shakily stood up and said, "I am sorry Tom but I'm not going to fly half way round the world for a holiday. I haven't seen much of this country yet and we can't leave the farm at short notice."

Hearing everyone laugh he looked to his wife for support, "We can't can we Louise?" but she was laughing too at the thought of Norman thinking he was going. She spluttered, "Absolutely dear, not us at all!"

Tom laughed "No, don't worry Norman the holiday is for we four but a holiday for you would be a very good idea." Norman sat down and chuckled.

"Tom you looked straight at me, how the devil was I supposed to know?"

Ben chirped in, "You gave Grandpa a right flight fright."

Again everyone laughed.

Louise looked at Norman and said, "It is time that we had a good holiday Norman; we haven't had more than a few days away for years. We have always talked of going to Ireland."

"Well let's go then love, while I am well enough to get around."

Grace had not laughed along with the others, she was appalled, and how could Dad book it without asking her. She would miss the school prom and she had made her beautiful oyster silk dress. She thought of Carl who had asked her to go with him, obviously that was not going to be possible now anyway.

When Tom looked at her expecting some reaction, he could see from her expression that she was miserable.

"Grace darling, it will be just what you need."

Rosie looked round at Grace who in a hardly audible whisper said, "The prom Mum."

With a horrible realisation of dates Rosie gasped, "Oh darling I am so sorry, the prom and your beautiful dress."

Everyone's eyes turned to Grace then Tom who felt as if he were the enemy. "Oh hell Grace I am sorry," and then trying to be optimistic said, "I am sure there will a dance we could go to in New York." Both Rosie and Grace glared at him.

Henry unhelpfully asked, "Why the rush Tom? Why not go in the school holidays they are long enough surely?"

Tom glared at his father, what could he say, he had wanted to announce his intention of going to work permanently in the States today but how could he now. The fact was that he had to make his decision as soon as possible. He needed his family to agree, he had already intimated that he was going to accept the offer.

"Dad, I am out there on business as you know and it makes sense to combine my work and the holiday, one following the other saves money and time. It is just easier this way."

"For whom Tom?"

Tom could bear this no longer, he felt a desperate need to get away from the emotions of Grace and the disapproving looks of his father.

Ben, it seemed was the only one of his family who was happy, he was busy chatting to Louise about the holiday and seemed oblivious to the emotions of Grace and his Grandfather.

Rosie looked across at Tom and mouthed to him. "Please tell them."

Tom looked away, now was the opportunity to tell them, he realised he should have done it before. He stood up and Rosie thought that he was going to make an announcement but he simply said, "Excuse me," and left.

Rosie watched him go out into the Hotel garden and decided after a minute or so to follow him but suddenly Louise gave an exclamation of delight. "How marvellous, Rosie you dark horse, why haven't you told us!"

Rosie was confused, "Told you what?"

"Ben has just told me that you are going to take part in a new TV series, how exciting!"

Rosie had no choice but to stay and tell everyone about the possible opportunity, explaining that she had wanted to wait until her appointment with Giles Barton before telling anyone.

It was another five minutes before she could get away, the coffee had come and she said she would go and tell Tom. She found him by the large natural pond at the bottom of the garden almost hidden by the huge weeping willow tree; its branches were dipping in the water. Tom was standing in its shade, arms crossed staring into the water. There was a pair of mallard ducks who were splashing around and diving in tails up. Rosie joined him slipping her arm in his.

"Aren't they funny?"

"Who's funny?"

"The ducks Tom."

"Oh I hadn't noticed."

She looked at Tom so preoccupied with his thoughts and wondered what he was feeling.

"Tom, you will have to be honest and tell them. It will be such a shock otherwise and that isn't fair."

"Tell them what Rosie? That I am moving to the States and you won't come with me?"

"That is not the case Tom, you must tell them that you have been given a choice and I can tell them that I am not happy about it, and the reasons why."

"Rosie other than the children's schooling the only reason is that you would rather pick flowers and paint pretty pictures in your English garden than support me, your husband."

Tom knew that he had overstepped the mark but he genuinely

felt that with Rosie he came a long way down her list of priorities.

"Tom there are many reasons why I don't want to move to America. One of them is that you have never taken my painting seriously and now I have the opportunity to."

Tom did not let her finish, "Oh for goodness sake Rosie you know that is just a fantasy, it is very unlikely to come to anything and there are probably other artists in line for it anyway."

She had never felt more like slapping him than she did at that moment, how dared he be so condescending.

"Tom I would like to remind you that one of the reasons you are so keen on this job is a certain girl called Polly," and then because she couldn't help herself. "Or perhaps with a name like Polly I should call her your little bird on the side," and then she giggled.

Tom was not amused and through gritted teeth said, "Don't you bring her into this equation and that is not remotely funny."

"No I know Tom." Rosie turned away from him. "I wish we could turn back the clock, we were happy a couple of months ago weren't we?"

He did not answer her, he did not know. What is happiness?

"Tom, answer me, we were happy. We were, I know we were. Since that day you came home early with the news things haven't been the same."

"Sometimes Rosie people grow apart, they just do. The fact is we have always been very different and this has just illustrated the differences."

"We have always enjoyed the differences Tom or at least I have."

"Rosie do not take this as a criticism but I have to tell you, your unrealistic airy fairy way of looking at things, your constant desire for everyone to be cosy and happy isn't life as it is. No wonder Grace can't cope with minor disappointments and Ben thinks that he will be a top footballer."

"Tom there is nothing wrong in being happy and optimistic and also there is nothing wrong in having dreams. Every football loving boy hopes to be a champion surely."

"Rosie I am driven, I want to move on and up and you are holding me back."

"Think about what are you driving away from Tom, your marriage, and your family, and to what? A big fat wallet or a new young business like girlfriend perhaps, is that what you want?"

Tom ignored her comments and replied. "Rosie before I settle into cardigans and slippers I want to move in a different direction, don't you see. I am sick of the same old dreary routine."

"It isn't for long once the children have left home we can have an adventure, go round the world even."

"Oh for goodness sake Rosie you are missing the point!"

Tom did not know where this conversation was leading; it felt as he was sliding away from her and his family.

"Tom, the point as I see it is that you no longer want to be with us, you are in effect rubbishing our life."

Exasperated by her choice of words he retorted, "We are not even on the same wavelength, are we?"

"Yes Tom we are but we have drifted away from each other and I am going to claw my way back, we have too much to lose. We must go back in they will be wondering why we are out here all this time. What will you say Tom?"

Tom turned to walk back in, "Nothing, absolutely nothing. I have decided to tell the children on the first day of the holiday. Our families will just have to accept what we do with our lives is our business."

THIRTEEN

Polly sat at the airport waiting for Tom's flight arrival announcement.

She felt sick with nerves; twice she had stood up to go and had sat down again. He did not know that she was meeting him from the airport and she had rehearsed over and over what she would say to him. Would he be pleased, she had no idea; she hoped she would know by his expression when he saw her waiting.

She had decided that if he was businesslike with her she would know what she had suspected was wrong. If he looked genuinely pleased then she would have hope that he might feel about her what she felt for him. The problem was she really did not understand her own feelings never mind understanding his. Since she had last seen him she had almost thought of nothing else, was it lust, friendship, or merely a longing to be close again with someone?

Without realising it, she said aloud, "Yes all of those."

The man sitting next to her eating tacos offered her one. "You may have one, lady, but not all of them!" Then laughed loudly at his own joke.

Polly noticed him for the first time. "Sorry, I was miles away."

"That's fine with me but each time you get up and change your mind and sit down again it makes me jumpy."

"I am sorry, I am waiting for someone."

"I'm a cab driver and have been for thirty six years, I wait for people all the time, doesn't give me the heebie-jeebies though."

Polly laughed at the open, friendly man with a smiley face and decided to confide in him.

"I'm nervous because I'm not sure if he will be happy when he sees me."

Polly half expected the cab driver to make some crass remark like, "A girl like you of course he'll be happy," but he did not. He said, "Well if you go you won't know will you?"

Polly nodded and gave him a weak smile.

Tom's flight announcement came at last, Polly jumped up and turned to say goodbye. However, the cab driver spoke first. "Lady let me give you some advice which has stood me in good stead. If you smile your widest smile believe me he will smile back."

Polly grinned at him. "Thank you."

"That's okay, any day."

The cab driver stood up and wandered over to the arrival gate, he could see Polly with a fixed smile on her face. He winked at her. He then walked over to the far side and held up a card with the name of his passenger on it in large print just as the swarm of passengers emerged through the gates.

After a few minutes of scanning every face, Polly saw Tom, smiled, and waved but Tom did not look at her but instead headed in the opposite direction.

Tom saw his name held high as soon as he entered the arrival lounge; relieved he made his way to the cab driver. He had asked his secretary to organise a cab for him, he knew that at eleven at night he would have had to queue and that was the last thing he wanted to do after a long flight.

He was exhausted, Rosie had kept him awake talking half the night and then had wanted to make love, he remembered her words. "Please make love to me and go knowing that I want you."

Guiltily he also remembered his feelings, he wanted to sleep and Rosie's melodramatic request had only infuriated him.

Tom reached the cab driver and shook the hand he held out to him in welcome. They began to walk towards the exit when the cab driver turned to look behind him and stopped, he had remembered Polly and out of curiosity had looked back to see if he could spot her looking happy and arm in arm with her chap. Instead, he had seen her alone, standing stock-still and looking directly at them. He left Tom saying, "Wait here a moment please Mr Holden." and went to her with his board held in front of him. When he reached her he said, "Something tells me we have come to collect the same man, here take this." He handed her his name board with Tom's name on it. Looking startled Polly took the board.

"I have been stupid, I didn't think. What about your fare?" She started to rummage in her bag.

"No need there will be plenty of takers, just take my card and if you need a lift remember me."

Smiling broadly Polly replied excitedly, "Oh I will thank you so much!"

"Keep smiling like that and he's yours."

Polly holding the board high in front of her walked towards Tom, it was not that far and yet it seemed to take ages. For her this seemed a momentous moment, a moment that could change her life.

Tom exhausted saw his name held high again and said under his breath. "What the blazes is that chap doing?" He held up his hand thinking that perhaps the driver had forgotten where he had left him.

When Polly reached Tom and lowered the board Tom was looking decidedly grumpy. Tom impatiently said, "Look I would be grateful if-" then realising who it was looked neither pleased nor unhappy just surprised.

They both started talking at once and then simultaneously laughed. Tom put down his bag and held out his arms and Polly relieved went into them and happily received a firm hug.

Rosie smiled to herself as she thought about indulging in a long soak in the bath with a glass of wine.

Having cooked dinner, cleared away, phoned her parents and helped Ben with his homework she at last had a chance to try and relax.

She filled the bath with hot water and added a generous amount of bath salts, put on her favourite Enya CD in the small player they kept in the bathroom, placed the glass of chilled white wine where she could easily reach it and then slipped gratefully into the welcoming warmth. "Oh bliss!"

Later in bed, Rosie made a mental decision not to dwell on her relationship with Tom, having fretted and worried all day she prayed and left it in God's hands. Then she decided that tomorrow she would spend the day painting, it was about time, and she had not painted since the day of the attack. It would mentally prepare her for her meeting with Giles on Wednesday.

Rosie could not relax, and had tossed and turned all night thinking about the previous night, they had talked and talked but had succeeded in simply going round and round in circles. Yesterday had been wretched, she and Tom had spent the morning at the police station filling in forms and answering endless questions.

After lunch at the local pub, Tom had left for the airport, earlier than he needed. It had been a fond farewell but Rosie knew instinctively that Tom was just trying hard to please out of a sense of duty and was desperate to get away. When she had said this to him, he had denied it but she knew.

When Tom hugged her goodbye, it was not the melting into one another sort of hug but a hug the sort her father would give her on occasions. Strong, loving and supportive, wonderful from her father but not the 'I am going to miss you like crazy' hug you have from your lover.

To cap the day Grace had come home upset, she had 'messed up' her final drama exam. She had known her piece well and had practised it countless times but in front of the external judges she had 'Fallen apart.'

Rosie tried to cheer her but was unsuccessful, Grace had stomped up the stairs and Rosie had heard her run a bath. When the children were young if either of them was upset or fractious she used to pop them in the bath, it had always had the desired effect of changing their mood and calming them down.

The next morning Rosie awoke early and seeing the sky already bright blue promising a warm and sunny day she got up.

She sorted her paints and packed her bag with all she would need for the day including a packed lunch.

She laid the breakfast table for the children putting a packed lunch beside each place then hearing the various noises of alarm clocks she went upstairs and knocking on each door in turn, she informed them of her painting expedition. Bidding them farewell and wishing Ben a happy day and Grace a successful English exam she left them to organise themselves.

She had a rising feeling of excitement as she packed the car with her easel and painting bag, and then put a delighted Charlie in the back of the car.

She had no idea where she was going but had planned to drive through the villages and stop when she spotted something she would like to paint. She had decided to do a series of colour wash sketches, which she could show Giles.

She headed east, towards the Waveney valley, an area she had never painted before. She drove for half an hour before seeing anything, which inspired her to stop; through the trees she had glimpsed what looked like a lake. As she got nearer she saw in fact that there was a large lake to the left of the road and a series of smaller lakes on the right, finding a place to park the car she put Charlie on his lead and together they set off to explore.

She decided to walk around the small lakes and find the best place to sit to do some sketches. She was delighted with her find; the steep sided pits now lakes, were an obvious haven for water-fowl. She saw coots, moorhens, ducks and two beautiful white swans gracefully gliding across the water.

She settled on a place to sit, in the shade of a hazel tree, where she had a good view of the waterfowl and a small island in the centre. The island had two young trees on it, which cast shadows on the water. She made a very loose water painting allowing the colours to mingle together, when dry she added a pen and ink definition. As she painted, an angler came to fish the opposite side of the small lake and she added him in to complete the picture.

Pleased she decided to move on to somewhere else, she wanted to find out of the way places that were unfamiliar and avoid the popular ones, painted by many artists before her.

She drove on a short way driving through the charming market town of Harleston where she noted an interesting looking gal-

lery and tea shop and promised herself a treat there on the way
home.

She saw a sign for Starston, never having been there before
she took it and after a mile or so came upon the small scarcely
populated centre. There was an old narrow bridge and a very attractive village sign, cottages with views of the valley and several
larger substantial houses. Looking up the hill, she saw the village
church half hidden behind the trees.

She walked around to see if she could fit the bridge, the sign
and a little of the church on the hill in one picture and decided
she could.

By three o clock, Rosie had done eight sketches of the area
around Harleston, Bungay and Homersfield. She had spent the
last half an hour sketching aircraft at the Flixton aircraft mu-
seum.

Remembering the gallery tearoom in Harleston, she began to
feel hungry and made her way there. Luckily, there was a parking
space just outside and in the shade. She gave Charlie a drink of
water and a bonio and leaving the windows half-open she locked
the car and went in.

Sitting on the inviting comfy sofas she perused the menu, she
chose a fruit tea and an apricot and almond cake with ice cream,
the smiling waitress assured her that it was home made and delicious.

While waiting for her tea she looked around the small gallery,
there was a delightful mix of contemporary art and assorted local
crafts. There were only two other people in the café who were in
the corner talking quietly together. Looking at the jewellery Rosie
saw a pretty shell necklace, which Grace would like, and decided
to buy it. The assistant, a stylish middle-aged woman took the
necklace from her and proceeded to gift-wrap it. "Do you live in
Harleston or are you visiting?" she asked. Rosie told her of her day

of sketching and found herself explaining about the forthcoming interview with Giles Barton.

"I would like to see your sketches if you are happy to show me them?"

"Yes of course you may."

"Have your tea first; I am being waved at so it must be ready."

"They are in the car which is just outside, I'll pop and get them and you can look at them while I have my tea if you like."

The cake was warm and delicious with the cold ice cream and just as she was finishing the gallery assistant approached her with the sketches in her hand.

"May I join you? Oh and by the way my name is Martha, I manage the gallery."

"Of course you may and mine is Rosemary but most people call me Rosie."

"Well Rosie, I like your sketches and I am sure they would sell well particularly as they are of local scenes. I would like to take them on a sale or return basis. I charge 10% commission. Obviously I need them framed."

Rosie taken aback, had not thought of selling them, they were just sketches. "Goodness, I will frame them and price them. Thank you, I must have been meant to come here today."

"Fate, I believe in it too."

They chatted for a while until Rosie looked at her watch, "I must go. I will hopefully get back to you with the framed pictures by Friday."

Martha watched her go and was delighted Rosie had accepted her offer; she was pleased with herself for spotting the opportunity. When Rosie became well known, via the TV programme, her pictures would fetch a high price and be a welcome boost for the gallery. It was providential for she very rarely worked on Tuesdays but her young assistant was unwell today.

When Rosie arrived home she was delighted to find both Grace and Ben busy in the kitchen, Ben was dressed in Tom's barbeque apron and chef's hat and Grace in Rosie's Aga apron.

"Am I to deduce from all this activity that you are the cooks for tonight?"

"Absolutely, we are giving you a night off," Grace replied with a grin.

"That is such a treat, you are wonderful"

Ben putting on a very formal voice said, "Now perhaps madam you might like a drink before dinner, if you go out into the garden I will bring one out to you."

Rosie laughed and happily entered into the spirit of things "That would be splendid, a gin and tonic please. I will just go and quickly wash and change for the occasion."

Rosie quickly changed into a long denim skirt and white t shirt and put on her colourful wooden beads; she twisted her hair into a French pleat and fastened it with a blue beaded clasp. She then rummaged in her wardrobe for her fuchsia pink wrap, just in case it turned chilly. As she dressed, Rosie wondered what Grace and Ben were so pleased about and felt infected by their obvious happiness.

She skipped downstairs realising that at last she could do so without aches and pains, she let herself out of the French doors and stepping out into the garden took a deep breath to breathe in the sweet heady aroma of the night-scented stock.

Seeing her drink on the garden table she went over to it and taking a long sip decided, she would walk around the garden with it.

She did not look for weeds to pull or faded roses to de-head but simply enjoyed looking at the numerous cottage garden flowers, which filled the island beds. She peered into the centre of a hollyhock marvelling at its hidden beauty, smelled the honeysuckle which was rambling through the apple tree branches, picked a small bunch of pinks for the table and felt her senses fill with the sheer intoxicating beauty of nature.

"Mum, it's ready!" called Ben as he walked towards her.

Rosie held out the bunch of pinks. "Here for you."

Ben took them. "Thank you, it is the first time I have been given flowers, they smell nice."

"I love them; they are one of your grandmother's favourites."

"Why are ladies given flowers and men wine when people come to visit?"

"Do you know I have no idea, silly isn't it, we will change that from now on, every time we visit a couple we will do the reverse. Give the gentleman the flowers and the lady the wine."

"I expect you will get some funny comments"

"I will say I am starting a new trend"

The table was set and Rosie sat at the head with Grace and Ben at either side. It felt strange sitting in Tom's place and with a pang, she wondered what he was doing at that moment. Grace must have felt it too for she said as she placed a plate of prettily fanned melon in front of Rosie.

"Oh by the way Dad has left a message."

"Oh good what does he say?"

Ben came in carrying a bottle of wine, seeing the label Rosie raised her eyebrows but said nothing. "I didn't know which one to choose but liked the look of this one. It is South African and I would like to go to South Africa, and the bottle was the dustiest so I figured it was about time it was drunk."

Rosie laughed, "Well Ben you have impeccable taste, it should be delicious."

Ben intuitively sensed that perhaps he had chosen a bottle that he should not have, looking worried, he said, "It is a special one for some reason isn't it, will Dad mind?"

"Ben it is special yes but this evening is special too, so please don't worry."

"Yes don't worry about Dad Ben," said Grace rather fiercely "He is away again after all."

Rosie surprised at Grace's tone, "Does it worry you Grace?"

Grace sat down and in an only just audible voice said, "He seems different Mum, he goes away more and when he is here he sort of isn't here. And you are left to handle everything on your own."

Ben looking cross said, "Shut up Grace!"

Rosie looked at her two children and felt guilty, why had they not told them what was in the air, why had they treated them as if they were babies and not the intelligent, intuitive young people they so obviously were.

Rosie reached out and with a hand on each of them smiled and said, "Right you two, first lets enjoy this delicious meal and after we have eaten I will tell you why Dad has been so distracted lately."

"You can't say it is delicious until you have tasted it, remember we have cooked it," said Ben in an already happier voice.

Rosie laughed as Grace stuck her tongue out at Ben.

The melon and passion fruit was delicious and so was the chicken stir-fry that followed. By the time they had finished Ben's ice cream bonanza, as he called it, they were all full.

It had been a happy meal and Rosie hated to spoil the evening but it was time Grace and Ben knew what could be in the offing.

Rosie chose not to prevaricate; she told them of Tom's dilemma, redundancy or move to America, and she felt unconvinced that she was telling them the whole story. The trouble was she did not think she really knew the whole story. What she was certain of was that any suspicions she had about Tom and Polly she would have to keep to herself.

Grace and Ben were so different but their reaction this time was exactly the same- outrage.

They angrily asked why they had not been told before and they both stated categorically that they would not move to America.

Rosie held up her hands to stop the tirade of objections. "Hey that is enough from both of you, let's be calm and talk this through. I understand that you feel you have been kept in the dark, I am sorry but rightly or wrongly we felt that we shouldn't unsettle you before we had to and especially with GCSE's looming."

Grace started to protest but Rosie stopped her. "Please Grace let me finish then you can speak. Your Dad didn't want us to make a decision either way before seeing America first, he felt that only then could we make an informed decision."

Ben said, "What if I like America and you don't or everyone likes it and I don't. I bet in the end whatever we think it will be Dad who makes the decision."

Rosie looked at her son and knew he was right but also felt a loyalty to Tom.

"Ben you may well be right but we have to remember that Dad works very hard to support us all."

Grace stood up and in a quiet voice said, "I think we have no choice you had better listen to the message Mum."

They all walked into the study without speaking as if their fate would be revealed by this one message.

"Hi there just ringing to say that I have arrived safely and it's really great to be back. I will ring you again soon. Love to you all"

For a moment, no one spoke they were all trying to make something out of the short message.

To Rosie it was a message just about himself and confirmation that he was happier there than here. It rankled that he had not wished her luck for her interview before he went nor in his message.

To Grace it seemed more like a message from an Uncle returning home after a visit rather than her Father away and missing them. She had felt hurt that he had taken so little interest in her exams and had expected him to help her as he had done in the past.

To Ben it was an encouragement; perhaps he too would think New York was great. He felt a masculine loyalty to his Dad and hated Grace saying anything derogatory about him. Although he had felt upset about Dad's impatience with him, he happily accepted his Mum's explanation.

"Well I expect he will ring again soon and we can have a chat, it is never easy leaving messages," Rosie smiled trying to believe it herself.

"Yep, I'm up for going to New York and I'll get to have a longer holiday from school"

"You have changed your tune Ben, don't forget you will have to go to school over there and what about your football?" said Grace furious with Ben for being so obtuse.

"What about Gran and Gramps and Granny and Grandpa don't you care that you won't see them? Ben you are just being selfish like Dad, that's just typical." She ran crying from the room and both Rosie and Ben heard her stomping up the stairs and slamming her bedroom door.

Ben looked utterly miserable and Rosie gave him a hug and keeping her arm around him said, "There is no point in getting excited, worried or upset until we know for sure what is happening. I do understand Ben you feel you need to support Dad and that is good. It is not that either Grace and I do not support Dad it is just such a huge step and we all need to make the decision together, weighing up the pro's and cons. The thing I worry about is whether Dad feels he has a choice and I think that is where we can help him."

"How?"

"Well the first thing I can do is to paint and sell more paintings; I found a new outlet today and there must be many more I can try."

"Why would that help?"

"It would help Dad because at the moment he is the bread winner Ben and the responsibility for a home and supporting a family can weigh heavily."

"Do you think that the TV programme will make you rich?"

Rosie laughed. "Well not rich but it would definitely help, so I must do my best to convince Giles Barton that I am who they want."

"If Dad does want to stay in America and you don't will you divorce like Jack's parents?"

Rosie felt her stomach knot, Ben had voiced what she feared. "Oh Ben your Dad and I love each other very much and this is just a bit of a blip, every marriage has them now and then."

There was a knock on the front door making them both jump. "Who could that be I wonder?" Sighing inwardly, Rosie did not feel like seeing anyone tonight. Ben went to answer it, Rosie with relief heard John's voice.

"Hi Ben, we were passing and I just thought I would pop in for a moment and wish your Mum luck for tomorrow."

As Rosie came to the door she wondered who we meant, whom had John bought with him?

"Hello John. Daniel how nice to see you, come in. I heard you say we and wondered who you had with you."

"I was just telling Ben that we were passing and thought it was an opportunity to say good luck and also an opportunity for Dan to see Grace if she is in?"

Rosie and Ben exchanged looks and Ben said, "If you want to

see Grace Dan it is you who will need the luck, she is in a bit of a mood. You would be better off playing footy with me."

Grace had heard the car and looking out of the window had seen John and Dan arriving, with a racing heart she rushed to the bathroom and washed her face in cold water and quickly applied some makeup in an attempt to disguise her red swollen eyes. Cursing to herself that life was just not fair, why did they come unexpectedly and when she had been crying. She was unaware how lovely she was and how her vulnerability would touch Dan.

Rosie silently thanked God and said, "Actually Dan you are just what she needs at the moment I am sure, why don't you have a kick around in the garden with Ben for ten minutes while I go and tell Grace you are here."

Dan obliged and he and a delighted Ben went into the garden.

Turning to John Rosie said, "John there is some rather good wine opened on the dining room table why don't you help yourself to a glass while I go and see Grace?"

"Sounds good to me."

Rosie knocked on Grace's door and went in, expecting Grace to be lying prone on her bed and was relieved to find her furiously brushing her hair. "John and Dan have come to see us."

"I know I saw them arrive and I look hideous."

"Oh Grace, you couldn't look hideous if you tried, Dan is in the garden with Ben and would like to see you. Before you go down Grace I just want to say that we must try to be fair to Dad and as I have just said to Ben I am going to paint more and hopefully help with the finances. I am sure that will ease the situation."

"Why, are we in debt or something?"

Rosie smiled and shook her head. "No Grace but I think it is time I contributed more to enable Dad to have a choice in what he does and where he does it."

"Oh I see, well I am going to get a job in the holidays and a Saturday job aren't I, I have been in to ask at the ceramic art centre by the way and they have put me on the list. I could then buy my own clothes and pay for my phone, and what is left over I could give to you."

"Oh Darling, that will be a wonderful place to work," and then she grinned at Grace and said, "You buying your own clothes and paying for your phone will make an enormous difference but if do you have any left over you could save that towards Uni. I will do for you what my father did for me, whatever I managed to save at the end of the month he would add the same amount and that was such a help, it was a real incentive to save and meant that I had lots of fun without getting into debt."

"Okay that's a deal."

"Good, now we had better go down and entertain our guests."

John was in the sitting room reading the paper when Rosie joined him "I am sorry John to leave you on your own but I needed to have a chat with Grace, she has been upset about Tom and America."

"Have you told them about the possibility of moving now?"

"Yes, tonight."

"Oh this was probably not a good time to call on you then."

"John it was the perfect time, believe me."

"I wanted to thank you in person Rosie for such a lovely evening on Saturday and for introducing me to Alice. Both Alice and I having talked on the phone for hours and have a feeling that this is the start of something special."

"Oh John I am so happy for you both, I couldn't be more pleased."

"Well, we will see. Now are you nervous about tomorrow?"

"I was but now I just feel determined to go for it. I had a stroke of luck today John, I went out for the day sketching in preparation for tomorrow and guess what?"

"Mmm goodness I don't know, you bumped into Constable and he gave you a hint or two."

Rosie laughed. "No a little less spooky than that. I had tea at the gallery in Harleston and got chatting with the owner and she having looked at my sketches wants to sell them for me."

"Well done, did you mention the possible TV programme?"

"Yes I did."

"Ah I think she is probably a very wise lady, she hopes your work will be in demand. I rather think she is right. I would like to see those sketches of yours."

Grace, popping her head around the door said, "Dan and I are just going out for a walk, bye."

She had gone before Rosie had time to reply.

"This John, is turning into a special day."

FOURTEEN

rriving at the Hotel Tom retrieved his luggage from the boot of Polly's car. Strangely, they had seemed almost shy of one another and after the initial welcoming exchanges had talked very little on the journey. He shut the boot and came round to Polly to say thank you and spontaneously said, "Why don't you come in for a drink Polly?"

"No Tom you are exhausted but thank you for asking."

"Suddenly Polly I don't feel as tired as I was and I really would like a nightcap and would appreciate your company."

"Ok Tom I will park the car and meet you in the bar."

When Polly entered the reception, the man behind the desk said, "Are you Polly?"

"Yes."

"Well I am afraid the bar has closed for the night, Mr Holden has asked me to show you to his room."

Blushing slightly she replied. "Oh I think it would be better if I just go home, I will see him tomorrow if you don't mind giving him a message for me."

"Mr Holden said that if you refused I was to persuade you. I am happy to ring his room though madam and give him a message?"

He could see, from the way Polly blushed, she felt awkward about it; having a daughter himself he felt protective towards her.

Polly did not answer for a moment, she had dreamed and fantasised about being alone in a bedroom with Tom but now that it was reality, she felt nervous.

Tom at that moment arrived bearing two glasses and two miniature bottles of wine.

"I thought that you might feel more comfortable in the lounge Polly so I raided the mini bar." Tom watched Polly for her reaction, Polly was relieved and disappointed at the same time and her face so full of expression went pink and she bravely smiled.

"The lounge I agree looks extremely comfortable, thank you Tom."

They found a comfortable leather sofa and both sat side by side. "Which would you like, red or white?"

"White please."

Having poured both drinks Tom laid back into the squishy leather folds and with a deep sigh said, "It is so good to be back."

Polly awkwardly perched on the edge turned round to look at Tom, he had his eyes shut and looked pale and tired. Without thinking, she said in a quiet voice "Is it so bad at home Tom?"

Tom opened his eyes but did not answer immediately as if trying to decide what he should say.

After a moment or two, he replied, "No it isn't so bad, it is strangely confusing. Do not ask me to explain because I cannot. What I do know for sure is that a couple of months ago everything was straightforward, ordinary, just jogging along."

Tom put his head in his hands and sighed deeply.

"And now?"

"Now everything is different."

Tom paused and then looking at Polly said, "Do you have dome shaped winter scene ornaments here, the sort that you can shake and all the snow whirls around and then settles?"

Polly laughed and said, "Yes we do, I had one when I was younger."

"Well that's what it is like; I feel as if my world has been shaken around but not yet settled."

"It isn't surprising Tom, you are planning to move job, house and country which must be very stressful."

"It isn't just that, I haven't even started organising moves yet."

Polly did not want to think of Tom's family but had to ask, she needed to know. "What about your family? How are they coping with it all?"

Tom again leaned back. "That is a difficult question, the children don't yet know about the prospective move." Seeing Polly's surprised look he defensively said, "I wanted them to experience New York first before I told them. They couldn't possibly make an informed decision before seeing it."

"Are you are afraid they won't want to come?"

"I am pretty sure they would definitely say no, but once out here and having fun hopefully they will want to come as much as I do."

"What about your wife? How does she feel about it?"

Tom did not want to talk about Rosie; it felt odd Polly mentioning her as if two different worlds were converging.

"She loves the house, her garden, her family why would she want to change it?"

"Does she love you?" Polly only wanted to hear one answer; she wanted him to be unhappy with his wife or her with him. Again, Tom did not answer and Polly was afraid of what he was going to say.

"Polly I am dogtired, I need to go to bed and get some sleep."

He finished his wine and put his glass down on the wooden coffee table and turned to Polly and took her hand in his and said, "Come with me."

"Tom you are tired, you need to go to bed and get some sleep. You have just said so."

"I also just said come with me, you must be tired and need to get to bed and need to sleep as well."

Polly felt confused. She longed to say yes but she was not sure what he was really asking of her. He had not replied to her question or perhaps he had in asking her to come with him.

Tom still holding her hand stood up, gently pulled her to her feet, and looked into her eyes as if searching for an answer, she nodded.

Together they walked up the stairs and along the long corridor to his room, neither of them saying a word.

He opened the door and led her in, he put the door card on the dressing table and took off his jacket and loosened his tie. He turned the bedside lamp on and switched off the main light. He then came over to her looked down at her and smiled. "Polly, I am going down to reception to book you in, I'll be back in a minute."

When the door shut behind him Polly looked around the room, it was large, comfortable but impersonal. Decorated in a masculine style, had deep blue and mulberry coloured check curtains at the window and matching upholstery on the two armchairs in front of a small coffee table, with two glasses placed invitingly on it. The king sized bed indeed looked inviting with a plain mulberry damask bedspread and two check cushions with a gold wrapped chocolate on each one.

Polly had not moved but as she looked at the bed with its now promise of carnal mystery with Tom she was galvanised into action. She quickly washed in the bathroom, hurriedly undressed, and then was undecided about whether to leave her underwear on. It was very pretty and she was glad that she had dressed with care. Would it look too promiscuous to be naked or would it look prudish to leave it on, she felt naïve.

At that moment she heard Tom's key card in the door, in a panic she dived under the cover, which she pulled up to, her chin, the cushions scattering and the chocolates thrown from the bed to land goodness knows where.

Tom closed the door behind him and turned to see Polly in bed and let out an involuntary laugh, then seeing her offended and worried expression said, "Sorry Polly I didn't mean to laugh but you look so tiny tucked up in that vast bed."

"Well I would hardly fill it would I?"

"I'll join you in a minute, it looks very inviting with you in it." Tom went into the bathroom.

Polly lay back on the pillows and felt a delicious feeling of expectation, she already was beginning to feel aroused at the thought of making love, and it had been so long.

A few minutes later Tom came out of the bathroom wearing only a pair of black boxer shorts. He had a good figure, quite toned but with just the hint of a thickening stomach.

Tom smiled at her as he approached the bed and said, "I have been longing for this."

That was not what Polly expected to hear, it sounded so unsexy, certainly not a seductive comment.

"Me too."

Tom lifted the covers, got in and turned towards her . He smiled warmly at her then drew her close to him. With her heart thumping, she gratefully nestled against him. She could feel the hairs of his chest against her face and hear his heart beating. After a few moments, she said, "I can hear your heart beating Tom."

Tom murmured, "Mmm that's reassuring."

Polly giggled and drew away from him slightly to look at his face but his eyes had closed and as she watched him, she heard his breathing change and she knew he was asleep.

Polly lay beside him for what seemed like hours unable to sleep and then slipped out of bed, quietly dressed and left.

Tom awoke at seven the next morning, groaned, stretched and with a slow awakening thought of Polly. The bed was cold beside him, he got up and saw that there was no trace of her, no note; it was as if she had never been there.

Tom cursed himself for his stupidity, what had he been thinking of. In the cold light of day, his actions astonished him. On the one hand, his betrayal of Rosie, he remembered his hasty phone call home from the hotel lobby last night and his relief when no one answered. He thought of the message he had left and how whilst leaving it he had also been thinking of Polly upstairs waiting for him in his bedroom

Polly, what an insensitive fool he had been to her. Laughing at her then getting into bed and falling straight to sleep.

He felt ashamed on both accounts; he was new to this game. Then the thought came to him and he voiced it aloud. "Why am I playing it anyway?"

When he arrived in the office and saw Polly blush and look at him, he knew exactly why he was playing it.

She was not alone so he mouthed. "Sorry," and went through into his temporary office, which he shared with three others.

On his desk was the list of local schools and several real estate portfolios, which he had requested. He glanced at them without much interest, try as he might he could not see Rosie and the children here, they belonged to another world.

He put them aside, promising himself that he would study them soon.

His role was already becoming less of an observer and more of an advisor. He had been asked to give a presentation on codes of conduct in the work place to the company directors.

He had not been able to judge whether this was part of an ongoing assessment of his capabilities or a genuine interest in the subject. Either way he needed to do a lot of preparation and was engrossed designing some overhead slides when Polly came in with a cup of coffee for him.

"I thought you might like a cup of coffee."

Tom looked up and smiled. "I would love one, will you join me?"

Polly looked straight into Tom's eyes and said, "Tom, I am not sure joining you would be very fulfilling, but thank you for the thought."

Polly then smiled at him and walked out of the office, Tom sat and watched her and thoughtfully drank his coffee, trying to think of a way to make amends.

A phone call from Mr Wilburn the HR director's personal assistant interrupted his thoughts. "Tom, I have prepared an employment package for you, perhaps you would like to read it and sign it when you have made your decision. You have theoretically six weeks but Mr Wilburn has asked for a decision if possible by the sixteenth of July."

Tom was surprised. "Can you tell me why?"

"Well I am not sure but all I can tell you is that I have been asked to advertise the post from the nineteenth of July, is there a problem?"

"Mr Wilburn does realise that I have a family to consider presumably?"

She ignored the comment and asked, "Would you like an appointment to see Mr Wilburn, he could see you next Tuesday at four."

Tom sighed. "No don't worry I will speak with HR in England first and get back to you."

He looked at his watch it would be five o'clock in the UK, he rang straight away and asked for Paul. Paul answered "Hello Tom how are getting on?"

"Fine Paul mostly observing and a bit of advising, it is the same just different people really. I have a query though."

"So what's the problem?"

"I have just been informed that I need to come to a decision by the middle of July, I was not expecting to have to do that until end of August."

"You have to realise that things move more quickly there Tom. I thought you were keen, that was the impression you gave me."

"It isn't that simple Paul, I need the family to agree."

"Tom, take a leaf out of my book, just tell them and make it sound as if there is no choice."

"I hardly think that's fair."

"Who brings home the bacon Tom?"

"Paul that is not the point and you know it."

Tom's temper was rising as he began to suspect he was being manipulated. "Is there something you haven't told me Paul?"

"Now you are being paranoid Tom." Tom ignored him and said "When are you next over here Paul?"

"I have no idea Tom; it is very unlikely to be in the near future."

"Oh really, you gave me the impression that you were dividing your time between here and there until the expansion was complete."

"Things have changed Tom."

Tom thought of Sally. "What about Sally, Paul?"

"Sally is none of your business but if you are so concerned you are welcome to take care of her, you might welcome a little female company."

Tom realised what Paul had done, he had obviously been having an affair with her and when she became a nuisance, he had brought her over to New York to get her out of the way

"I will treat that with the contempt it deserves."

"You know Tom I always thought you were a self righteous little prick."

Tom slammed the phone down on Paul and went directly to see Mr Wilburn's personal assistant. He knocked on the door and went in. "Hello Peggy, could you get me a copy of all information and correspondence regarding my transfer please. I also would like to see the procedure file on redeployment. I hope that is okay?"

"No bother at all Mr Holden, I will bring them to you as soon as I can."

"Thank you Peggy, there is just one more thing. Who is going to handle all the new recruitment if I decide not to stay?"

"Well as I said earlier we will be advertising for a HR manager in time for the recruitment drive in October."

"I find it a little puzzling that the Company is willing to relocate me and my family at great expense unnecessarily. I had been given impression that only someone with extensive knowledge of the Company could manage the expansion."

Peggy looked thoughtful for a moment and said she was sure that she had the minutes of the meeting where the post had been discussed.

"I will find out all I can, once I find the Minutes I may be able to help you."

"Thank you, you are an angel."

"Definitely in disguise," laughed Peggy.

Tom was just about to leave when he had a thought "Do you know if the Company has a policy of compulsory redundancy?"

"I think Polly would be able to help you more than me Mr Holden, she deals with the legal and financial ins and outs but if you would rather I look it up for you I can. The bigger the company gets the less I understand it."

"How long have you been here?"

"Fourteen years and I will retire in two years time hoorah! In the meantime is there anything else I can help you with?"

"Not as long as I have then. No Peggy I have bothered you enough for one day and do call me Tom by the way."

Peggy smiled at him, "Okay Tom here is the employment agreement for you to look at. You are obviously keen to get to know everything about the post; does that mean you have made up your mind?"

"I can't do that until I am fully aware of my position, but I like it here Peggy far more than I expected."

"Good, I know we would be happy to have you here and when your family come to visit you must all come and have dinner with Jo and I."

Tom looked for Polly in the large open plan office; she was not at her desk and was told that she had gone home with a migraine. Tom felt guilty He had no idea how much sleep Polly had the previous night but suspected from the dark circles around her eyes it had been very little. Suddenly he could not stand to be in the office any longer; he looked at his watch and discovered that it was nearly one. He would take his employment portfolio, his bagel, bought from the snack trolley and have a working lunch in the small park nearby.

FIFTEEN

Rosie was in the bath with soft music playing and a glass of wine at her elbow trying to relax in preparation for her interview the following day.

She was going over in her head what she would say to sell herself and her art to Giles. Her conversation with Tom an hour previously had disturbed and delighted her and she could not concentrate.

Tom had rung, he said, in time to speak to everyone before they went to bed but both Grace and Ben had gone to bed early and so Rosie had him to herself.

Tom had sounded different somehow, she wasn't sure how. He had told her about Paul's behaviour, and suggested she meet with Paul's wife Jane, something she had been meaning to do any way but it seemed odd of Tom to suggest it.

He had wished her well for her interview and had given her some hints on interview techniques; he even suggested she should have bought herself a new outfit. She had already decided what to wear for the interview but would enjoy going shopping afterwards for the holiday, as either as a celebration or consolation depending on the outcome. He rarely suggested she buy clothes so she would very happily oblige.

Rosie was pleased he had shown interest in her interview but it puzzled her, why would he want her to get the job if he was planning for them all to go to America? He had been rather dismissive of it previously and had even implied that it had been an unrealistic fantasy.

It was his last rather ambiguous comment that now bothered her most, he had said America was another world away and in the world that she was in he loved her very much.

What had he meant by that, was he being romantic or did he feel along way away and somehow detached from her there or, as she began to fear, that he meant that in America he loved someone else?

She now wished that she had asked after Polly, she had thought she might but somehow by saying her name she became a reality and she didn't want to think of her in any way at all.

Something had definitely changed for the better, his voice sounded less depressed and more like the Tom she used to know.

Sighing she took a large gulp of wine and consciously put Tom out of her mind, she had to prepare herself for tomorrow.

At breakfast, both Grace and Ben were excited for her, Ben particularly. Thankfully, she felt calm, the day had come and she just had to go and do her best. She had dressed casually in cream linen trousers and a brown and terracotta wrap top, one of her favourites, and tan leather sandals.

She put on a green amber pendant and earrings to match. She applied light makeup and twisted her hair up on top, she was ready.

She had promised the children a lift to school, which would ensure she was there on time; she could not afford to be late.

Having dropped the children at school she had made good time. In fact, she was horribly early. She parked in the hotel car park and decided to take a wander along the cobbled streets, she loved this old part of Norwich with the lopsided buildings and old crooked roofs. She was the only one who was wandering, at this time in the morning everyone seemed to have an urgent purpose as they hurried past her. With more time to kill time she popped into the Cathedral book shop, where she had done some voluntary work before her accident. She bought a birthday card for her Goddaughter Ruth and a wooden holding cross to replace the one she had given Carl.

Then she returned to her car and collected her artwork, it was five minutes to ten when she walked into the hotel foyer. The extra time made her feel relaxed and prepared, it was a good feeling and she vowed to try to be punctual more often.

Going up to the reception desk, she asked one of the efficient looking young receptionists if she knew where Giles Barton might be.

"Are you Mrs Holden?"

"Yes."

"Mr Barton has asked me to take you up to the conference lounge."

She led the way and Rosie dutifully followed.

Feeling nervous for the first time, she felt perspiration breaking out on her hands..

She envied the efficient little figure hurrying along in front of her, dressed smartly in black and white and appearing totally in control. As they reached the door, she hoped she was not too casually dressed and began to regret her casual outfit.

She need not have worried, Giles, a tall tousled haired young man came across the room clad in jeans and an open necked polo shirt. He greeted her warmly with a loud cheery hello and a wide smile. Turning to the receptionist he asked for more coffee and plenty of biscuits.

There were three other people, two older men and one young woman, sitting around a low coffee table in the blue upholstered bucket shaped chairs.

"Welcome to the team, what do you like to be called?"

"My name is Rosemary but everyone calls me Rosie," she smiled, trying to look relaxed.

It obviously had not worked as Giles said "Don't worry we are a relatively friendly bunch, we only bite when there is a full moon," he then laughed loudly at his own joke.

Rosie laughed too and quipped, "When there is one, I hope you find me tasty."

Each member of the team rose from their chairs and introduced themselves and told her of their role in the enterprise.

Then Giles said, "I gave you an outline of what we have planned on the phone the other day but David will tell you in more detail and then perhaps you can tell us about yourself and show us your work. How does that sound to you?"

"Yes fine."

"First let me say that we have looked at two other local artists and neither was happy with the commitment needed for the filming. It is intensive I am afraid and will invariably involve long days. The problem, as I initially explained, is that a pilot programme may never get past the planning stage if it doesn't appeal to the big shots."

Rosie felt suddenly that this was going to happen, being there with this group of interesting people felt right.

"Oh I am sure it will happen, I think it is a marvellous idea. I am very ready to commit to it."

There was laughter all round and David, the Producer winked at her and said, "Great, an enthusiast, just what we need." He proceeded to outline his plans for the programme, telling her that initially it was for local viewing but had high hopes that it would then be broadcasted nationally.

Having heard all about it Rosie felt even more excited at the thought of being involved.

It was then her turn. She told them about her degree and experience, emphasising the fact that she had sold many paintings over the years. Finally, she showed them her sketches and the three paintings she had chosen to bring along.

It was midday before she emerged from the hotel, on a high; the whole experience had exhilarated her. They had agreed she should be the artist and she was officially aboard. Longing to share her good news, she rang John, who worked nearby, and asked him if she could meet him for lunch.

"I am meeting Alice at one, why don't you join us?"

"I would love to if you sure I won't spoil a romantic lunch?"

"How could you spoil it Rosie, it is thanks to you that we have met. We went out for a romantic meal last night so I am sure we will survive."

"Oh good, I am so delighted. I will ask Alice all about it."

"I certainly hope she won't tell you *all* about it."

Rosie laughed, delighted that John and Alice were obviously getting on very well.

Rosie had an hour to kill and decided to buy herself something new in celebration. She went into Monsoon and after trying on various skirts and tops settled on a delicate eggshell blue skirt, which cut on the bias, hung beautifully, and had beaded detail. She chose a pale biscuit coloured embroidered blouse, which contrasted well with the blue. They were feminine and pretty and showed off her light tan beautifully. She also chose a t-shirt for Grace, which she knew, would look good on her.

She then had to run all the way to the restaurant and arrived ten minutes late and out of breath. So much for the pleasure of being on time she thought as she breathlessly said, "Sorry I am late."

"You are always late, it doesn't matter. We have ordered you the same as us, today's special, crab salad," smiled Alice.

"Yummy, just right thank you."

"If you aren't in a hurry Rosie we could spend the afternoon together, I am free for the rest of the day."

"I would love to; I have a mound of things to do at home but none that can't wait. I thought you two were not meeting until next Sunday, I distinctly remember you telling me that." she said with a grin.

"We couldn't wait," both John and Alice said in unison and grinned at each other.

Rosie felt like an interloper but was so pleased for them and with a pang realised how much it contrasted with her own relationship now.

Alice must have noted her change of expression for she asked, "How are things at home Rosie?"

Rosie hesitated, she didn't want to spoil the lunch by sharing her concerns so replied, "Things are on the up." She laughed naughtily at the inference despite the painful thought of it and added, "Well for Tom anyway." Before any questions could be asked she said, "I have good news; I am to be the resident artist on a proposed TV programme."

It was a very merry lunchtime and Rosie found herself chatting animatedly about her plans for her part of the programme. It was not until John asked, "How will this fit in to Tom's plans for America?" that Rosie saw that there could be obstacles in her way.

"I just don't know John, Tom was very supportive last night, rather strangely actually because he hadn't taken it seriously before."

John realising it was time had to go back to work, kissed them and insisted on treating them both, he waved at them as he hurried away.

Rosie and Alice then stayed for another hour drinking coffee and chatting, Rosie telling Alice about the phone call from Tom and Alice telling Rosie about her blossoming romance.

They enjoyed sharing the joy of friendship, one accepting of the other with total trust, true friendship.

After this, they went shopping, and with a lot of laughter being in turn, the others style guru.

When Rosie eventually arrived home, bearing gifts and supper she felt happily exhausted. The children were waiting knowing from the cryptic message she had sent them that they would be celebrating.

After dinner Rosie rang her parents and parents in law to tell them the good news, they were delighted for her but Lillian asked her about Tom's reaction. Rosie cursed inwardly and admitted that she had not told Tom yet, she gave the excuse that the time lapse was awkward.

Lillian had replied, "Face things head on Rosie, for yourself and Tom."

Rosie had always admired Lillian's ability to be wisely intuitive but at that moment felt unbalanced by it, not knowing how to reply she simply said, "I'll try."

She waited until nine to ring Tom when she thought that he would be back from work and in the hotel.

The problem was she had no idea how he would react after last night's conversation and where this would lead. She had the weird sensation of being on a cloud, blown about, first one way, and then another and she had no control. She even found herself looking at her feet to check that they were on the floor, they were.

Taking three deep breaths and trying to stay calm, she rang the hotel. As she waited for someone to answer, she remembered Alice's words to her.

"Hold your head high, stick your chest out, you can make it." She smiled at the thought and stuck her chest out, Tom would be impressed.

The ringing stopped and Rosie heard the clicking sounds of the phone being put through.

"Hello Tom, I am sticking my chest out just for you."

"I am sorry madam, I think you must have the wrong number this is the Madison Hotel."

Rosie put down the phone hastily without saying another word, she laughed at her stupidity then rang back saying very formally, "Would you please put me through to my husband Mr Holden's room?"

The hotel operator recognising her voice said, "Certainly madam, he is a lucky man."

Rosie laughed and said, "I hope he thinks so."

After a few clicking noises, Tom answered.

"Hi."

"Hello Tom, it's me."

"I know it is you." Tom sounded impatient. "You told him you were my wife."

"Well I just asked if he could put me through to my husband, is that a problem Tom?"

A sigh. "No of course not, sorry. How did you get on today?"

"I got the job and they are hoping that it will go from local to TV to national TV, so it is very exciting!"

"It is definitely happening then?"

Rosie heard an edge to Tom's voice and almost fearfully replied, "Yes Tom, they said they were 99% sure."

"Right, good for you," the edge was still there.

"Tom how do you feel about it? You wished me well last night but today you sound funny."

"Oh ha ha," in a sarcastic tone.

"Tom please tell me what you want or what you feel?"

"How do I feel? Let me see, I feel hungry at this moment."

Rosie with rising frustration ignored the comment, "For goodness sake Tom, this will give us more options don't you see?"

"Oh yes, Rosie it will give us options, you in England following your career and me in the States with mine. It is obviously what is going to happen, what is happening." Tom replied with a hint of bitterness.

Rosie felt that she had fallen off her cloud and was spiralling to earth; she could almost feel the air rushing past her.

Desperately she tried, "You don't understand. This will enable you to stay in England Tom. With your redundancy money and me earning, you can take time to find what you want."

"Redundancy is no longer an option Rosie."

"Why not?"

"Because I found out that weasel, Paul, has deliberately organised it all in an attempt to get rid of me."

"I don't understand."

"In England we have a non-compulsory redundancy policy; over here they can make you redundant if you have worked for less than ten years for the Company."

"But you have worked for the firm for years!"

"Rosie you are being dense."

"Tom don't be insulting, just explain."

"Paul wanted me to go; I had succeeded in managing the Linkston merger and was in line for promotion which would have put his nose out of joint. Added to that I knew of his little fling with my secretary, remember? He didn't expect me to transfer, he is trying to put the boot in here for me. I read a letter he sent to the HR here, he stated that I had been offered a transfer as a legal formality but was an unsuitable candidate and unlikely to take up the option."

"I thought he encouraged you to take it?"

"Only because he didn't think I had the guts apparently, but when I look back on it he continually stressed how difficult moving the whole family would be and at the same time seemed to encourage me."

"Why not take the opportunity of going for heavens sake and blow the lot of them?"

"You are joking Rosie? I have given years of my life to this firm and I am not letting Paul dictate what I do. I have agreed to a transfer, they have already seen my worth. Once all the new recruitment has been done, they will need me to manage the department." Tom rushed on, "Anyway it is too late, I signed today."

Rosie felt numb. "What now then? Does that mean we have to move over there?"

Quietly and gently, as if he was talking to a wounded animal he said, "Rosie it is over, our marriage can't survive, you and the children are rooted in England, I feel driven to succeed over here."

Rosie had crash landed.

"Succeed Tom, with the job or Polly?"

Tom hesitated for just a moment too long. "We have grown apart Rosie, you are following a career without me now."

Angrily Rosie retorted. "Oh very convenient, no wonder you suddenly wanted me to get the job. How could you Tom? Nothing matters more to me than our family staying together."

"So you would be prepared to move the whole family lock, stock and barrel, leaving your parents and friends behind?"

Rosie now hesitated for just a moment too long and Tom noted it.

"You see, your silence says it all, you wouldn't would you?"

Rosie now crying, tearfully managed to say, "I would try, it would be hard but I would try, for us!"

"You would hate it, you would grow to resent me, you all would."

"Tom what upsets me is that you haven't even contemplated trying to find work here, you have chosen to go away!"

Tom knew that she was right there, he did not truly understand why; he just felt that his only option now was the States.

"Rosie, please stop crying I can hardly hear you. I am so sorry, really I am. I can't explain why but it feels right here. You know I didn't choose to go away, believe me please."

Rosie could not believe that he really thought he had no choice, that in some way he felt it was his destiny. Her anger returned and she almost shouted.

"How can I Tom? You are there and we are here. You have just told me our marriage is over, just like that. A few weeks ago everything was happy and you *have chosen* to leave us and go and start a new life, face facts Tom!"

"You are obviously overwrought. Why don't you go to bed and I will ring you tomorrow?"

"Do you actually expect me to be able to sleep?"

Rosie had an idea and before he could answer said, "Tom you are right I am exhausted. I need to get to bed. Tell me your room number so that I can ring you."

"I will ring you Rosie, tomorrow."

"Please Tom I don't want to be waiting for your call, if you give me your room number at least I can just ask for that instead of having to explain."

Tom did not want to argue and gave her his room number.

"It is room 22, but you will have to remember the time lapse if you are determined to ring me."

"I do realise that Tom and it was me who rang you tonight, remember?"

"Rosie please don't be upset, go to bed have a good night's rest and then perhaps you will be able to think calmly about everything."

Rosie would like to have said something very offensive to him at that moment but restrained herself and just said, "Good night Tom," and put down the phone.

She wrote 22 on the jotting pad, noticing as she did so that the written number looked like two people curled up together, the irony of it hit her. Would Tom and Polly be curled up together later while she inevitably lay wide-awake and alone?

She stamped her foot in frustration and then liking the sensation stamped it again and then with both feet jumped around angrily shouting, "Ahhhhhhh!"

"Whatever are you doing Mum?"

"Oh Grace," said Rosie coming to an immediate breathless stop. "I am having a tantrum, it feels good, no wonder you and Ben enjoyed them so much."

Grace laughed, "You used to put us out in the hall, I remember. Anyway why are *you* having a tantrum?"

"Well Grace unfortunately Dad has had to make an instant decision."

"About his job?"

"Yes amongst other things. I need to go straight over Grace, so I am going to have to arrange a flight and sort so much out," as Rosie spoke, she was formulating her plan.

"What about the weekend Mum, we were going to the farm?"

"I know darling; I think I can be back in time to go on Saturday instead of Friday."

"Why do you have to go now Mum? We will be there on holiday in a couple of weeks!"

Rosie hugged Grace to her and said, "I have to go darling as this is a decision that both Dad and I need to make together. Grace, I will ring Lillian to see if she could come over and stay with you."

"Mum I am seventeen and quite capable of sorting Ben out and looking after things for a couple of days."

Rosie looked at Grace who despite the occasional teenage angst was growing into such a mature young woman.

"I know you are, but you have exams at the moment and have quite enough to worry about without having to think of Ben and animals and food etcetera but thank you for being so helpful when I need it."

"Okay but what if she can't come?"

"Well, I will have to think again. Anyway I must ring the airlines and book a flight, I hope I can get one straight away, I would like to arrive in the morning."

"I thought it took about eight hours?"

"It does but they are five hours behind us."

Rosie worked it out and realised that the very earliest she could feasibly be there would be about seven allowing for travel and airport waiting times. She would arrive in time to catch him before he left for work.

She rang Norwich airport and it was providence, there was a place available for her on the one fifteen flight arriving in New York at local time at five in the morning. By the time she was through customs and after a taxi to the hotel it would be about seven, perfect. "Thank you, thank you, thank you God!"

She quickly rang Lillian; after all, it was she who advised her to face things head on.

Lillian sounded surprised but promised to be at the house in the morning to look after things. Rosie felt grateful, she knew how busy Lillian was with all sorts of things.

She rang for a taxi next, that would cost a fortune but would save her from having to drive and park. She planned to give Tom's firm the bill for all her expenses or perhaps Paul, she grinned to herself.

Rosie rushed around packing a small bag with her new clothes and essentials, then just had time to give the children some essential cash, a hug and a few do's and don'ts before hearing the beep beep of the waiting taxi. As she went downstairs she glanced around the house and seeing the muddle regretted not doing more housework, but there was no time now.

Then with an awful panicky thought, what if something happens and she didn't ever come home again, she yelled up the stairs. "I love you so much, goodbye darlings. Be good, be happy!"

There was a chorus of "You too!"

Grace appeared at the top of the stairs, "Don't worry Mum we will be fine and tell Dad that I miss him!"

Ben called out "Tell Dad I would like to see the Bronx Bombers!"

Rosie smiled, "Okay will do."

The taxi hooted again.

SIXTEEN

R osie watched from the small aircraft window the lights of Norwich diminish into a nothingness of dark, she then pulled down the blind, rested her head back and closed her eyes. She did not want and could not cope with conversation with the stranger sitting at such close proximity by her side. They had already exchanged the usual polite pleasantries and Rosie had closed the beginnings of what she had feared would be a long conversation by saying how tired she was. The elderly woman, on her way to visit her family, was smiling and friendly but Rosie did not have the energy for the swapping of life stories.

How strange it felt to be doing something that she had no intention of doing when she woke that morning, finding herself on an plane jetting across the world to her husband who she may find is sharing a bed with another woman. How would she react if he were? How would they react if they were?

What if he was not there, he could be staying the night with her in some apartment somewhere? What if he was just on his own and was innocent? How would she know anyway?

She would know, he would be different, he would be defensive, detached but dear God please not out of reach. Please let the invisible cord which held them together be intact and not severed forever, just frayed a bit.

She could feel the tears pricking her eyelids, she screwed her eyes tight, she did not want to cry.

She must plan something to say or do depending on which scenario she met, a sort of script but with planned ad-libbing. Can you plan ad-libbing? No, it would all be impromptu, how can you plan? She would stay calm though and be irritatingly polite to the pretty Polly, even kind and understanding. She laughed at the thought of it.

"Thinking of something funny dear?"

Rosie turned to the smiling and enquiring woman but could not share the joke; after all, it was not funny.

"I am sorry I must have been dreaming."

"I expect you have a lot on your mind, I will be quiet unless you want to talk of course and then I promise I won't go any-where for a few hours!" She laughed and Rosie laughed too.

"Thank you."

Tom was angry with himself, angry with Rosie, angry at life in general. It was as if a huge blanket of resentment had settled on his shoulders. He felt guilty and desperate to try to think of ways to justify his actions. He could hardly believe he had suggested to Rosie that their marriage was over, he had voiced what he had feared but did he really want that? He had felt cornered, trapped into the decision he had made but who had trapped him? Who had put him in that corner? Had he, as Rosie suggested, selfishly thought only of himself?

Polly had intimated last night they were very alike, in tune as she had put it and he had believed her and then realised he did not feel in tune with Rosie anymore, perhaps he never had been. He smiled ruefully and thought of the well-used cliché *she does not understand me.* What was there to understand, was he so complex? He doubted it.

He sat on the end of his hotel bed thinking of home, his family and Rosie and with his head in his hands, he felt an ache so strong in his heart that he cried out.

He sat feeling broken until the phone went; startled he jumped up and reached for the phone knocking it on the floor as he clumsily tried to be quick. There was a peal of infectious laughter on the other end and Polly exclaiming, "I do have an unusual effect on you don't I?"

Tom picked up the swinging phone and with a wave of self-pity said, "Polly I need to see you."

"Tom whatever is the matter? I thought we had decided to have a rest after last night or have you had just about enough of me to make you want more?" She giggled expecting Tom to laugh with her.

"I have just told my wife that our marriage is over."

He heard a sharp intake of breath. "I will be right over."

"Have you eaten?"

"No, not yet."

"I will organise for something to be brought up, I don't feel like going out."

"I will be with you in half an hour."

Tom picked up the phone and ordered two crayfish salads and a bottle of white wine to be served in his room in an hour and a half.

He then quickly undressed and showered and as the water poured over him imagined all the emotion and anxiety washing away from him. He watched the water swirling around the plug hole and began to feel a sense of heady freedom.

It was nearly time for her to arrive, he dried and put on the thick white robe provided by the hotel.

There was a knock on the door exactly half an hour later, as Tom knew there would be, Polly was always punctual.

When he opened the door she fell into his arms and held him tight.

Tom chokingly said as he buried his head in her hair. "Thank you for coming."

They stood there holding each other for a minute or two and then Tom released her, closed the door and led her to the bed. Without saying a word he started to undress her, undoing the buttons on her silk blouse, sliding it over her soft brown arms where it fell on the floor. He undid the zip of her cotton skirt and let it slip over her slender hips. She reached up to help undo her bra but he stopped her and expertly did it for her, then he slipped her panties down to her feet where she stepped out of them.

Compliantly she stood there while he looked at her, "You are beautiful," he murmured then gently he traced her contours with his fingers, from her neck over her shoulders, down her arms and up again over her breast, circling her erect nipples, over her perfectly flat stomach and reaching down to the triangle of soft brown hair between her legs, she moaned and whimpered and reached for him.

They made love tenderly and silently, afterwards they laid in each others arms until they heard a knock then a voice at the door calling, "Room service!"

Polly got up and smiling at Tom scooped up her clothes and went into the bathroom to shower. While she was there Tom dressed in jeans and a t-shirt and then poured the wine that the waiter had delivered. It was only when Polly appeared out of the bathroom a towel around her head and another wrapped around her that they spoke for the first time.

"You look wonderful," smiled Tom.

"I feel wonderful and hungry," said Polly eyeing the delicious looking salads and smelling the hot rolls.

While they ate Tom told Polly of the conversation with Rosie.

"Tell me about your marriage Tom."

Tom sighed. "I don't know Polly, do you really want to hear about it?"

"Yes Tom I do but only if you want to talk about it."

"I don't know how to describe my marriage, I suppose it was an ordinary sort of marriage. We met at university, married, bought a house with a hefty mortgage, had children quite soon after marrying and suddenly you are busy and just get on with the business of working and child rearing. We settled into a pattern I suppose. The children are great but seem closer to Rosie than I am to them. We aren't alike, she is arty and very much a country girl, religious too, all the things I am not."

It felt very odd talking about it in the past tense and a well of sadness started to overflow inside him.

"No I can definitely see that you are not a country girl!" She tried to make a joke but felt an unreasonable jealousy. What Tom had just described is what she had hoped for, still hoped for. Tom smiled but said nothing.

"Did you argue?"

"We didn't argue much, I suppose you could say that it was comfortable. We have probably argued more just lately but we don't normally. Doesn't sound very exciting does it? I am afraid there isn't much to say about it, I am not very good at analysing relationships."

"Perhaps you didn't have much to talk about if she didn't work?"

Tom shrugged. "She was always doing something, painting classes or gardening, sometimes she did voluntary work for the hospice and church, never anything that brought in much money, that was left up to me."

"You sound as if you resent that?"

Tom thought, "If I am honest I suppose I did." He realised that it had been a resentment that rankled.

"I resented the way she had choices and I didn't. Rightly or wrongly it would bug me that she didn't try harder to make more of a career of her art, she was good enough."

"I thought men like to be the providers?"

"It isn't that I didn't want to provide. I did, I do and will."

"What did your mother do Tom?"

"You are sounding like a counsellor," said Tom getting up to pour more wine.

Polly laughed. "Oh dear sorry."

"Don't be sorry Polly, you are trying to help. You would like to know about my mother. Before she married my father she was an accountant but gave it up to have my brother and me and to be with my father who was in the RAF. She is now a fund raiser and treasurer for various organisations, all voluntary. She and Polly couldn't be more different but they get on well enough, they admire each others skills."

"Do you still love your wife Tom?"

Tom saw the look on Polly's face as she asked that question and thought about his answer carefully.

"Yes I do, but we have grown apart, we are going in different directions."

Polly needed to know whether she had been an instrument in Tom's marriage breakdown, she so hoped not.

"Have you been unhappy for a long time Tom?"

"No in fact I can't really say that I have been very unhappy, just a growing restlessness as if I was searching for something else and not knowing what, a sort of emptiness."

"Has your wife seemed the same?"

Tom laughed but without humour. "On the contrary, she was always happy, always looking on the bright side of things. One of her favourite sayings was; Oh what a wonderful world and how wonderful it is to be alive in it." Tom covered his face with his hands not wanting to visualise Rosie miserable or to reveal his anguish to Polly.

Polly came and stood beside him and stroked his hair. "I think just as we find ourselves falling in love we also find ourselves falling out of love and there seems to be nothing we can do about it."

Tom didn't answer, he wanted at that moment to be alone but didn't have the heart to ask Polly to go after he had asked to come and then made love to her.

He thought he might cry, he never cried about anything, no that wasn't true he had cried when both his children were born. He pushed the thought of that away, it was too painful. He stood up and turned to Polly.

"I am afraid I'm not very good company, I don't feel I have been fair to you asking you to come here, taking all the comfort you have to offer and then being maudlin. I am sorry Polly, if you want to go I do understand."

Polly stood looking at Tom then in a brisk voice said, "We are going out for a walk, then we will come back here, have a large whisky and go to bed where we can try and comfort each other again." She winked at him and he found himself rising, literally, to the challenge.

Rosie tried to rest but so many thoughts were chasing around in her head and she knew it was hopeless. She opened her eyes and saw that the air stewards were serving drinks again, she thought that perhaps a hot chocolate might help.

"Can't you rest dear?" Asked the elderly lady.

"No I think perhaps a hot chocolate might help. My name is Rosie by the way."

"How pretty, I am just plain Jane. Why don't you have a whisky it is what I will be having? Then I will put on a film and fall happily asleep watching it."

Rosie laughed "Yes I think I might, not that I normally drink whisky but then I am not normally flying at three in the morning trying to sleep." Rosie looked at the elderly face smiling at her, she had soft skin, wrinkled in the smiley places and twinkling eyes. "I think your mother must have called you Jane because she could see that you were beautiful."

"Thank you, but you are wrong there I was named after the young nurse who found me on the hospital steps seventy nine years ago."

"Oh gosh! I am sorry, did you ever find why your mother left you, she must have been unwell or desperate?"

"Yes they found her but she had eight other children and just couldn't cope with another. I never met her and I thank her because I was brought up by a wonderful childless couple who always told me from a young age that my mother had loved me too much too keep me. I never questioned it but when I had my own children I realised how painful it must have been for her."

Rosie was fascinated, "Do you know anything about your father?"

"I know very little, only that he died of Tuberculosis a year after I was born. I have tried not to think about it too much but as I get older I find myself wondering more and so my daughter Mary and I are going to do some research when I return from America. It is she who wants to know about her ancestors, all those 'Who are you?' programmes on TV have stirred her curiosity and mine too."

"How fascinating, my family are very straightforward, on my father's side anyway. I grew up on a farm where my father's family have farmed for more than three hundred years and lived in the same house."

"That must be very stabling for you."

"Yes I suppose so, I have to say I took it for granted I am afraid."

"But you are troubled now and while we have our whisky you can tell me all about it."

Rosie smiled, despite having previously wanting to be quiet she found herself needing to confide.

The air stewards arrived at that moment, bringing the astronomically priced whisky and then Jane said in the direct way that many elderly people have of cutting to the chase as if they had pussy footed around enough in their lives. "Come on I'm listening."

Rosie thought for a moment and decided that she too wouldn't preamble.

"I am pretty sure my husband is having an affair with a girl called Polly, I am going to confront him or, as my perceptive mother in law advised, face it head on."

"Is it a shock or is it something you have long suspected?"

"Oh everything has been turned upside down in the last couple of months. If I am truly honest I have probably taken him for granted, I have been perfectly happy you see and haven't looked at him closely enough to see if he was too."

"What makes you so sure that he is playing away?"

"He is different, distant in more than miles. He has been bored at work, apparently he has been saying it for ages, but again I think I have only been listening with half an ear."

"I think we are all guilty of that."

"Yes, I think so too but Tom has been given the opportunity to work in New York and he has accepted without my agreement. We, that is my two children and I, are supposed to be going over to the States for a holiday and to decide if we like it enough to stay."

"Very dangerous, it is inevitable that out of four of you at least one will not want to and then what will you do? Disregard their wishes as unimportant?"

"What do I do then, not ask them if they want to leave England?"

"Exactly. If you and your husband decide together that the best option is to move you have to tell the young ones and then support them if they mind. Children can't be expected to see the wider picture."

"Well they are both teenagers not little ones."

"Very tricky but it still applies. You can not stand behind the children you have to stand in front and lead the way."

"But their schooling is at a critical stage and I do feel they have a right to an opinion at least."

"They have schools in New York, my grandchildren go to one of them and they seem to be surviving. Nothing is insurmountable if you want it badly enough but you don't want it do you?"

"No I don't, I love my home and life in England."

"Do you love your husband?"

"Of course I do."

"There is no of course about it, either you love him enough or you don't."

Rosie felt rather irritated, she had expected empathy not a cross-examination. "I think you are on his side, as if it is all my fault."

"I can either sympathise with you and have you in tears or I can help you see the situation clearly, so that when you *confront* your husband you are prepared. When you arrive at his door may I suggest you greet him as lovingly as you would normally and if you find a young lady with him don't be afraid to be shocked and upset because it is how you are feeling and if she is half decent, which I am sure she is as most people are, she will have compassion for you. This will make her think twice perhaps and certainly won't put your errant husband in a good light."

"What a wise old owl you are or have you had the same experience?"

"Not so much of the old, no not quite the same but I'm a novelist and some of my good friends have," smiled Jane.

"A novelist, you are full of surprises, I must read one of your books."

"We must exchange addresses and I will send you one. Things will work out for you they always do one way or another."

"I have been praying so hard for something to come up in England for Tom and for our marriage," said Rosie miserably, now close to tears.

Jane took hold of Rosie's hand and smiling reassuringly at her said, "Have hope and trust."

Rosie smiled back knowing that Jane was right.

"Yes I know Jane, you are right. I must have trust. I feel so tired now I think I will try and sleep."

"That's right you must rest and I must too."

Rosie was amazed to find she had slept for three hours when she awoke to the sound of drinks and food being served. She looked at her watch and could not believe she had slept so heavily. She stretched and rubbed her stiff neck, she would have liked to get out of the confined space and stand up but Jane was still sleeping and she did not want to disturb her. When the flight attendants arrived at their seats to offer breakfast Jane stirred and opened her eyes and for a moment looked startled before realising where she was.

"Good morning," said the stewardess cheerfully. "Would you like a continental breakfast or a bacon and mushroom omelette?"

Both Jane and Rosie said simultaneously with feeling, "Continental please."

"I can tell that you have had the omelettes before."

"Once too often," laughed Jane.

Rosie was not hungry but found the distraction of eating comforting.

After they had eaten Jane suggested watching an in-flight film, Needing to take her mind off everything Rosie readily agreed. The film being shown at that time was 'Mr Bean's holiday.' Rosie silently groaned, she was not a great fan of Mr Bean but determined to engross herself in it actually found it very funny. Laughter therapy was just what she needed she realised when the final credits rolled that her spirits were altogether lighter.

When at last they arrived and went through all the paraphernalia of passport control and baggage collection, she bade farewell to Jane, thankful that she was on the last leg of her journey and near to Tom.

She quickly found a cab despite the milling crowds of travellers and gave the driver the address of the hotel. The cheery ruddy-faced man having established that it was her first visit to America treated her to a description of New York's highlights all the way to the hotel.

When she alighted from the taxicab and stood on the pavement in front of the tall, many floored hotel building she began to feel tense and wondered what Tom's reaction to her unexpected arrival might be? She looked down at herself and saw how crumpled her clothes were, the same she had worn for her interview, which seemed like days ago. She felt grubby and decided that she should find the cloakroom and change into her new outfit, the only other clothes she had with her, except for a pair of jeans and t-shirt she had packed to travel home in.

She walked with purpose into the hotel foyer and without even looking towards the reception strode down the nearest corridor which looked as if it might house a loo. It did, a very spacious one with proper towels and sweet smelling soap and hand cream.

She stripped off quickly hoping that no one would come in to disturb her and dipping a corner of one of the fluffy white towels into some hot water gave herself a strip wash, then with an ample helping of hand cream smoothed it all over her hands, face and neck. She brushed her hair and twisting it into a knot and fastened it on top of her head. She then slipped into her new outfit and looked at herself in the vast mirror. She was delighted with the outfit but she looked very pale. She quickly fumbled in her handbag for a lipstick, used it on her lips lightly, and rubbed a little on her cheeks, she did not want to look clown-like but certainly, she looked a little healthier. She knew it would give her courage if she felt she was looking her best. She hoped that when Tom saw her he would notice.

She was ready, she stuffed her old clothes into her bag and taking a deep breath opened the door. The corridor was empty but she heard the ping of a lift door opening at the end of the corridor to her right and saw a man emerge.

She had no idea where she would find room 22 but hopefully the lift would have floor numbers and that would help.

She was right, there was a helpful sign saying rooms 12 to 29 were on the first floor. Her heart was thumping with nerves or excitement she was not sure which, either way adrenaline was coursing through her and she could feel her hands and feet tingling. The lift opened with a ping and she stepped out into a wide corridor, rooms 12 to 20 to her left and 21 to 29 to her right. She glanced at her watch; it was seven fifteen local time, perfect. Taking several deep breaths to calm herself she knocked firmly on the door marked 22. Tom's voice called out croakily, "Yes?"

Rosie hadn't expected him to speak only answer the door, she thought for a moment in panic then grinning to herself pinched her nose and in a nasally twang she called out, "Room service!"

Then she very clearly heard Tom groan, and say, "Oh perfect timing," then a feminine giggle, and a mumbling of voices.

Waves of emotion swept over her and she knocked again more loudly, Tom's voice called out, "Okay, okay."

A moment later, the door opened to the sound of more giggles behind him and Tom stood there dressed in a white bath robe.

Rosie didn't give him time to say anything but loudly and in the happiest and most excited voice that she could muster said, "Surprise, surprise!" and flung herself into his arms.

Rosie letting go of Tom quickly entered the room laughing, despite the pain of hurt threatening to engulf her, and said, "Tom you look so shocked."

Tom grabbed her hand and as he swung her around said, "What are you doing here for pity's sake?"

Rosie ignored him as she looked at Polly sitting white faced in the bed; for an instant, she felt sorry for her.

In a quavery but firm voice, she simply said, "I am here because I love you and because I am your wife."

Rosie saw Polly looking desperately around for something, she presumed her clothes. She was tugging at the sheet which, in all the best romantic movies, just lift off and wrap fetchingly around but this was obviously tucked firmly in at the bottom.

Tom was saying something under his breath and making some kind of hand signal to Polly.

"Tom fetch your stranded girlfriend something to put on for heavens sake and I am in desperate need of a cup of coffee please." She went and sat with her back to the room in the comfy seat by the window and looked, with tears now, out at the blur beyond.

Tom looking deservedly embarrassed replied, "Rosie I think it best if I met you down in the lounge in fifteen minutes, order what you like at reception."

Rosie was about to do what he asked but emotion and survival instinct took over and she simply said, "Tom this is where I belong, just here with you, not waiting in the lounge like an unwanted visitor."

She was aware of Polly getting up and going into the bathroom and Tom following her. Within moments she emerged dressed, Rosie expected her to leave but instead she saw from the reflection in the window Polly making a drink. After several minutes with only the sound of Tom showering and the kettle heating Polly brought over a cup of coffee and handed it to Rosie and said, "Here, you must be exhausted, I am going now."

Rosie smiled weakly, took the cup and said, "Thank you."

Polly turned to go and then stopped, turning back to Rosie she said, "I am sorry."

Rosie looked at Polly directly; she was shocked to see how young she was and miserable to note how beautiful she looked tousled and vulnerable. "This feels very surreal Polly, but I find myself sorry for you too. Goodbye and I truly hope you find happiness with someone else."

They both knew that whatever happened in their lives in the future they would never forget this moment.

Polly picked up her bag and left, closing the door quietly behind her.

Tom emerged from the bathroom and glancing around the room turned to Rosie and with a look of contrition said, "I am sorry you saw me with Polly but you should have told me you were coming," then went to the wardrobe and dressed.

Rosie did not trust herself to say anything but thought rapidly about what she should do or say next, she was not normally lost for words but sensed that what she said now could affect her whole future. She felt her anger rising, she could almost taste it, how dare he say that. If that was an attempt to make her feel in the wrong, well it had failed miserably.

Tom, now dressed, came over to her and sat in the opposite chair, "I am leaving for work in five minutes what will you do?"

"Tom, you said that when you are in England you love me, well I am here now and I am the same person here as I am in

England. So if you love me you will cancel your work for today and we will spend the day together trying to repair our marriage and plan our future," and then with a determined emphasis, "Together."

Tom sighed in an exaggerated fashion, "Rosie you don't understand."

"I don't understand? How dare you be so condescending and so bloody predictably self pitying!" She then stood up and threw the remains of her coffee over him; it gave her a small sense of satisfaction seeing the furious glare he gave her as he stormed into the bathroom. She followed him, her voice rising, "I understand only too well, you are completely blinded by Polly but Tom you are deluding yourself she is too young for you, she will want marriage, children."

"If you must know I am only twelve years older than her and my relationship with Polly has nothing to do with you." Tom had flung his clothes in the bath and pushed past Rosie to go to the wardrobe for more clothes.

"Nothing to do with me, are you mad? It affects our relationship, our marriage, our family Tom for heavens sake!"

"Don't bring the children into this, what ever happens they will be fine."

"Fine? You are evidently in some weird state of denial Tom." He did not answer her. She watched helplessly as he dressed in a business suit again. She thought desperately what she could say that might make a difference, she decided to appeal to him, remembering what she had voiced to Jane only hours earlier. "Please don't go to work Tom I am only here until tomorrow and I have so much that I want to talk to you about."

Brutally he replied, "You have two minutes. I have arranged to meet Polly at a café and I am already late, she will be in a dreadful state. We can talk over dinner tonight."

The fact that he was obviously more concerned with the state of Polly and apparently indifferent to her own feelings hurt her deeply. In her agitation she just blurted out what she could, hoping still to move him somehow. "I am so sorry that I have taken you for granted I didn't mean to. I know that I was happy and wasn't taking your discontent seriously. But things will be different I promise, I will be working and-"

Tom stopped her by putting his hands on her shoulders and said with a note of compassion in his voice, "Hey look Rosie you are understandably overwrought and I am sure exhausted as well. Why don't you go to your hotel, have a rest and I will take the afternoon off and we can discuss things then. Where are you staying?"

Rosie was incredulous, "Here of course, with you," she saw him glance around the room his eyes resting for a split second on the bed. With a quivering voice she continued, "Nothing would make me sleep in that bed, I will have to change our room." Rosie could not believe he would think that she would be staying in another hotel, it was bizarre. The whole situation she found herself in was bizarre and she realised what he was doing, he was putting Polly first.

"Tom please look at me, look at me long and hard. I am your wife, the mother of your children, your lover."

Tom at least had the good grace to look at her but he was obviously struggling to keep control. "You are wearing new clothes, they suit you and I do know you are my wife Rosie, I hardly need to be told."

Tom sighed exaggeratedly and looking down saw that his hands were shaking with pent up frustration, he wanted to go to find Polly. Thrusting his hands in his pockets, he looked up and curtly said, "You do not belong here, you have made it perfectly clear that you would rather stay in England. I know you say you love me but they are just words Rosie, the trouble is you don't love me enough to want to make any sacrifices at all," he then cruelly added, "Polly does."

"Tom, you have only known her for five minutes, you don't love her, you just think you do, you are in lust with her."

"How would you know how I feel? You have just said yourself that you took no notice of my feelings."

"All families are busy doing their own thing and are not always aware of each other, you could at least have talked to me about it."

"I tried Rosie but you were always dismissive and tried to treat me like a child who needs cheering up after falling over, *'there, there get up and forget about it, here's a chocolate'*, or in my case a quick bonk, that will keep him happy."

"How dare you, that is so untrue and unfair, I have never used our lovemaking as a bribe, comfort perhaps but that is loving isn't it? I thought you liked to make love? I do," she wanted to add especially when he remembered foreplay, but didn't dare.

Tom looked at his watch and in a firm voice, which defied any argument said, "Find somewhere else to stay and meet me in the foyer here at two." He then saw Rosie with tears now spilling down her face unchecked and with a lump in his throat said, "Rosie I am so sorry that you have put yourself through all of this, believe me I hate hurting you. I didn't plan to have an affair, I can't believe it myself."

With that he left her, standing in the room of adultery, alone.

SEVENTEEN

Tom raced down the stairs and along the road feeling the heat of the morning sun already warming the pavements; he knew that it would be suffocatingly hot and airless later as the sun bounced off the concrete and the endlessly tall buildings.

As he hurried to meet Polly he could not get the image of Rosie's distraught face out of his mind. He tried to replace it with an image of Polly but all he saw was her look of shock and resentment as she hurriedly dressed in the bathroom. He pushed both images out of his mind, and tried to concentrate on what he should say to Polly. She had agreed to meet him at the Bagel Bite Café, which was convenient for work, but regretted suggesting there now, as it would probably be busy with people grabbing a quick breakfast.

He recalled how she had pushed him away when he had tried to embrace her and how she had whispered through her teeth, "Your wife is the other side of the door or had you forgotten," and then she had left. He now wondered if she and Rosie had said anything to each other.

He could see the café ahead and broke into a trot realising

with the ease that he was running that he had left his briefcase in his room. "Shit, shit, shit!"

He received a reproving look from a mother with a child and apologised.

He at last reached the café and entered, desperately looking around for Polly, she was not there. He found a seat and waited wondering if she had gone to the loo or perhaps she had not waited thinking that he had changed his mind. A waitress came up to him, "Are you Tom Holden?"

"Yes."

Handing him an envelope she said, "A lady has left a letter for you, she said she had to go, she seemed upset about something, perhaps she had recieved some bad news." She hovered waiting for him to open it obviously hoping to be enlightened. He disappointed her by getting up and saying simply, "Thank you," and walked out of the café.

Tom walked a few paces away then ripped open the cheap brown envelope; in it was a slip of notepaper headed with Bagel Bite Café. It only took a moment to read the note, which had written diagonally across it in untidy capitals *GO HOME WITH YOUR WIFE.*

Tom stuffed it into his pocket and felt his stomach lurch and tighten, he felt sick, he had lost her and the pain of it made him cry out in anguish, "NO!"

A rising fury at Rosie for coming and destroying his relationship with Polly gripped him. He stood in the street, with people hurrying to work either side of him, wondering what to do. Should he go back and have it out with Rosie or go into work and hope he could see Polly on her own. He could take her in his arms and tell her it was she he wanted, tell her that everything would be fine once he had moved to the States.

Yes, that's what he would do he decided, as he hurried the

short distance to the office, bounded up the ten steps passing several staff members one of whom called after him.

"Hey what's the rush, you are going *in* to work remember?"

Feeling hot and decidedly bothered Tom was relieved to feel the cool of the air conditioning hit him as he entered, taking a deep breath to steady his nerves he strode over to the lift hoping against hope that Polly would be at her desk when he arrived at her office.

She wasn't, he asked Jacky her assistant if she knew whether Polly would be in today.

"She has been in, but has a migraine so she said she would work from home today. She did look ill so I don't think she will be able to do much work but you know Polly, a dedicated perfectionist."

"Yes I know Polly and she is perfect in every way."

Jacky gave him an astonished look, her women's intuition telling her that there was obviously more to that comment than mere flattery.

"If you are falling for Polly Tom, you had better be careful, she lost her fiancé on nine eleven, she doesn't deserve any more heartache."

Tom could have kicked himself for his stupidity. "Heartache is the last thing I have in mind for Polly but promotion might be." Tom hoped that his spontaneous lie would deflect any romantic ideas. It was not much of a lie; he wanted her as his right hand woman.

Jacky, not fooled said no more.

Tom seeing her expression said, "Jacky, I will be out of the office this afternoon my wife has come over for a couple of days and I obviously want to spend as much time with her as possible."

"I should hope so; you should have taken the whole day off. You didn't say she was coming."

"No it was a shock, I mean a surprise," with that Tom walked out of the office and cursed.

It was only when Tom was at his desk that he realised guiltily that he had left Rosie to organise somewhere to stay, tired, distressed and in a strange city. He quickly rang the hotel and explained that his wife had arrived unexpectedly this morning and his room was not suitable and he would like to change. He had to think of an excuse as to why it wasn't suitable. It was only afterwards he remembered he had booked Polly in as his wife only the day before.

Lying seemed to be coming too easily to him and he shamefacedly remembered only a few weeks ago telling Ben off severely for lying and telling him that deceit has a way of coming back to haunt you.

Rosie stood at the window looking out, watching the people below hurrying about their business. There were so many it reminded her of a disturbed ant's nest, all scurrying around and going in different directions.

She did not know what to do. Should she stay in this room with Tom or should she move them both to another room or even find a different hotel just for herself, which Tom had suggested. Suddenly blind rage hit her, how dare he treat her like that, how could he be so cruel?

The phone rang and made her jump so much in her heightened emotional state that she began to tremble. She stumbled over to the phone and in a shaky voice said, "Hello?"

"Good morning Mrs Holden and welcome, Mr Holden has requested a change of room. I have put you on the seventh floor the other side of the building; it has a distant view of central park. I hope you will feel less claustrophobic there."

Rosie frowned at what was obviously Tom's fabricated excuse, claustrophobic? How typical of Tom to blame it on her thought Rosie, her anger fuelled even more.

"Would that be acceptable to you?"

"Oh sorry, yes thank you."

"A porter will be up to help you with your cases in ten minutes"

"Thank you and could I also order some soup and a salad sandwich"

"Soup? I am sorry madam breakfast is still being served."

"Oh sorry it is the middle of the day for me."

"Of course I will see what I can do."

"No please don't worry, a bacon roll and some coffee would be fine."

Rosie looked around the room, she would have to pack Tom's clothes, still trembling she opened the wardrobe and just seeing his familiar clothes and smelling his familiar smell made her dissolve into painful tears. Holding one of his jackets to her, she sank to the floor in racking sobs.

It was the loud knock on the door, which roused her from her numb wretchedness. Wiping her eyes she stood up stiffly and called through the door, "I am sorry, could you come back in ten minutes please?"

Galvanised into action she hastily packed Tom's clothes, unceremoniously throwing them into his suitcase. Going into the bathroom, she saw beside Tom's toothbrush an assortment of feminine toiletries.

Staring at them for a moment she angrily scooped them up and flung them into the waste paper bin. When the knock on the door came she was ready and gratefully allowed the porter to take the bags and lead her out of the room.

When he showed her into the new room, she was thankful that it was not identical in arrangement and décor as the last.

The room was larger and had soft pale blue walls with cream

accessories, the bed faced the huge picture window from which she could see between numerous skyscrapers, as promised, the distant view of the park.

Moments later, her brunch arrived; a full coffee pot, a bacon roll, and as a surprise, a chocolate bagel which she doubted she would be able to eat. She ate it all, both the roll and bagel proved to be delicious and the coffee aromatic and heartening. Feeling replete but exhausted, she eyed the bed which looked comfortable and inviting. She thought she would lie down for half an hour before going out to explore until it was time to for Tom to return.

Needing the loo, she peered into the all white bathroom to see no bath but a large s-shaped shower obviously designed for two. Suddenly the need for a shower to wash away the travel grime and ragged emotions overwhelmed her. She stripped off her new clothes and carefully hung them up then stepped into the shower and let the gloriously warm water rush over her. Using the complimentary shampoo and shower gel she washed her hair and body vigorously then just stood luxuriating in the sensation of the water until the overwhelming need for sleep enveloped her. She wrapped herself gratefully in the huge fluffy white bath sheet, twice the size of the ones they had at home. Giving her hair a cursory dry with the powerful hairdryer, she padded over to the bed and slipped into the crisp clean sheets and with blissful relief hoped for immediate oblivion.

The bed was too big and too empty, she tossed and turned, she missed Tom. She got out and opened Tom's suitcase and took out a soft fleece, it would have to do. She held it to her and climbed back into bed and curled herself around it, snuggled down and slept.

This was how Tom found her when he returned to the hotel. Tom stood beside the bed and looked down at his sleeping wife, she looked so at peace that he could not bear to wake her, knowing that due to him she was far from at peace. He then saw that she was holding what appeared to be his fleece, the sight of that hit him more forcibly than any words could. In a whisper he said, "My poor Rosie what have I done to you?" He let out a choked sob as he saw himself for what he was, for what he had become. He had hurt, by his wanton selfish desires, two special people, neither of whom deserved such careless cruelty. The shame of it made him want to crawl into a corner and stay there.

He thought of the conversation he had just had with Polly, he had tried to phone many times during the morning to no avail and then finally she had answered. Through tears, she had told him that he had destroyed her love and respect for him. When he had tried to protest and ask to be understood, she had replied, "Tom I do understand you, I thought you were a man who was escaping an unhappy life and searching for something better but you are not. You may have lost the most precious thing in the world by turning your back and running away, turn round and open your eyes Tom."

In his desperation to try to make amends, he had begged her to meet him but she simply said before putting down the phone, "Goodbye Tom."

He had known then that it was over for they never said goodbye. It was painful but also surprisingly he felt a sense of relief. He also knew she was right.

A shrill ringing disturbed the troubled peace, before Tom could reach the phone Rosie woke with a start.

Tom, picked up the phone wondering who it might be, it was Grace.

"Hi Dad I had to ring, we, it was addressed to us all, have had a letter from Carl's probation officer and a letter from Carl and a whole lot of bumph about Probation Service, I haven't read that yet. We can go and see him. We can also-" said Grace in an excited breathless voice.

Tom interrupted. "Hello Grace, how about saying that again

more slowly and perhaps it might be a little more coherent if you read the letters to us."

As Grace talked, Tom sat on the edge of the bed, took Rosie's hand in his, and smiled at Rosie's sleepy enquiring face.

Grace read out the letters to Tom and Rosie put her ear next to Tom's in an attempt to listen too.

When they had heard the contents of the letters Rosie took the phone from Tom and said, "Grace that is wonderful news Darling and you know what we must do don't you? We must forgive him."

Rosie looked piercingly at Tom and he nodded and while she was still listening to Grace Tom mouthed with tears in his eyes, "I am so sorry."

Grace must have asked to speak to Tom as Rosie said, "Yes Dad is still here, I don't think he is going anywhere, have a good day and see you soon," and she handed the phone to Tom.

"We are both coming home Grace, yes together tomorrow as long as I can get the flight. No I don't think so. Why? Well all I know is that suddenly I have come to my senses. Yes, of course we will still have the holiday. No Grace I hope that will never happen. Yes, yes I am sure that things will be fine but I have some very important things to do today and must go now."

Tom put down the phone and turning to Rosie who was looking nonplussed said, "I have been a completely selfish bastard to you, to the children and to Polly and if you will let me I want to spend the rest of my life making up for it," with that he enfolded Rosie in his arms.

Rosie did not say anything just allowed herself to be hugged and then withdrew from him and looking up directly into Tom's eyes asked, "What are you intending to do Tom?"

Not sure by Rosie's non-committal tone whether he was being presumptuous by assuming that she would still want him said in a less than confident tone, "I have decided where my priorities lie

Rosie and I know that I have been a fool. I will refuse the job, take the redundancy package and hopefully find something else."

Rosie got out of bed, wrapping the bathrobe around her went over to the window, and stared out unseeingly then said intuitively, "She has given you up then?"

Tom shamefully acknowledged that that was true. "Yes, she has. She told me to look at what I had and warned me that I could lose what I held most dear. She made me see Rosie."

"You have hurt her too; I could see the pain in her eyes."

"Yes."

"Why Tom? That is what I find hard to understand. Why decide to drop us all and turn to someone else? What had we done to deserve that?"

"Nothing Rosie I lost my way, I can't understand it myself."

"I know that you hadn't been particularly happy at work and I also know that I didn't take your discontent seriously enough but I thought that we were ok, I thought that we were happy weren't we?"

Tom came to join her at the window. "Yes we are or were happy I think but suddenly America and a new relationship seemed exciting and became all consuming, I am sorry, so sorry Rosie."

Rosie didn't comment but asked instead, "What did you mean when you said to Grace you had something important to do today?"

"I meant that I had to try and put things right, hand in my notice. Take you out somewhere special and woo you back to me if that is possible."

"Just like that and you expect me to forget everything and take you back with open arms?"

"No I don't, I can't expect anything of you Rosie, I just hope."

Rosie again did not comment but peered out of the window searching for something.

"What are you looking for?"

"I am looking for the site of the twin towers, there is a beautiful chapel there, and a lovely lady on the plane told me about it. Please Tom will you make the phone calls to work and the airport while I get dressed. Oh and my plane leaves at nine thirty tomorrow night. Then we are going out together to some where very special, St Paul's chapel, I would really like to go there, I believe it has been a place of sanctuary for so many. Is it far from here?"

"St Paul's Chapel? It is very near the site of the twin towers we could walk."

The phone went again, "Who on earth will that be now?" Tom strode across the room and snatched up the phone "Yes?"

"Hi Dad, Grace put down the phone before I got a chance to speak"

"Hi Ben how are you?"

"I'm Good thanks but I have something vital to tell you," Ben said seriously.

"Right fire ahead, I'm intrigued."

"Are you going out for a meal?"

"Yes we will be, why?"

"Well don't choose the lobster."

"Lobster? Why not?"

"They mate for life."

Tom flinched, "Ah right, I hadn't realised what intelligent creatures they were. Where do you find these interesting facts?"

"I watched ocean life on TV last night. Did you know that dolphins are the only creatures besides humans that make love for fun? Tell mum and say Hi, I've got to go now."

"Bye Ben, see you tomorrow."

The irony of Ben's snippet of information was not lost on Tom and he groaned inwardly.

Rosie called from the bathroom. "Was that Ben is he alright?"

Tom laughed, "Yes fine, I think hormones have hit him."

Twenty minutes later Rosie was dressed and ready and Tom had made his phone calls, he had been lucky there was a seat available on the flight home. The phone call to the Company director had been harder, he had told them he had changed his mind and would take redundancy, apologising for the decision. Without preamble he now told him how impressed he had been with Polly's work and recommended her for the post he was refusing. Just talking about her made him want to punch the wall in anguish.

He sat for a moment taking in the enormity of what he had done, he could hardly believe it; he had felt a physical pain at the ending of his career, as he had known it. What a surreal day this was turning out to be.

Rosie broke into his reverie saying, "I'm ready Tom."

Wearily Tom stood up and smiling weakly said, "Right, let's go."

Rosie looked up at him and asked, "What happened Tom, what did they say?"

"They were surprised but I'm not indispensable, no one is."

"What reason did you give?"

"I simply said I had changed my mind and apologised."

"How do you feel?"

Tom felt irritated by her cross examination but tried not to show it.

"I feel like showing you a little of this amazing city."

Rosie knew that his evasive answer meant that he felt wretched and did not want to talk any more about it.

"I won't ask you anything else Tom, about anything or anyone, I just want us to move forward from here. I want us to start a new chapter in our lives; let's try and make it an exciting one."

Tom replied, his voice thick with emotion, "I know that it's more than I deserve, I am afraid I lost sight of you and the children for a while."

"Tom, I lost sight of you too, I am so sorry."

They held each other tightly, both of them with a lighter spirit.

"Let's go to St Paul's and pray together Tom and light a candle for our marriage."

Knowing that it would take him a long time to put Polly behind him and think of her only in the past. He took a deep breath and replied, "Yes let's do that Rosie, then later I will take you to a restaurant I have heard about which apparently is supposed to be one of the best in New York."

Polly had not gone home after leaving the office but had taken a cab to central park, choosing the Northern Park in an attempt to avoid too many people. She had always enjoyed the Southern Park best with all its varied attractions and many people to watch but today the quieter ,wilder, natural beauty of the Northern Park suited her emotions.

Her head throbbed in unison with her footsteps as she walked along the myriad footpaths, not choosing any direction to walk in but choosing the shady side out of the full glare of the relentless sun.

She went over and over in her mind the events of the morning, knowing without a shadow of doubt she would remember forever the shame and humiliation of facing Tom's wife.

She remonstrated with herself for falling for Tom; she felt anger at herself for going out with a married man. In her own defence it had not been like that, she had not consciously made the decision. It had unexpectedly happened; she had awakened from the dulling ache of grief she had been carrying with her since 9/11.

Being honest with herself, she had not asked Tom about his wife and family but had wanted to assume his marriage was over.

Thinking about how wretched he had looked when she had informed him that his wife was in hospital she should have known he still loved her. Why had he given her the impression that he was unhappy on his return to the States? She knew that they were both to blame, they had been tempted and selfishly succumbed.

She flushed remembering the note behind the picture she had given him; it had been thrilling to tempt him. Why had she done it? She did not have an answer.

Aware suddenly of her sore feet that walking in high heels in the heat with no stockings were causing, she sat down underneath the nearest tree. She eased her shoes off and stretched her toes, wincing at the pain of the broken blisters on both heels, knowing as she did so that it would be hard to put them on again. She leant back against the wide trunk of the tree feeling the ridges of bark through her thin blouse. She glanced down at her feet twisting her ankles round to have a good look at the damage. "Damn, I am an idiot."

A woman walked by with a child in a pushchair and gave her a look of sympathy. She wanted to call out to her, "I don't deserve your pity."

She painfully recalled the look of compassion for her on Tom's wife's face and felt a deep regret for the hurt she had caused her. She felt sorry for herself too and anger at Tom for treating her like his little American diversion, she didn't want to be and wasn't going to be a bit on the side.

Bitter tears of guilt, pain and loss trickled down her face when suddenly a large hairy dog of indeterminate breed with a wet nose and rough tongue excitedly bound up to her and with furiously wagging tail licked the salty tears from her face knocking her sideways in the process.

"Chuck, Chuck come here!" yelled a young male voice as Polly laughing stood up and held the dog by its collar, feeling his great shaggy tail thudding against her legs.

Panting an apology as he approached a tall young man in baggy shorts and a t-shirt jogged up to her.

"Sorry, are you okay?"

"Yes I'm fine, just thoroughly licked," smiled Polly

The man bent down and attached a lead to Chuck, who had turned his enthusiastic attention to her feet. "Chuck you bad boy. He is harmless but rather too exuberant. Ever since my girlfriend left he accosts all likely females who might act as a surrogate mistress." Looking up at her at the same time as taking Chuck's collar he said "sit" firmly.

"No thank you I have just got up," teased Polly glad of the friendly diversion.

They both laughed.

"May I buy you a drink by way of an apology? They do a really great iced tea at the lake tea house."

Polly looked at his open honest face and smiley brown eyes and felt safe and just a touch intrigued.

"Thank you I would like that."

EIGHTEEN

Feeling a little jetlagged but pleased to be home Tom was reading his post sitting at the kitchen table. With increasing interest, he read the information on the Probation Service which had come with Carl's letter. Carl's short letter of remorse had touched them all and the recommendation from his probation officer had moved Tom to read the information leaflet. At the end was a request for people willing to train for the Probation Service. Tom felt a feeling of excitement and a dawning of a future, it was if at last, a light had switched on and he could see clearly. For the moment he decided not to share this with anyone, he needed to think it through but he was determined to ring the number provided on Monday.

Rosie was busy packing for the weekend away with her parents so Tom decided to take Charlie for a walk, he called up to both Grace and Ben to see if they wanted to come, predictably neither did. He did not try to persuade them with his usual extolling of the benefits of fresh air, as the weekend ahead on the farm would afford them plenty of opportunities for that.

He walked up the village street towards the fields and looked from side to side appreciating the picturesque cottages and gardens. He found himself waving to various people he recognised but hardly knew.

During the last few months, he had been detaching himself from his home and the village but today he seemed to see things more sharply as if he had put on a pair of new spectacles and made everything bright again.

The previous day's events and emotional upheavals had required him to do more soul searching then he had ever previously done. He had felt emotionally exposed, had seen himself, and had not liked what he had seen.

Rosie's honesty and desire to find a reason why he had done what he had made him realise how much she cared. He had just blundered into the situation without any true thought or awareness of the consequences.

He and Rosie had stopped communicating on anything but a superficial level lately. He knew he had distanced himself from her and his family, something that he remembered consciously doing.

He had hurt her deeply and for that he felt remorseful and ashamed but her willingness to try to forgive had moved him.

Yesterday, as they had sat side by side in the beautiful chapel he had listened to her whispered prayer asking for the grace to forgive and to love him more deeply. He too had prayed for the same, haltingly but wholeheartedly and had felt an overwhelming feeling of love envelop him. He could only describe it as a feeling of completeness, fullness to overflowing. He knew as tears slid down his cheeks that he felt forgiveness. He just knew that he had communicated with God and the knowledge had brought him greater joy than he had thought possible. Rosie had slipped her small hand in his at that moment and he had known too that they would be closer than they had ever been before.

As he walked along the footpath with Charlie yapping with

excitement at a disturbed rabbit, the sun warm on his bare arms and the sweet smell of wild honeysuckle he felt a truly happy man. The unexpected sense of freedom from work was exhilarating, he would not return and was pleased the Company had an instant departure policy after redundancy acceptance.

The thought of Polly was the only cloud but even she, all those miles away, seemed somehow blurred. He had left a letter for her on her desk when he had gone in to finalise his departure. Rosie had read it, he did not want any more secrets from her.

He had written that she had been like a beautiful gift to him and that he bitterly regretted hurting her. He wished her happiness and hoped her dreams would come true. He had signed it simply Tom.

Rosie, despite feeling tired after the emotional rollercoaster she had experienced, felt blessed for she had her husband back and with absolute assurance knew their marriage was secure. She had not had to fight for him or win any competition, she had just been given the opportunity to show her love for him and be grateful.

Lillian had sweetly cleaned the house in her absence, washed and ironed all the items in the linen baskets and everything looked tidy and gleaming. She had even persuaded the children to tackle their rooms, something Rosie rarely achieved.

Lillian had left before they arrived home so Rosie rang Lillian's local florist and asked her to deliver her an orchid, her favourite, with a message saying, *All is well, Thank you so much.*

By the time Tom returned with Charlie she and the children were ready to leave for the farm.

The children unconsciously absorbing the improved atmosphere were in good spirits and enjoyed the united family occasion.

Grace remembered Uncle Matthew had said that he had a surprise waiting for them and the excitement rose as they neared the farm. When Tom drove into the farmyard, he tooted the horn and a cacophony of noises resulted; the farm dogs barked, the geese honked, a farm bell rang and Norman appeared waving his stick and shouting to the dogs to be quiet.

Charlie and the children tumbled out of the car calling to Norman to show them the surprise.

"Hang on a minute you two all in good time, Matthew will show you, it's his idea and his responsibility. Now how about a hug for your grandfather?"

Rosie was gratified to see that although her father was obviously not strong he looked a little better; the new medication was obviously working well.

At that moment, Louise came out of the kitchen door, the delight of seeing her family obvious on her smiling face. "Hello one and all, lunch is almost ready."

Charlie was beside himself with excitement and was rushing round and round in circles barking, delighted to be on the farm where some of his favourite smells were.

Rosie ran to her mother and gave her a hug. "It is so lovely to be home Mum and you and Dad look so much better."

"Well your Dad is certainly coping better than he was and I have a Mrs Tandy helping in the house and garden"

Ben overheard and chanted. "Handy Mrs Tandy was too handy with the brandy. It made her very randy, shocking poor old Grandy!"

"Ben for goodness sake, stop it," admonished Rosie laughing.
"Why?"
"You know very well why!"
"He's only having a bit of fun, she's not here to take offence," smiled Louise indulgently.

Ben was close to his grandmother; in her eyes, he could do no wrong. Grace was closer to her grandfather and from an early age had pottered about with him wherever he was on the farm.

But to Ben now Louise said, "Go and be a good lad and find everyone, including your Uncle Matt, and tell them lunch will be ready in fifteen minutes please and I don't want anyone under my feet until then."

When Ben had left, Louise turned to Rosie and held her arms out to her and she gratefully received one of her mother's enfolding hugs "Now something tells me that you and Tom have been going through a rocky patch, and then you go rushing off to America. What's happening love?"

Rosie smiled at her mother. "You and your mother's intuition. Well we have had a rocky patch you are right but we are working through it Mum and everything will be okay. The fact is we are talking now more than we have for ages. Although it has been really painful we are both committed to each other and Tom has some good news which he will tell you himself."

"Well good that's what I wanted to hear. Most marriages have their difficult times but you know I am here if you ever want to talk."

"I know Mum but you have had a terrible time just lately yourself remember. How are things really with Dad?"

"He will never be the man he used to be; he has good days and bad days, that is the nature of the beast. Parkinson's Disease is degenerative so he won't get better just gradually worse"

"Oh Mum it must be so hard for you both?"

"Yes there is no denying it but his medication does help a lot as long as he remembers to take it on time."

"He seems more cheerful."

"Yes we both are now we know what we have to cope with. The Parkinson's Disease Society have given us lots of information and helped us realise we are not alone. We also have more help around the house and farm that has made all the difference. It wasn't easy getting your Dad to admit he couldn't cope. Anyway enough of the glooms we are going to have a happy weekend."

"Yes we are and I am going to help, I'll do some gardening while I'm here and anything else you want. Is Eve coming to lunch Mum?"

"Oh glad you reminded me, give three rings on their phone and she'll know to come."

Rosie did as she was bid then smiling at her mother said, "I have a surprise for her and Matt. While we were in America the painting I had done for Eve to give to Matt was returned by the Police."

"Where was it found?"

"I don't know, Lillian didn't think to ask. Perhaps Carl had kept it and told the Police. We had a letter from him and his probationary officer."

Noisy chattering was heard which was a sure indication everyone was about to arrive for lunch.

Lunch turned into a very merry event. Both Grace and Ben were delighted with Whisper, the new pony and Ben was ecstatic at Matthew's offer to teach him to drive the tractor.

The day passed happily and quickly, everyone was busy doing tasks in various corners of the farm. Tom helping Matt with renewing fences, Rosie with her mother in the garden and both children with the new pony.

It was not until Rosie was in bed in her old room that an overwhelming feeling of insecurity swept over her. As she watched Tom strip off his clothes and climb into bed she thought someone else has seen and has caressed my husband What had they said to each other while making love? Had she been better in bed than Rosie was?

Both Tom and Rosie had previously had a long-term relationship before they met, but since they had together her body was exclusively for him and his had been exclusively for her.

Tom broke into her thoughts. "It has been good today being in the fresh air and doing some hard labour. I feel physically tired, I bet I will feel it in the morning. I have really enjoyed it." He chatted on unaware that Rosie wasn't listening.

Rosie hardly heard what he was saying she was lost in her private thought, she knew that if he touched her she would find it intolerable and yet she longed to be held and reassured that he still wanted to touch her. She wondered when he would want to make love to her again or whether he ever would truly desire her as he once did or whether she would desire him in the same way.

"You aren't listening, are you alright?"

In a small hardly audible voice she answered, "No," tears slid down her cheeks.

Tom, turned towards her and leaning on his elbow looked at her, "Tell me, is it your father or is it me?"

"It is me Tom, I don't know how to feel, I don't know how you feel. Seeing you naked makes me think of you with someone else, you gave away what I thought was mine for ever," she sobbed.

Tom took her in his arms and Rosie, despite her misgivings, was comforted.

"What can I do Rosie; I can say sorry which I truly am. I can promise that for the rest of my life all that is mine is yours."

Rosie said nothing for a moment then moving away from him said in a hushed tone, "Describe me Tom, who am I?"

Tom hated this kind of conversation, he was not good at it, and he did not know what she wanted him to say.

"You are my wife, whom I love."

"No Tom who am I? What am I like? I want the good and the bad."

Tom groaned inwardly, he looked at her knowing he had to

play along "You are attractive, with eyes that sparkle and a face that crinkles up when you laugh."

"Thank you I like that, what else?"

"You are optimistic, a bit unrealistically I have to say, intelligent but rather too opinionated at times."

"I have a strong opinion on that," laughed Rosie.

Encouraged Tom continued, "You are a successful and soon to be well known artist, you are, as you know, scatty and forgetful so hopefully you will remember where and what you will be painting." Rosie dug him in the ribs "Ow, have I said enough now?"

"No Tom."

Groaning Tom thought, "What does she want to hear?"

"Umm you are a good cook, a loving mother," Tom then added hurriedly, "A wonderful wife of course. Am I doing okay?"

"Am I sexy Tom?"

Tom realised that what he said now was what she had really wanted to hear. Did he find her sexy? He supposed he must do, he certainly had when he had first met her. He recalled his first clumsy attempt at seducing her, he had sung in her ear in the student café.

"All I want is the air that I breath and to love you."

She had replied, "You won't be wanting your pizza then?" and laughing had taken it off his plate and shared it amongst her friends. Much to Rosie's disappointment it had been several months before he had plucked up the courage to ask her out.

It was hard to analyse how he felt now, she was still attractive of course, and he had always enjoyed their lovemaking.

Hurt by his inability to answer Rosie said turning away from him, "I am not obviously."

Gently turning her back towards him he said "Rosie, I do find you sexy but-"

"But what Tom, have you grown bored?"

"Rosie, as you know I am not good at analysing things, what

I can tell you is in no way did I go looking to find anyone else it just happened. I think it was a symptom not of our marriage at all but of my general restlessness."

"Tom, you told me that you had found her a temptation but had no intention of doing anything about it, I understood that, could identify with that but you chose to pursue it. Nobody forced you did they?"

Tom with a sigh said, "We are trying to put it all behind us and move on."

"I know, I am trying, believe me, but seeing you naked just reminded me. Tom, how would you feel if it were me who had gone to bed with someone else?"

"I would hate it of course, in fact I did think at one time that you and John had a thing going since you seemed so in tune and pally"

Rosie felt her face flush as she remembered how she had felt when John had made a pass at her, she had felt tempted, flattered. It could so easily have been her. After a moment's silence she said, "I am attracted to John and I know he is attracted to me. We have art in common and I like him and felt sorry for him when he became a widower but I am so glad that Alice and he are now together. I must be honest with you Tom, he did make a pass at me and although I didn't respond I was tempted."

Tom lay back on his pillow with his arms behind his head and asked in a flat, resigned, voice, "Do you think monogamy is possible, or is it unrealistic?"

"Yes I do Tom if both parties want it and are committed to it, surely you want that?" and with a hardness to her voice said, "don't you?"

"Yes I do, honestly I do. The fact is, as I said to you, I lost sight of us and seemed to leave reality and go to another world. I ran away in effect. Do not ask me to explain Rosie, all I know is that you are my wife and that is how I want it. I have returned back to our world."

Rosie reached for his hand and squeezed it, not trusting herself to speak.

"I am so tired, shall we sleep or try, I had forgotten how this bed dips in the middle."

"Yes Tom, do you remember when we first slept in it just after we married and we laughed and you said it was a perfect conjugal bed?"

Tom now half asleep said, "Yes I do and it is."

"When will we want to do it again Tom?"

Tom was asleep and did not hear her, she turned on her side away from him and tried to sleep thinking why was it men could always sleep whatever was happening while women tossed, turned and fretted.

On Monday morning, after the children had left for school and Rosie had left for another meeting with Giles Barton Tom sat down to ring the number on the Probation Service leaflet. The more he heard, the more he was convinced it was what he wanted. He arranged to have an informal interview with the training officer for the following day. He was in such an optimistic mood he decided that he should ring Paul and not put it off. He rang but Paul was out of his office so Tom left a message.

I am taking redundancy, out of the rat race hoorah. I am on to much better things. Do not keep in touch. Tom.

Feeling very satisfied with himself he then called to Charlie, "Come on Charlie you and I are going for a walk."

They were just out of the door when the phone rang, Tom toyed with the idea of leaving it but letting go of Charlie's lead he dashed back in and snatched up the phone just as the answer phone clicked in.

"Hello, I am here" he called over the irritating lady's voice stating that '*we are unavailable to take your call please ring back later or leave a message after the tone*' beep. "Sorry."

"It's me Tom; I am just ringing to tell you that it is all going ahead, the programme is on. I feel so excited about it!"

Tom felt genuinely pleased for her and it was so good to hear the excitement in her voice. "Well done that is good news, when do you start filming?"

"In September for real but we are doing some dummy runs first. Tom, I realised when I was discussing schedules that we will be on holiday and I feel panicky at the thought of New York. Can we change the holiday to somewhere else? I don't think I could go there just yet, perhaps in a couple of years time."

"I did wonder about it, also of course the firm were paying for it, they won't now. How about I look up on the internet and find us a last minute holiday bargain somewhere else, perhaps Grace and Ben could help choose. I will speak to them about it when they get home."

"Thank you Tom, I don't know what time I'll get home as we are going to the pub to celebrate."

"Okay have fun, remember you are driving."

"I don't need alcohol I am on a high as it is. Bye Tom."

By the time Rosie got home, it was after nine, a holiday destination had been chosen, and the holiday booked.

Grace met Rosie at the door with a squeal of, "We are going to the Seychelles and Daniel is coming too!"

Tom watched Rosie as she received this news and smiled as she looked at him with raised eyebrows and teased Grace. "Really why on earth would we want Daniel with us?"

Ben chipped in with, "So that he can play footy with me."

"As a treat for us all I have booked us in for snorkelling lessons, the coral and marine life is supposed to be fantastic.

"Sounds bliss."

Rosie then told them all about her day and as she chatted animatedly Tom saw a glimpse of the Rosie he first met. She looked vibrant, radiant and full of enthusiasm.

Not to be outdone he decided to share his news. "Guess what, I too have something new and exciting ahead."

Everyone turned to look at him "What is it then? Don't hold us in suspenders," laughed Rosie.

"I am going to train to be a Probation Officer."

There were surprised looks all round. "Goodness Tom, that's quick, when did you decide on that?"

Tom put his arm round Grace's shoulders, and looked down at her. "It was when I read Carl's letter and Mr Gough's, his probation officer's letter and info. Somehow something just clicked and after talking to the training officer today I know with absolute certainty that this is what I want to do."

"I think it is fantastic Dad," smiled Grace who gave him a kiss, "It is so weird Mum, perhaps what happened to you was meant to happen, in a funny kind of way."

Rosie made a grimace. "Well who knows darling but I can think of funnier ways. What I do know for certain is that life is like a jigsaw puzzle, so many misshapen pieces all eventually fitting together creating a picture."

Ben asked, "What training will you have to do Dad, and if you have to go into prisons may I come?"

Tom laughed and ruffled Ben's hair.

"I'll go and make a coffee and then you can tell us all about it," said Rosie as she turned to go into the kitchen.

"I'll come and help," said Tom as he followed her, watching her familiar bottom wiggle slightly as she walked in her thin cotton dress. He felt aroused at the sight and an overwhelming tenderness towards her. When they were alone Tom came up behind Rosie and putting his arms around her waist and his lips to her ear he sung quietly in a voice full of emotion, "All I need is the air that I breath and to love you."

ISBN 1425146872